Peri drew a shuddering breath. "I was lying in bed. I couldn't stop thinking about you. Since the other night. And this afternoon. And I had to come."

"I was thinking about you, too," Asha said huskily.

"I can't cope with being like this, wanting to touch you, needing to feel your lips on mine. I've thought of nothing else." Peri's voice broke on a sob.

Stepping forward, Asha gently drew her into her arms, holding her close as she cried. Asha murmured soothingly.

"I've never felt like this before," Peri said into Asha's shoulder. "I've never wanted anyone as much as I want you. Don't send me away. Please."

"Never." Asha found Peri's lips and kissed her softly, gently. Then their kisses deepened as passion took hold of them.

Somehow they were on Asha's bed and Peri's fingers and lips were moving over Asha's skin, setting her aflame. She reveled in Peri's touch, the taste of her, the familiar scent of her.

Visit

Bella Books

at

BellaBooks.com

or call our toll-free number

1-800-729-4992

Past Remembering

LYN DENISON

Bella
BOOKS
2007

Bella Books, Inc.
P.O. Box 10543
Tallahassee, FL 32302

Printed in the United States of America on acid-free paper

First Edition

Editor: Cindy Cresap
Cover designer: S. Webber (Canada) & S. Tester (Australia)

ISBN-10: 1-59493-103-8
ISBN-13: 978-1-59493-103-1

For Glenda
My LT
With soft eyes
and thanks for the great 20 years

About the Author

Lyn Denison is an Australian who was born in Brisbane, the capital city of Queensland, the Sunshine State. Before becoming a writer she was a librarian. She's not fond of composing her own bio as she's a Libra and, well, there's so much to choose from . . .

Her hobbies include genealogy, scrapbooking, photography, travel, reading, modern country music and her partner of nineteen years. (Saving the best for last.) Lyn's partner works in an art gallery and they live in an inner city suburb of Brisbane.

CHAPTER ONE

Asha pulled her Holden Astra into the last parking niche in the riverside lay-by. With relief, she switched off the engine of her small sedan, unbuckled her seat belt and tried to relax her tensed muscles. Because she was unfamiliar with this side of the city, she'd left early in case she had trouble finding Mrs. Chaseley's home. Now here she was with twenty minutes to kill before her appointment with the elderly woman.

She was glad of the time to calm the flutter of nervous anticipation she always felt when she was stepping out of her comfort zone. And taking on this project for such a well-known pioneering family left her feeling ambivalent. There was the anticipatory excitement she always felt with her research, but this time there was the unaccustomed fear of failure, that she wouldn't quite measure up.

Asha tried to push away her feelings of inadequacy, feelings she told herself were unfounded. She had Tessa to thank for that. While part of her acknowledged she was being irrational blaming Tessa, she knew deep down she was the one responsible for her own feelings, her own actions, but her confidence in herself had taken a battering, along with her vulnerable heart. Tessa had had some input into that, surely?

With a sigh, she glanced over the wide expanse of the Hamilton reach of the Brisbane River. From this distance, the buildings on the far bank looked almost modest for their considerable real estate value, but the yachts bobbing on their moorings gave far more indication that these were very affluent suburbs. It was a lovely picture-postcard area of the city, and now that developers and the City Council were cleaning up the old wharves, the area had taken on a renewed and trendy outlook on life.

These up-market suburbs were a far cry from the part of Brisbane where Asha had grown up. Her stepmother and half sister still lived in the solid working class suburb with its mixture of older people and the influx of young families. Not so Asha's father. After divorcing her stepmother and then marrying his secretary, he had moved into a prestigious inner city suburb to reflect his continuing business success.

It wasn't that Asha begrudged her father his new life or his obvious wealth. He'd certainly worked for it. As an ex-cricketer who had played for Australia, Sean West's small sports store had expanded into a state and then a national chain. As a sportsman, and now as a businessman, he was lauded and well liked. It was simply a pity, she contemplated wryly, that it had all been at the expense of his marriage to her stepmother.

Laura West was the only mother Asha had known. Her own mother had died when Asha was just four years old and her father, left with a small child to raise, had married Laura a year later. Asha had desperately missed her mother and had warmed to her gentle and loving stepmother. When her half sister,

Michelle, was born two years later, Asha had been ecstatic to have a baby sister to play with.

The thought of Michelle brought a smile to Asha's face, as it always did. Her sister was an amazing young woman, a free spirit who was studying Arts at the University of Queensland. Asha knew Laura sometimes wondered at the bright and bubbly personality of her biological daughter. The quieter Asha was more akin to her retiring and somewhat shy stepmother.

For the last three years, Asha had been living down at the Gold Coast, working in the Gold Coast City Council's library service. Asha had loved the job, and through her work in the library, she had furthered an interest in genealogy that began in her teens with a school project on ancestry.

What had started with curiosity about her late mother's family had blossomed from a hobby into a fully-fledged business. Asha obtained a Diploma in Family Historical Studies, and from there she'd been asked to construct and hold courses on genealogy at local colleges and schools.

She so enjoyed her subject and knew she passed on her enthusiasm to her students. And one of her students . . . She reminded herself she wasn't going to think about Tessa, but Tessa had meant so much to Asha it was difficult not to do so, and she sighed in resignation. Although she knew she shouldn't dwell on the past, Asha couldn't help revisiting her first meeting with Tessa, and that wondrous, frightening, freeing time.

Asha had met Tessa not long after she moved to the Coast, at just the second course she had taught. A couple of months later they were sharing Asha's pleasant little unit with its view of the mountains.

The familiar heavy weight of betrayal and despair settled on Asha. She'd fallen for Tessa the first moment she'd seen her. Dark, dangerous, so exciting Tessa, with her sleepy-lidded, sensual eyes and her athlete's body. However, Tessa's athletic body was due more to genes than any working out on Tessa's part, but

3

the forbidden promise in her dark eyes had been so very true.

Asha had fallen under Tessa's sybaritic spell, and their physical relationship had been so much more than the conservative Asha could have imagined. Tessa had been Asha's first love and Asha had thought she was Tessa's. She bit back a painful, self-derisive laugh.

Asha had begun to suspect she was a lesbian when she was still in high school, but that was a secret she had kept buried deeply inside her. Too shy to broach the subject with anyone, she had done her own surreptitious research, read as much as she could on the so-called "alternative lifestyle." Even so, she was half-convinced her secret crush on her English teacher was simply part of growing up, but deep down she suspected that wasn't the case with her. When she met Tessa, she knew without doubt those feelings were not just an adolescent stage she'd gone through.

At thirty, Tessa was eight years older than Asha, but the age difference hadn't been an issue with them. In fact, Asha often felt years older than the vivacious Tessa.

When Tessa boldly asked Asha to go for a cup of coffee after the second week of Asha's eight-week course on genealogy, Asha had barely hesitated before accepting the invitation. Part of her, the part she usually kept hidden, recognized and exalted in the promise in the depths of Tessa's liquid, knowing eyes.

Two cups of coffee and three hours of talking later, they'd parted. Tessa had taken Asha's hand, leaned closer and kissed her softly, slowly, on the cheek. Asha had sailed along in a daze of sexual arousal for a very long week before the next class.

When Tessa came in late Asha felt herself flush with relief, relief that was almost palpable. She had been filled with terror that the other woman might have sensed her more than friendly interest and been so repulsed by it Asha would never see her again. Tessa slipped into her seat, her full lips lifting in a knowing, enticing smile, and Asha knew she'd fallen in love for the

4

first time in her life.

When Tessa suggested coffee again, this time at her unit, Asha had willingly agreed. They had barely closed the door on the outside world before Tessa pulled Asha into her arms and kissed her, a deep, sensual, lingering kiss that took Asha's breath away.

They didn't have the proposed cup of coffee until morning. Making love with Tessa had been fantastic, and Asha fell more deeply in love. No. It wasn't love, she berated herself. What she'd felt for Tessa was more like plain and simple lust. Now, three years later, sitting overlooking the picturesque riverscape, and with the comfort of that famous, or infamous, hindsight, Asha could see that the cracks in their relationship had appeared less than six months after Tessa moved into Asha's unit. There were the drinking binges followed by the tearful apologies. Then there were the nights Tessa didn't come home until the early hours of the morning and the spurts of anger when Asha questioned her.

Tessa worked as a travel consultant and often went away on work-related trips. When she began staying away for weekends, Asha accepted Tessa's explanations. She was in love with her and trusted her completely.

One afternoon when Asha couldn't reach Tessa on her mobile phone, she'd rung the office. Tessa's boss told Asha that Tessa had taken their new travel intern to a travel expo in Brisbane. Surprised that Tessa hadn't told her about the expo, she'd been about to hang up when Tessa's boss inquired about Asha's recent illness. They'd been so sorry Asha was too ill to come along to the weekend at Cooran Cove.

Asha had hung up in a daze. Tessa had said she was going away on a working weekend to Cairns. Why had she lied? Asha had been hurt and she'd confronted Tessa when she arrived home at midnight.

"Why did you lie to me?"

"About what?"

"For a start, you told me you were going to Cairns when you were really going to South Stradbroke Island," Asha said tersely. "I don't understand why you felt you had to lie to me."

Tessa shrugged and then disappeared into the bathroom while Asha sat on the side of their bed. They'd barely spoken to each other all week. They hadn't made love for ages. Coming to a decision, Asha stood up and walked into the en suite. For once the sight of Tessa's lean body barely registered.

"We have to discuss this, Tessa," Asha said earnestly. "I really can't cope with lies."

"You're overreacting." Tessa sauntered into the bedroom. "I only made up the story about you being sick because I knew you wouldn't want to go. I thought it was easier all round."

"Tessa—"

"You know you never want to go to my work promotions."

"Once." Asha raised her hands and let them fall. "Once I didn't want to go because it was my stepmother's birthday."

"If you told her you were a lesbian, that we were together, she wouldn't expect you to run every time she calls," Tessa remarked cuttingly.

"Yes, well, we're not talking about Mum, are we? We're discussing us, specifically why you're never home these days." Asha took a steadying breath. "Are you having an affair?"

"Oh, for heaven's sake!" Tessa exclaimed. "The travel business is shaky these days. It's not a nine to five thing anymore. I have to make contacts. Who knows when I might need them? What if the agency closes down?" Tessa appealed dramatically.

"Is that likely?" Asha knew it was a family-owned business and she was concerned.

"Who knows in this climate?"

"But your boss told me they've just put on a trainee consultant. Why would they do that if business was bad?"

Tessa turned away, the low light picking up the curves of her lithe, naked body.

"Your boss said you'd taken the new staff member up to Brisbane today."

"So?" Tessa pulled back the bedclothes, not meeting Asha's gaze.

"If you feel you have to tell me lies about it then why wouldn't I think you had something to hide?"

"I didn't lie."

"It was a lie by omission, wouldn't you say?"

Tessa rolled her eyes. "My, what big words you use, my little librarian."

"Tessa! I'm deadly serious. Are you having an affair with her?" Asha asked, swallowing nervously as she waited for Tessa's reply.

"Get real, Asha!" Tessa turned from the bed and grabbed a cigarette out of a pack in her bag. She lit up, knowing Asha hated her smoking in the unit.

"What else can I think? You're never here."

"I work. Remember?" She walked over to the window and stared out into the night.

"You don't work twenty-four hours a day."

"I told you the travel industry is in a slump."

"If that's so then logically you should have less to do," Asha remarked dryly.

"How would you know?" She spun back to face Asha. "You've got that cushy job in the library. You wouldn't know what it was like out in the real world."

"I put in the same hours you do," Asha said. "If you add my genealogy classes, probably more."

Tessa gave a snort. "That's exactly it. You live in a fantasy world with your nose in your books. And if it's not your books, you're stuck in the past with other people's ancestors."

Hurt, Asha stood and gazed at Tessa as though she'd never seen her before. "When we met I thought you were interested in

7

genealogy, too," she said softly.

"I *was* interested. I was curious about my grandparents. You found them for me." Tessa shrugged indifferently. "And that was that."

"You moved on," Asha remarked, knowing it was true. Tessa rarely kept an interest longer than a few weeks. Is that how she regarded Asha? Interesting for a while and then to be discarded for something, or someone, new?

"I prefer to live in the present," Tessa continued, pacing back and forth. "Life's for today. Not yesterday."

"Yesterday? *Our* past means something to me. I thought it meant something to you, too." She shook her head. "What happened to us, Tessa?"

Tessa exhaled in exasperation and stubbed out her cigarette. "We've had some good times, but things, life, doesn't stand still. It moves on. You must see that, Asha."

"Is that what you're trying to tell me? That you want to move on? Why can't we do it together?"

"I really don't think you're into moving on, Asha. That's your problem."

"*My* problem? I can't see that I could do anything more than I'm doing. I don't understand what more you want from me."

"If you don't know then there's not much point, is there?" Tessa moved her shoulders irritatedly. "Anyway, I'm tired of this conversation. Let's go to bed." She sat down, patting the bed beside her. "You know talking's not my thing." She gave a sly grin. "I'm more of an action person."

Asha gazed at the queen-sized bed, at the attractive woman looking at her with her sensual dark eyes. And suddenly that bed, lying beside Tessa, was the last place Asha wanted to be. Quietly she collected her things from the en suite and took her pillow. "I'll be in the spare room."

"Suit yourself. But you know where I am if you get lonely."

The next morning, after a sleepless night, Asha told Tessa she wanted her to leave. Tessa flatly refused. This unit suited her, no matter that it had been Asha's, that most of the furniture, although not new, was Asha's too.

Two weeks later, two weeks of arguments, recriminations and then heavy silence, Asha took a day off work, found a small, barely habitable flat, and moved out. As the weeks passed, she grew thinner and paler and all the joy she'd felt seemed to have seeped out of her. Her job didn't hold the appeal it once had. When her senior assistant took her aside one morning, asking her what was wrong, she knew she had to get her life together.

Later that evening, sitting alone in the shadowy dullness of the dingy, one-roomed unit, she tried to take stock of her life. She missed Tessa, and it seemed their friends were Tessa's friends. Asha had never felt more alone. Her job was a chore rather than the joy it used to be.

Resolutely, she made herself get dressed, walk down to the little street of cafe's around the corner and order a meal. She had to put Tessa and all she'd meant behind her and get on with her life. In fact, she had to snap out of it, sort herself out, be like Tessa and make a fresh start. On the way home she bought a newspaper and pored over the positions vacant columns. She chose a couple of promising jobs, and after an afternoon spent updating her résumé, she sent applications off before she could change her mind.

The interviews she found more than a little harrowing, but surprisingly, although she didn't get the job she'd applied for, she was offered a position that would be available in four months time. It involved research and that was her forte, after all. It would also mean moving back to Brisbane, and she knew that was the change of scene she needed. She accepted the position and handed in her resignation at the library. After working out her month, she packed her things and headed home, feeling better than she had in months.

Her stepmother and sister were thrilled to have her at home

again. Laura West wanted her to move back into the family home, but Asha gently but firmly refused. She'd stay a while and then find another flat. Asha prized her independence. Disappointed, her stepmother agreed she could store her things in the garage until she found the flat she insisted on getting.

She had barely been back a week and had only just started flat-hunting, when a contact from the Genealogical Society rang to ask if she was interested in doing some family history research for a well-known Brisbane woman. The woman had specifically asked for Asha and would Asha care to contact her? Asha agreed, and Mrs. Chaseley rang back almost immediately.

Apparently, she had seen the book Asha had compiled for a friend's family reunion and was impressed. She wanted Asha to research and write a history of her husband's family as a birthday gift for his son, her stepson. The Chaseleys were a well-known pioneering family, Vivienne Chaseley told Asha, and the area where they lived, Chaseley's Hill, was named after her husband's grandfather.

There were papers and photographs that had just come to light when Mrs. Chaseley was clearing out her attic, and she was very excited about them. They had sparked the idea for a similar book on their own family history.

Asha smiled as she recalled meeting the eighty-six-year-old at a café in the city. Vivienne Chaseley was tall and thin, her only deference to her age being the carved walking stick she carried. She'd dressed with care in an obviously expensive suit, stockings, shoes with a sensible heel, and light gloves covered her hands. She wore a pearl necklace that peeped from behind the silk scarf she'd wrapped around her neck and tucked into the collar of her suit coat, and she smelled faintly of roses.

"Miss West," she greeted Asha after the young waitress led her to Asha's table. "How do you do? I'm Vivienne Chaseley."

"Call me Asha, please," Asha said when they'd settled and ordered Devonshire teas.

"Then you must call me Vivienne."

"Oh, I don't know—"

The elderly woman waved the gloves she'd just removed. "Mrs. Chaseley makes me feel like my mother-in-law, and she was quite old." Her bright blue eyes twinkled.

"All right." Asha smiled back. "Vivienne it is."

Their pots of tea and scones with strawberry jam and whipped cream arrived.

"I saw the book you prepared for Betty Peterson, and I thought it was absolutely wonderful."

"Thank you." Asha sipped her tea, pleased by the compliment.

"Betty couldn't stop talking about it at our Ladies' Guild meeting, and when I saw it I could understand why."

"It was an interesting story. Her great-great-grandmother was an extraordinarily resilient woman."

Vivienne nodded. "They certainly knew how to survive in those days."

They discussed some of Asha's other projects, and then Asha asked Vivienne Chaseley what time frame she had in mind.

"You see, it's my stepson's sixtieth birthday at the end of the year, and I wanted something special for him." Vivienne frowned for a moment. "He's always been a good boy." She stopped and gave a soft laugh. "I suppose it's strange to hear me refer to a sixty-year-old as a boy, but when I married his father, Richard was barely four years old." She shook her head. "Such a sad little boy, losing his mother so young."

She sipped her tea genteelly. "Dickie and I were so happy when Richard found dear Sara to marry. They desperately wanted a family, but it didn't happen. In those days, that was back in the Seventies, they didn't have the knowledge about such things that they have today, so Sara and Richard adopted Timothy. And would you believe, ten years later Sara fell pregnant and Megan was born."

"That's great," Asha said with a smile. "They must have been pleased."

"Absolutely. They were over the moon. We all were." Vivienne sobered. "Then four years ago my husband and Sara were driving back from the city. A truck overturned on Kingsford Smith Drive and they were both killed." Her lips trembled and she fought for control. "Not far from home."

"I'm so sorry," Asha said softly, unconsciously taking Vivienne's hand.

"Yes. Although I still miss Dickie every day, I try to carry one. But Richard, he's never quite recovered from losing Sara, and I despair he ever will. Oh, he works and sleeps and eats, but the life seems to have gone out of him. I know he makes an effort for Timothy's and Megan's sakes, but—" She shook her head. "I keep telling myself it will take time."

"I suppose it will," Asha murmured inanely.

Vivienne nodded. "When we found the old box in the attic filled with so much of the Chaseley family history, I was so excited I rang my daughter to tell her. Rosemary, my daughter, lives in Melbourne, and when she was home on a visit a couple of weeks ago, I showed her the book you wrote for Betty Peterson. It was Rosemary who suggested I contact you and ask if you'd be interested in doing something similar for us. Richard's always been interested in history, and I think seeing his own family's presented so nicely will cheer him up. So what do you think, my dear?"

"It sounds interesting," Asha said.

"I know you live down at the coast. Would it be a problem driving up here? Because I wouldn't care to have the papers and photographs leave the house."

"I understand that." Asha felt the same way about her own family heirlooms, and Vivienne Chaseley's sounded priceless. "I've actually moved back to Brisbane. My new job doesn't start for a few months, so I'll be staying with my stepmother while I look for a unit here in Brisbane."

"Now isn't that amazing?" Vivienne smiled. "It's as though it's meant to be, don't you think?"

Asha laughed. "So it would seem."

Vivienne held up her thin hand. "Goodness gracious, I've had a wonderful idea. You could stay at Tyneholme."

"Tyneholme?"

"Our home. It was built by the first Richard Chaseley and named by him after Newcastle-upon-Tyne, where he came from in England. The house is quite large, so there's plenty of room. We rattle around in it these days. You could do your research in my late husband's study and use the bedroom opposite. It has an en suite and it's self-contained. There are cooking facilities, although we'd love to have you share meals with the family, so we could get to know each other. What do you think, my dear?"

"Oh, I don't think I could presume on your hospitality," Asha put in quickly.

"It's almost a private suite, and we'd ensure you had as much privacy as you want. Apart from that, the photographs and family papers would be right on hand."

Asha hesitated.

"I could provide references," Vivienne began, and Asha felt herself smiling.

"Having me, a perfect stranger, living in your house, don't you think it should be me providing references?"

"I think I'm a reasonable judge of character, Asha. I can see you have integrity." She smiled and her blue eyes twinkled. "And, all that aside, you come very highly recommended by the Genealogical Society. I think it would work out perfectly."

"I'd have to pay you for my accommodation," Asha said hesitantly.

"I'm sure we could work that out."

"And I'm not sure how long it would take me to do the work. It could be months."

"I'm sure it will be, my dear. But I see no problem with that."

"What? Didn't you say you wanted to surprise your family? How will you explain my presence?"

Vivienne waved her hand again. "That will be fine. Richard's away at the moment, and anyway, I'll tell them you're working with me on a project connected with the Ladies' Guild. It's not exactly a lie, just a stretched truth. And to tell you the truth, the family gets quite bored when I talk about our Guild's money-raising ventures. They won't dare ask for fear I'll tell them in great detail."

Asha laughed. "Well, it would certainly save me time commuting."

"Good. It's all settled. Now, let's discuss the price."

When Asha told her stepmother and sister about these arrangements, Laura and Michelle were disappointed that Asha wasn't staying with them for as long as they'd hoped she would, but she promised to visit them often.

"Who are these people? Are you sure they're bona fide?" Laura asked worriedly.

"Of course they are, Mum. Stop worrying. I've checked them through the Genealogical Society." Asha was interrupted by the ringing of the telephone. "That'll be Dad. He said he'd call." She went to answer it.

"At least we've got your stuff in the garage to remind us of you," Michelle called after her and Asha chuckled.

After talking to her father for a while, Asha returned to the living room and gave her stepmother a quick hug. "As I was saying, Mum, try not to worry. You know how much I enjoy family research. It'll be a good winding down period for me. I was pretty jaded. With my job and all that," Asha said carefully. "And I feel I need some breathing space before I start the new job. This is ideal to tide me over until I do."

Laura nodded. "Asha, I don't mean to pry, you know I don't, but are you sure there isn't anything you're not telling me?

About why you left your job and your flat?"

Asha felt her muscles tense, and she shot a quick look at her sister. "What could I not be telling you?" she asked as lightly as she could.

"You never talk about . . ." Laura paused slightly. "Boyfriends. Did you have a bad breakup?"

"Mum!" Michelle rolled her eyes. "Give Asha a break!" She turned to her sister. "Boyfriends *can* be the pits though, can't they?"

"It's not that. I just got tired of my job," Asha shrugged, "and I wanted to come home."

Laura looked unconvinced. "What about your flat mate? Will she be able to find someone else to share the unit?"

Asha nodded. She had no doubt Tessa wouldn't let her bed go cold for long. "I believe she already has," she said vaguely.

Laura sighed and went into the kitchen to make dinner, refusing Asha's offer to help.

"Was Mum on the right track?" Michelle asked softly. "About the broken heart?"

"I don't think I want to talk about it, Chelle."

"Oh." Her sister gave her a level look. "How come you never talk about the guys who take you out? I mean, I'm always talking about Danny."

"But that's because Danny's so wonderful," Asha teased, and her sister took her statement on face value.

"I know he is, but I was talking about you, Ash."

"Maybe I just don't date," Asha said, striving for humor.

"Yeah, right! Look at yourself in the mirror. You're decidedly sexy, and you're cute. No guy would *not* notice you. Even Danny said you were hot for an old broad."

"Young Danny is so romantic. And for the record, I don't consider twenty-five to be old either," Asha added dryly.

"Maybe not," her sister conceded. "But seriously, Ash, guys must be falling all over you."

Asha gave an exasperated sigh. "This has nothing to do with a guy. All right?"

"If you say so, then okay." Michelle put her arm around her and gave her a squeeze. "I was just sort of teasing you. Tell me you do sometimes have fun though, Ash. And I don't mean delving in old books and things."

"I like old books and things."

"Sheesh! Give me strength," Michelle appealed. "I've just had a thought! Maybe this old woman you're working for will have a handsome grandson. I'll keep my fingers crossed for you."

Asha laughed. "No sister could do more."

Michelle looked at her suspiciously, but their mother called them before she could comment.

Asha sighed as she looked out at the river. If she simply told her stepmother and her sister she was a lesbian, it would save the periodic cross-examinations, but . . .

It was all so difficult. She had no earthly idea how her stepmother felt about homosexuality, and Asha knew she was a coward for not discussing it with her. She was fairly certain Michelle would be okay with it. Her sister would probably see the fact that Asha was "different" as exceptionally cool. Oh, the joy of being so youthfully tolerant. Maybe she *was* getting old, as Michelle had implied, Asha reflected ironically.

Glancing at her watch, Asha reached for her seat belt. Time to go. Although she was a little nervous, she was also excited about her new project.

She backed carefully out of the car space and rejoined the traffic along Kingsford Smith Drive. At the lights, she turned right and wound her way up the steep hill, Chaseley's Hill, named after the Chaseley family, to the address Vivienne had given her.

Number 78. The gate in the high privacy fence stood open,

and with a sense of nervous anticipation, Asha drove inside, pulling the car to a stop at the entry to the circular driveway so she could sit and stare at the gorgeous old home.

Consisting of three stories, including the attic, the grand old house had been kept in immaculate condition. Stately was the first word that came to Asha's mind. The main part of the house was built of large blocks of sandstone, with wide timber verandas on both floors in deference to the hot climate. On the upper floor the veranda had timber posts with carved wooden brackets, and the railings were of intricate wrought iron, featuring a floral design. The steep, multi-gabled roof was made of weathered red corrugated iron that curved over the upper verandas.

Asha slowly continued around the circular driveway and stopped before the ornate front door. She got out of the car, walked up the age-worn wooden stairs and crossed the wide veranda. Pushing the buzzer, she heard the tinkling melody of the door chimes, the sound muted by the thick door. As she stood waiting she glanced back over the immaculate lawn and gardens to part of what appeared to be a large, double story garage around the corner of the house.

Then the sound of the door suddenly being opened made Asha turn back to the house. She was expecting to see Vivienne Chaseley, but this certainly wasn't the elderly lady. She found herself swallowing, her throat suddenly dry, as she gazed up at the attractive woman standing in the doorway.

CHAPTER TWO

The woman was tall, at least a couple of inches taller than Asha's five feet eight inches, and she appeared even taller as she was standing a step higher than Asha. Asha's gaze rose slowly from her long, well-shaped legs, moving upward. Although the woman was slender, the plain dark blue dress she wore couldn't disguise her compact feminine shape. A gold chain belt encircled her narrow waist above the curve of her hips, and the rounded neckline of her dress rested above the swell of her small breasts.

Asha's eyes moved higher and she paused, her nerve endings suddenly singing, filling her with an acute physical awareness. The woman's hair was fair, pulled severely back into a tidy chignon, and not a stray strand had broken free. She wore no makeup and her skin was a little pale, as though she was a stranger to sunshine.

Asha took in the woman's features. It wasn't a conventionally beautiful face, but there was an arresting quality to her beauty, with a high brow, classical cheekbones, a firm chin and a generous mouth that Asha sensed hadn't done a lot of smiling.

But it was the woman's eyes that held Asha's attention. They were clear and gray, like a stormy, unsettled sky, and they were regarding Asha expressionlessly.

Then the woman raised one fine, imperious eyebrow.

"Can I help you?" she asked, her slightly husky voice neither welcoming nor unwelcoming.

Asha couldn't believe she'd so openly ogled the woman, and she felt the heat of a flush of embarrassment color her cheeks. Who was this woman? Did the Chaseleys employ a housekeeper? Although the woman certainly didn't look or act like a maid.

Asha nervously cleared her throat. "I have an appointment with Vivienne, with Mrs. Vivienne Chaseley. At two o'clock." Asha glanced disconcertedly at her watch. Only five minutes late. "I'm Asha West."

The expressive eyebrows came together in a frown.

Then there was a movement behind the woman and the sound of a cane on the polished parquetry floor. "Asha!"

Asha's attention shifted as Vivienne Chaseley appeared in the foyer. She came forward until she stood beside the tall, thin woman, and, by contrast, the elderly woman's smile was warmly welcoming. Only then did Asha relax just a little.

"Nice to see you again, my dear," Vivienne Chaseley said. "I've been so looking forward to your arrival. And I see you've met Peri."

"Ah, well, we haven't exactly—" Asha shot a quick glance at the still unsmiling Peri. Her expression hadn't warmed all that much. "I've just arrived," Asha finished weakly.

Vivienne laughed. "Then we'd best make the formal introductions. Asha West, meet my sort of adopted granddaughter, Peri Moyland. Peri's grandmother and I have been best friends all our lives." She turned to the woman beside her. "And Peri, this is Asha. Asha—such a pretty name—Asha is going to be working on a secret project for me." She lowered her voice, her eyes sparkling, and put her finger to her lips. "Very hush-hush. So we'll be telling everyone she's here on Ladies' Guild business."

Peri Moyland's eyebrows rose again.

"You know, Asha," Vivienne continued, "Peri may be able to give you some help. She's been staying with me for a while, having a little holiday before she returns to work."

The idea of helping Asha didn't seem to please Vivienne's adopted granddaughter so Asha made herself smile. "That's something we have in common, Ms. Moyland. I'm having a break from work myself. I guess you'd say I'm between jobs, so Vivienne's project came at an opportune time."

A fleeting expression of pain crossed Peri Moyland's face, but she recovered quickly and the mask fell back into place. "I see," she said noncommittally.

"Now, come on in, Asha," Vivienne said brightly. "I suppose your bags are in your car?"

"Bags?" Peri Moyland repeated, obviously taken aback.

"Asha's going to be staying with us. I thought I mentioned that. Oh, dear. It must have slipped my mind. Things do these days. Not to worry. I thought she could use Dickie's study, and I've given her the room opposite. I thought it would be easier for her to work on our little project. I'll get Joe to bring in your things, Asha."

"Oh, I can manage." Asha felt in the pocket of her dress jeans for her car keys. "I travel fairly lightly. Oh, and where shall I park my car?"

Vivienne stepped down onto the veranda, and Peri quickly took her arm to steady her.

"Now, where is that young man?" Vivienne scanned the immaculate gardens.

"I'll get him." Peri Moyland strode along the veranda and disappeared around the corner of the house.

"Tsk! Tsk!" Vivienne made a clucking noise. "Peri has a heart of gold, but she worries too much about me." She lowered her voice again. "She's had a bad trot just lately. Her wretched young man ran off with her best friend. That was a year ago now, and she took the breakup very badly. It even affected her health."

"Oh, dear," Asha said.

"As I said, her grandmother, Grace, is my best friend. We went to school together as young girls, and we've been close all through our married lives." Vivienne sighed. "I know Grace has been very worried about Peri. She's such a self-possessed, private sort of person now, so different from the bubbling child she was."

Then Peri Moyland was returning, striding purposefully along the veranda, followed by a young Adonis.

"Oh, Joe. Good. We need your help," Vivienne said, and Joe's handsome face broke into a grin.

"Sure thing, Mrs. C."

Asha felt her own eyebrows go up in reluctant admiration. Joe was a very handsome young man. She guessed he was a few years younger than she was, his sleeveless top showing his bulging biceps while his short shorts and work boots displayed long, muscular legs. As Asha's gaze ran up over his torso to his rugged face, Joe's eyes met hers and he gave her a cheeky half wink that made her smile reluctantly. Asha's gaze then moved to Peri Moyland and the other woman's lips pursed in disapproval.

Ah! Asha reflected. Was there some history between Peri Moyland and the young Adonis? Asha almost laughed. If Peri only knew. Her toy boy was as safe as the Bank of England with Asha.

"Joe's uncle has been keeping our gardens magnificently for years," Vivienne put in. "And Joe's filling in for him while he's off on sick leave. You might recognize Joe," she continued. "He's something of a celebrity."

Asha looked back at the smiling Joe and frowned. He did look vaguely familiar. "Joe Deneen," she said as recognition dawned. "You play for the Broncos."

Joe inclined his head. "You follow league?"

Asha nodded. "Yes. I've been to a few games, but lately my young sister has been pressuring me to attend some soccer matches. Her boyfriend, Danny Cleary, plays for City."

"I've seen him play. Wouldn't be surprised if he gets an offer from the UK." Joe chuckled. "But don't tell anyone I even know what soccer is, though. They might drum me out of my league team."

Asha laughed too. "It'll be our little secret."

"So. What needs doing, Mrs. C?"

"Could you bring Asha's cases upstairs and then park her car around by the garage?"

"Sure thing."

"I'll just get my notebook." Asha opened the front passenger side door and took out her computer and her small backpack before handing Joe her keys. "There's just one case in the boot."

Joe flashed her another grin. "Consider it done. Nice to meet you, Asha." He went around to the back of the car and lifted the boot lid.

"Come on inside," Vivienne said, "and I'll show you to your room."

Asha followed her into the house, fancying she felt vibes of displeasure from Peri Moyland as she walked in behind her.

The foyer opened into a wide hallway with an equally wide staircase leading upward on the left. Through an open door on the right, Asha glimpsed what appeared to be a formal dining room, with a rich, dark polished wood table and high-backed carved chairs. An ancient intricately carved grandfather clock ticked away by the dining room doorway. Asha exclaimed at the wonderful house and Vivienne smiled, obviously pleased.

They crossed the beautiful parquetry and Vivienne sat herself down on the elevator seat that had been installed on the staircase. "Not that I can't walk up the staircase," she told Asha. "It just takes me forever. My old bones are slower these days. That's the definite downside to being over eighty. I have to live with my limitations."

"You seem to be doing fine to me," Asha said as she started up the stairs beside her.

"No sense complaining. Oh, Peri, are you coming with us, my dear?"

"No, Viv. I need to make a few phone calls. I'll do that in the living room."

Asha watched Peri Moyland walk down the hallway to the right of the stairs. When she'd disappeared, Asha turned back to catch up with Vivienne Chaseley as her chair slid upward. At the top, Asha took her arm to steady her as she stood up.

"Thank you, dear. Now, I've put you down here." She led the way down a short hallway on the left, pausing at the sound of footfalls behind them.

Joe Deneen came toward them carrying Asha's case with ease.

"That was quick, Joe. In there, please." Vivienne indicated the door on the right, and Joe gave Asha her car keys before carrying her case inside.

Vivienne opened the door on the left and Asha followed her into a large comfortable room. Bookcases and cabinets hugged the free wall space and natural light poured in through the two sets of open French doors, one in front of Asha and one to the side.

"This used to be my husband, Dickie's, study." Vivienne indicated the painting on the right wall. "That's us not long after we were married."

Asha walked over for a closer look. She recognized Vivienne's features. She was a pleasant-looking young woman and the same smile lit her face. Her husband was only just taller than she was with a thickset build, and his compelling dark eyes drew Asha's attention. Although his expression was serious, he looked as though he was happy with his life.

"No matter how hard he admonished me, the painter couldn't get me not to smile." Vivienne stood beside Asha, looking up at the portrait. "I was so happy. I felt my aimless life had taken on some purpose. Richard, Dickie's son, needed me, and I needed Dickie and Richard. My life had been so empty for so long. I had the family I'd yearned for, and then we had Nicolas and Rosemary to complete it. Dickie wasn't my first love, nor I his, but we loved each other and had a good life."

"You make an attractive couple."

"Go on with you! Dickie and I were hardly attractive, but we were comfortable." She turned away. "And he loved this room. It's only fitting you write his family's story here."

Asha ran her hand over the rich polished wood desktop. "This is just beautiful."

"It was Dickie's father's desk." Vivienne smiled, her expression reflecting a visit to the past. "That desk was something Dickie treasured." She gave a sigh. "I feel so close to him in this room. And as I said, it seems just fitting somehow that you work in here. And if you want a break to relax a little, I've had Joe put a couple of loungers out on the veranda." Vivienne led Asha through the open French doors.

Asha murmured appreciatively as she gazed at the view.

"The veranda wraps right around the house and the view is three hundred and sixty degrees. Back there are the mountains, and around there we have the river sweeping toward the city center. When my grandson was a boy, he'd chart the ships on the river. Now, come on back in and I'll show you your room."

Asha followed her back through the study and across the hall. Joe had left the door open and they walked inside.

The room opposite the study was large and equally as airy and light. It was furnished with a comfortable looking double bed covered by a handmade quilt, a chest of drawers with an ornate mirror and two equally comfortable lounge chairs. Joe had set her suitcase on a stand. The French doors were open and the curtains moved in the breeze blowing in across the veranda.

"In here is your own en suite"—Vivienne indicated one door—"and in there is a closet for your clothes. Behind those doors you'll find a microwave and a small refrigerator. We've had the house modernized over the years. No point in living in an uncomfortable mausoleum, Dickie used to say. When our son was married we built an extension out over the garage for him and Sara so they could have a little privacy. Richard and his daughter, Megan, still live there. Richard's son, Timothy, has his own flat in the city and he comes and goes. But they're all in Melbourne on a holiday at the moment, so it fits in having you work on our project while they're away. So, what do you think?"

"I think it's wonderful." Asha smiled. "And I can't wait to get started."

Vivienne beamed at her. "I think you should get settled in first. I'll leave you to get unpacked and in, say"—she looked at her small gold wristwatch—"half an hour, we'll have some afternoon tea. Just go back down the stairs and turn left down the hall. The morning room is on the right after the living room. I'll be there." She reached out and patted Asha's arm. "I'm just so excited to have you here."

"And I'm happy and grateful to be here."

With that, Vivienne left Asha alone. She gave a sigh of pleasure as she glanced around the room again. What an incredible house it was. She couldn't wait to describe it all to her stepmother and Michelle. And Vivienne Chaseley was so nice. Asha's thoughts turned to Peri Moyland. Vivienne might be pleased to have her here, but Peri Moyland obviously wasn't. Oh well, she reflected, one out of two wasn't too bad. She bit off a chuckle and began to unpack.

Asha put her clothes in the closet and carried her computer

and her little upright scanner into the study. Then she returned to her room to wash her face and comb her hair. She paused to regard herself in the mirror.

Her short, dark hair, cut in what her stepmother called a shaggy cut, was her best feature, in Asha's opinion. It was thick and kept its style with little attention. And her eyes were brown and unremarkable. A pleasant face, also pretty unremarkable, Asha thought ruefully.

She wrinkled her nose at her reflection and then smiled. A small dimple appeared in her left cheek and she sighed. It might have been nice to have a matching one in the other cheek. Kissed by an angel, her stepmother always told her when she was a little girl.

Asha straightened her cream short-sleeved knit shirt over her jean-clad hips. Not svelte-like but passable, she decided. She ran her hands over her breasts, wishing she were a little less curvaceous. She pushed that out of her mind. Her figure hadn't bothered her until Tessa had drawn her attention to it.

Tessa had been stretched out on the bed one morning critically watching Asha dress for work. "You know, if you got a breast reduction, you'd have the perfect figure," Tessa had said lightly enough.

"A breast reduction?"

"Mmm. You're a bit top heavy, don't you think?"

Asha had cringed, feeling her shoulders instinctively round in an effort to disguise her breast size. "Apart from the cost I don't think I could cope with that," she said defensively. "I'm not that big anyway. Am I?"

Tessa shrugged and gave a slow smile. "Maybe Dolly Parton's record is safe. Just."

Asha straightened her shoulders, reminding herself she wasn't going to give anything Tessa had said any credence. She turned away from the mirror as a blanket of depression began to settle over her. She stepped out onto the veranda and crossed to the railings. On this side of the house leafy suburbs stretched away to the mountains. She moved around the corner, in front of the study, and the riverside suburb was spread out below, skirting the wide Brisbane River. It was a beautiful scene.

Suddenly Asha wished she had someone to share it with. Would Tessa . . . ? Asha stopped her wayward thoughts, knowing Tessa wouldn't take the time to get any pleasure from the peace, the beauty. Asha sighed.

Love, she thought wryly, could lift you up or tear you down. In retrospect, Tessa had gone about her destruction with the subtle chipping away of Asha's self-esteem. And it had almost worked, Asha knew. Sometimes, in low moments, Asha felt Tessa had been more successful than Asha wanted to acknowledge.

She drew herself up to her full height. Tessa was the past. This was now. The new Asha. An Asha who wouldn't let anyone close enough to cause such pain again.

For some reason the serious face of Peri Moyland came into her mind. Vivienne had told her Peri had had a bad relationship breakup, too. Asha's lips twisted. As much as the idea might horrify the disapproving Peri, it would seem Asha and Peri had more in common than Peri knew.

Asha realized she was smiling and admonished herself. Misery apparently did love company.

She took one last look at the view, knowing she would enjoy describing it to her stepmother and sister. She'd even take some photos to show them. She turned away and retraced her steps to her room. It was time to rejoin Vivienne for afternoon tea.

Asha walked down the staircase and turned toward the sunroom where Vivienne said she'd be waiting. As she approached the end of the hall, following the soft murmur of voices, her footfalls silent on the thick carpet, she stopped in surprise as she heard her name mentioned.

"Who is this Asha West anyway?" asked a familiar husky voice.

"I told you, dear. She's a researcher," Vivienne replied. "She's going to do a family history for Richard for his birthday. It's his sixtieth, something of a milestone. I can't believe he's that old. It seems like yesterday he was a little boy."

"Does she have any credentials?"

"Who, dear?" murmured Vivienne.

"Asha West," said Peri Moyland patiently. "Did you check her references?"

"Of course I did. She's highly respected by the Genealogical Society, and I told you I've seen the book she produced for Betty Peterson. It was wonderful. Beautifully done."

"She seems far too young to be a fully qualified genealogist."

"She's twenty-five, only three years younger than you are."

"Oh." Peri paused. "She looks a lot younger. Did she actually show you her qualifications?"

"Yes, she did. And apart from that, Peri, I like her."

"But to have her stay in your home? Isn't that risky when you don't know a thing about her?"

"I don't think so. And I know a lot about her. She's a librarian, you know, as well as a genealogist."

"I just think there are some unscrupulous people around these days and you're far too trusting, Viv."

Asha knew she should make her presence known, but she held back.

"You worry too much, Peri," Vivienne said. "Besides, don't you think I've learned a little bit about human nature in my eighty-plus years? You take my word for it, Asha West is trustworthy. We had a lovely chat before we decided to work together. She told me all about herself."

"I'm sure she did," came the quietly sarcastic comment.

"Peri!" admonished Vivienne Chaseley.

Asha felt herself straighten her spine. She was rapidly deciding she and Peri Moyland had absolutely nothing in common.

"So what did she tell you, Viv? You know anyone can manufacture a background."

"Not Asha," Vivienne said firmly. "This suspicion is so unlike you, Peri." She sighed loudly. "All right. If you insist. She told me her parents are divorced. Her father's a famous cricketer. She has a young sister. And she's spent the last couple of years working down at the Gold Coast."

"A famous cricketer? West. You mean her father is Sean West, the fast bowler?"

"Yes, dear. I believe that's his name. Asha's his daughter. And as far as being a genealogist, Rosemary had heard of her. In fact, it was Rosemary who suggested I contact Asha after I saw Betty's book."

"Rosemary did?"

"She did," Vivienne repeated.

"I suppose if Rosemary checked her out. But I think perhaps your idea that I offer to help her is a good one, Viv. That way I can keep an unbiased eye on her."

Unbiased? Yeah, right! Asha thought.

"I'm telling you, Peri. Asha is ethical. She's intelligent. And she's an attractive young lady."

"Beauty is as beauty does," Peri stated dryly. "As you always told us when we were young."

"I did, didn't I? But, love, it upsets me to see you so cynical. Put Lance and all that behind you. Your ex-fiancé was a poor excuse for a man. Pay no heed to anything he said to you."

"I don't, and I wasn't talking about Lance and the past," Peri said even more coolly. "I was referring to Asha West."

"She's a nice young woman. I must find out if she's single. If she hasn't got a boyfriend at the moment, maybe we should introduce her to your brother. It's time Jackson settled down."

"Viv! You're incorrigible," Peri said with an exasperated laugh. "And Jack's more than capable of finding his own partner."

"I know. I was just teasing you. And I was trying to make my

29

point that Asha's a nice young woman."

"Yes, well, we'll see. But I still intend to keep an eye on Ms. West."

Asha pursed her lips as she heard Vivienne Chaseley's spontaneous chuckle. Asha didn't need watching. Not by Peri Moyland. Without warning, a spiral of awareness took hold of her and she stiffened.

"I'm sure you will, Peri," Vivienne said lightly. "You're nothing if not tenacious. You were even as a child. Remember when Jack was trying to teach you to ride a bicycle? You'd fall off and get right back on."

Peri gave a soft laugh and the sound played over Asha, making her feel hot and then cold. "That probably had more to do with downright stubbornness."

"It's so nice to see you smile again, Peri," Vivienne said softly.

"I've told you I'm fine, Viv." Peri's husky voice dropped lower. "I just have to, I don't know, perhaps find my new path."

"I know, my dear. You know, if I were a violent person I could just slap that ex-fiancé of yours and your friend Janet quite senseless."

"Ex-friend," said Peri flatly. "And let's say they were both senseless to begin with."

Vivienne laughed again. "I don't think you'd find a soul to disagree with you on that score."

There was a moment of silence, and Asha could hear the faint sound of movement coming from what must be the kitchen.

"I wouldn't have believed it of Janet," Vivienne said. "She seemed so—"

"Sensible?" Peri put in, emphasizing each syllable, and Vivienne chuckled again.

"You have a wonderful sense of humor, my dear. And I'm so pleased to see it again. You've been so serious these past months." There was the sound of movement. "I wonder if Asha's lost her way. Maybe you should go and find her, Peri."

Asha drew a quick, steadying breath and continued along the hallway. As she stepped into the doorway, she made herself smile.

"Asha! There you are! Peri was just coming to look for you. Come on in, my dear."

Peri Moyland stood across from Vivienne, leaning on the high back of another of the antique chairs.

"Sorry I'm late," Asha said evenly. "I could barely draw myself away from the fantastic view upstairs." She focused on Mrs. Chaseley, making sure she didn't make eye contact with Peri Moyland, in case she gave away her antipathy toward the woman.

Vivienne Chaseley beamed at Asha. "That view is wonderful, isn't it? I never tire of it." She indicated the comfortable-looking chair opposite her. "Now, make yourself comfortable, dear. Margo's just delivered the tea." She turned to Peri. "Come and sit down, too, Peri. Would you like to do the honors and pour?"

Peri Moyland walked around and sat in the third chair pulled up around the coffee table. As she lifted the antique silver teapot, Asha glanced around at the enchanting room. Vertical boarding covered the lower half of the walls. A silky oak dado separated it from the rest of the plastered walls, while the cornices and ceiling rose were beautifully patterned. She turned back to Vivienne and exclaimed over the beautifully furnished room.

"All family pieces," Vivienne said, "but we like to use them. It's our home, after all, and there's no point in turning the place into a museum."

"Viv tells me you've been living on the Gold Coast, Ms. West," Peri Moyland said, handing Asha an eggshell-thin china cup and saucer.

"Thank you." Asha took it, as carefully as Peri was obviously being to ensure their fingers didn't touch. "And yes. I've been living down there for a couple of years."

"And you worked in a library?"

Asha laughed quietly to herself. It seemed the distrustful Peri

Moyland was going to conduct her own third degree. "Yes again. I was in charge of one of the Gold Coast City Council's branch libraries."

"Did you enjoy library work?" Peri sipped her tea.

"Very much." Asha made herself smile at the other woman. "Besides a large retiree population, we had a number of schools nearby, which meant lots of young families as well. So the library was used by very diverse groups of people."

"Libraries are so technical these days," said Vivienne, "what with their computers and everything. I had to get the young staff members to help me out for a while until I got the hang of it. But I still yearn for the old card catalogue and the more personal face-to-face service."

"I think a lot of the members of my library felt the same way. I know my stepmother says as much every time she visits her library."

"So why did you leave your job there?" Peri Moyland asked, not to be deterred.

"Now, Peri," Vivienne admonished lightly. "I told you Asha just wanted a change of scene."

Asha turned to look at Peri Moyland and she levelly held her gaze. "That's right. I felt I needed a change of scene."

Peri raised her eyebrow, and Asha read skepticism in every line of her body. Asha mentally drew herself up to her full height. She saw no need to tell Peri she already had a job to go to.

"Actually, I'd wanted to come back home for a while," she found herself adding. "I always planned to anyway, after I'd gained a few years experience. Then I felt it was time to move on." Asha looked down at the cup in her hands. Breaking up with Tessa had only precipitated her move. "So I decided to come back to Brisbane." She raised her eyes and gave a little shrug. "Now I guess you could say I'm taking a sabbatical."

Peri set her own cup and saucer on the coffee table. "So you've given up your job before you found another one. That's taking something of a chance, isn't it, in today's employment climate?"

Asha shrugged again and smiled at Vivienne. "Well, I have this job at the moment, thanks to Vivienne. And afterward, I'm sure something will come up. What about yourself, Ms. Moyland? What do you do?" Asha put the ball firmly back in Peri's court, and again Peri's eyebrow rose.

"I'm taking a little sabbatical myself," she said carefully.

Vivienne reached over and patted Peri's knee. "Peri owns a very successful temp agency."

"Oh." Asha took a sip of her tea. "As in, you find positions for office staff?"

"Yes. Mainly. But we fill other positions as well."

Asha could see Peri wasn't keen on sharing information with her. That was mutual.

"I know!" Vivienne's eyes crinkled with amusement, and she winked conspiratorially at Asha. "Maybe you could find a job for Asha, Peri."

Asha knew Vivienne was aware she had a new position to go to, and she tried to prevent a chuckle escaping. She somehow thought Peri Moyland wouldn't find Vivienne's suggestion, even though it was made in jest, at all palatable. In fact, something along the lines of *Not bloody likely!* was probably hovering on Peri's tongue. Asha slid a glance at her.

Peri's expression was difficult to read. Her gaze seemed to have settled on Asha's lips, and all at once, Asha drew a shallow, slightly flustered breath. Suddenly, the politely formal equilibrium of the air between them changed almost imperceptibly and was replaced by a totally different tension.

Asha felt a dull flush color her cheeks, and she knew she should look away. But she couldn't seem to.

Then Peri's startled eyes met Asha's, and Asha watched with fascination as a myriad of emotions fluttered across her face, settling so fleetingly Asha was hard-pressed to interpret them. Just as suddenly that same icy barrier fell into place and the familiar cool, withdrawn Peri Moyland stared back at Asha. Asha struggled with a rush of bewilderment. Had she simply imagined that ephemeral moment? But no, why would she have?

"But not until she's finished my project," Vivienne continued, and Asha and Peri both looked at her in surprise. "Getting Asha another job," she elaborated. "Not until she finishes my research."

"Oh." Peri absently passed Asha a plate of delicious petit fours. "And how long will that take you, Ms. West?"

"Asha. Please." Asha took a tiny fruit tart. "I won't know until I see what information Vivienne already has. People can spend a lifetime researching their family history," she said, and watched with satisfaction as Peri's eyes widened a little. "So I guess I could be here for oh, what, twenty years or so, Vivienne?"

Her eyes twinkled again, as she too watched Peri's expression.

This time Asha couldn't prevent herself from chuckling. She took pity on the so-serious Peri Moyland. "It depends on how far back you want to go and how easily researchable your family is. It shouldn't take me all that long to do what Vivienne has in mind, I don't think, as she just wants to concentrate on the Chaseleys since they arrived in Australia. According to Vivienne she's found a lot of family birth, marriage and death certificates, which will help immensely."

"Ah. The chest we found in the attic." Peri nodded and gave Vivienne a quick smile. "Viv was very excited about that."

"And rightly so. Every family historian would kill for such a collection."

"So how do you go about writing such a book?"

If Asha hadn't known better, she would have thought Peri Moyland was genuinely interested. "Basically, I weave the personal family history in with the history of the times." Asha forgot Peri's suspicions as she warmed to a subject she found so fascinating. "For instance, my mother's family immigrated to

Australia and settled in Gympie, north of Brisbane, in the late 1860s, in time for the discovery of gold and the subsequent gold rush, so my family's history paralleled the history of those times. It's absolutely mind-blowing to put people, people who came before me, into that scenario. My ancestors played their small part in the history of those days."

"Were they gold miners?" Peri asked, her eyes watching Asha's face.

"Two of the boys tried their hands at mining, not all that successfully, but the family were farmers. Descendants of the original family still are."

"And all our ancestors played their small part in history, too," Vivienne said. "In fact, we today are doing the same."

"Mmm." Peri murmured dubiously and Vivienne tut-tutted.

"I think we're going to have to work hard to convince our skeptical Peri, don't you think, Asha?" she said, and Asha just smiled.

For the next couple of days Asha worked with Vivienne Chaseley sorting out the contents of the family chest from the attic. It was certainly a treasure trove of official certificates, a few letters and lots of old photographs. In the evenings she dined with Vivienne and Peri, the meal prepared and served by Joe Deneen's Aunt Margo. Peri continued to remain aloof, and Asha told herself that was fine by her. The more grating Peri Moyland was, the easier it would be for Asha to convince herself the spark of awareness she felt toward her was the acknowledgment that Peri was simply a very attractive woman, and nothing more.

One morning Asha was working in the study doing some preparatory work on Vivienne's book when there was a light tap on the open door. She looked up to see Peri standing in the doorway. She wore tailored dark slacks and a very pale pink, long-sleeved, cotton knit shirt. Her fair hair was neatly coiled on her head.

"Hi!" Asha said, struggling with that same disconcerting frisson of awareness Peri seemed to stir inside her. Being attracted to a straight woman had Asha faltering in uncustomary confusion. Yet if Peri hadn't been straight, Asha knew she could have . . . Could have what? Made a move on her? Asked her out? But Peri had been engaged to be married, and what could be straighter than that? She was definitely heterosexuality personified.

"Vivienne suggested I might be able to help," Peri said without conviction.

"Actually, I'm doing quite well," Asha told her. "There's so much information already collected"—she indicated the piles of birth, death and marriage certificates—"it makes my job so much easier."

Peri reluctantly stepped into the study and sank down in the chair opposite Asha.

"That's all the stuff from the old chest Viv and I found in the attic?"

"Yes. Apparently someone knew how valuable they'd be and kept them safe." Asha smiled. "I know I would have given my eyeteeth to uncover such a box of treasure relating to my family."

"I suppose you need a lot of information before you start the book." Peri was perched on the chair, not exactly at ease.

"The more information I have the easier it is. Vivienne has all the relevant certificates, saving me lots of time researching, and of course, there're all these wonderful photographs I'm in the process of sorting out." Asha warmed to her subject. "There are photos of Richard Chaseley and his wife and children and their children. And there are even photos with this house in the background, showing how it's evolved over the years. For example, this one"—she indicated a very old photograph—"has written on the back, 'Richard's cottage before building began.' I suspect it may be the original building where Tyneholme now stands. It's very exciting."

"But it's so faded," Peri said as she leaned forward to look at the photograph Asha indicated.

"Not so badly that I can't fix it up a little. I have a couple of amazing computer programs to help me restore old photographs like this one. Just wait till you see the finished product." Asha smiled and Peri held her gaze for long moments before she looked quickly away.

"Viv seems to have been very impressed by the book you did for her friend Betty Peterson," she said after a moment

Asha wondered derisively how hard it was for the reserved Peri to voice what was, for her, a positive comment. Then she told herself she was being ungracious. She simply had to win this disapproving woman over. Although why she felt compelled to do so she couldn't, or wouldn't, have said.

"Well," Asha began enthusiastically, "the book I did for the Biddle Reunion, that's Betty's family, was such an interesting project. Betty's English great-great-grandmother Eliza was the daughter of a very well-to-do landowning family. She fell in love with James, a gardener working on her father's estate. Of course, Eliza's father forbade her to see him, so they eloped and escaped to London.

"Amazingly, her father didn't catch up with them, and they returned to the small village where James was born and got married before setting sail for Australia. Their first child was born on the ship during the voyage." Asha stopped, embarrassed. "Sorry. I get a little carried away when I get onto my research projects."

"No. Please go on. It's interesting," Peri said, and Asha decided to take what she said at face value.

"Can you imagine anything worse than being cooped up on a small, small by our standards that is, on a small sailing ship, let alone being pregnant as well?" Asha shook her head. "They were incredible women."

"How long was the voyage?" Peri asked.

"Usually three months or more. The Biddles arrived in

Brisbane in the eighteen sixties. Queensland was only proclaimed a separate colony in late eighteen fifty-nine, so it must have been very 'last frontier'. James eventually acquired a considerable amount of property in the Brisbane Valley. Eliza worked alongside him and had ten children, seven surviving to adulthood."

"Her life out here in the colonies must have been so different from the life she'd been used to if she came from a wealthy family," Peri reflected.

"Ah, the things we women do for love." Asha laughed and then sobered, hoping she hadn't stirred up painful memories for Peri. "Betty has a portrait of James and Eliza," she went on hurriedly, "taken when they were in their mid-thirties, and it's easy to see why James swept Eliza off her feet. He was a very handsome man."

Peri made no comment, that closed expression on her face again. She picked up a glass paperweight from the top of the wide desk, turned it over in her fingers, then set it down again.

"Actually, not a lot of families have as many photos as Vivienne has," Asha put in.

"I suppose not. Viv tells me your father is the famous cricketer, Sean West. He's considered by some to be Australia's best fast bowler, isn't he?"

"Yes," Asha replied carefully. "That's right."

"It must have been," Peri paused, "interesting growing up having a famous parent."

"It was. Sort of." Asha was reticent talking about her father. Her stepmother had instilled in her right from the start that it wasn't wise to talk too freely about their family. Not that there was the pressure from reporters on them when Asha was small, but by the time Michelle was born, her mother had often had to fend off zealous media people. That was one thing she didn't envy her father and Karen having to deal with. For Sean West and his new family it was a day-to-day battle. "I was pretty young when Dad was playing for Australia, and in those days families of sports personalities were kept pretty much in the background. I remember he was away a lot."

"Was that difficult?"

Asha shrugged. "My stepmother and I, well"—Asha smiled—"I had her undivided attention. What more could a child want? In fact, I remember being very put out when Dad came home and demanded some of my stepmother's time, spoilt little brat that I was."

"Viv said your parents divorced. Do you think that was because of his career in the public eye?"

Asha hesitated and Peri looked a little concerned. "I'm sorry. I didn't mean to be rude," she said quickly.

"It's okay. As long as you're not a newshound in disguise. Even now I'm usually loath to talk about Dad, just in case."

"No, I'm not. Scout's honor. Just interested," Peri said, and Asha saw her flush a little. "I—My brother Jack has always been mad keen on cricket, and under some sufferance in the beginning, I watched cricket matches with him. Then I found myself enjoying the game, especially the One-Day matches. Just recently I watched a cricket special that included highlights of your father's career. He was pretty impressive, and I know your father is one of Jack's heroes."

"He is to a lot of cricket fans. I guess I didn't realize that until I grew up." Asha shrugged again. "As to why my parents divorced, I suppose Dad was never really there. In the beginning he was away playing cricket, and when he stopped playing he was concentrating on building up his business."

"He's been very successful. He remarried, didn't he? Do you see much of him?"

"Every so often. Chelle, that's my sister, Michelle, and I go over for dinner now and then. I get on fairly well with Karen, his new wife. She's more . . . I suppose she's the sort of wife my father should have had. Mum just wanted a quiet life. She hated the socializing Dad wanted her to do. Karen seems to thrive on it. Although when she has time with the children, I don't know."

"Your father has a second family?" Peri asked and Asha laughed.

"You could say that. And I take it you haven't seen this month's *Australian Women's Weekly*?"

"No." Peri shook her head.

"There's a story coinciding with the opening of another of Dad's sports stores and the birth of the new baby. Their fifth."

"They have five children?"

"Oh, yes. All boys. Andrew, the eldest, is eight."

Peri raised her eyebrows and Asha grinned.

"Chelle calls them the alphabet kids. Let's see. There's Andrew, Brendan, Christopher, Devin and the baby's Ethan. She's even choosing names for the next one. I think Frederick and Fritz were the last possibilities. She also thinks Dad's trying for his own cricket team."

Peri laughed softly and the sound played over Asha's skin, the feeling confusing and thoroughly disconcerting her. This attraction Asha had to Peri Moyland, no matter that she kept telling herself she didn't even like her, was getting out of hand.

She also tried to convince herself again that it was purely physical, because Peri was so attractive. Along with that thought came the recognition that she was fairly susceptible at the moment. Her self-esteem had taken a beating when she'd realized that Tessa was tired of her. Having recently broken up with Tessa, Asha had to concede she could be vulnerable. And she could understand that Peri Moyland, after suffering a broken engagement, was probably in the very same position.

Still, by any standards, straight or gay, Peri Moyland was attractive in a cool, come-melt-my-ice sort of way. Tall, slim, great figure, self-assured, intelligent. Not to mention a strong, beautiful face.

Asha wondered about Peri's ex-fiancé. What sort of man

would Peri choose? And why would a man leave her for another woman? It was unbelievable. But regardless, Asha told herself, this purely physical attraction she felt to Peri wasn't something Asha wanted or needed at this moment in time. Especially an attraction to an obviously oh-so-straight woman. There would be no future there.

"And your mother," Peri said. "How does she feel about your father's new family?"

Pulling her thoughts into some semblance of order, Asha made herself concentrate on Peri's conversation. "She seems okay. She once told me she should never have married anyone, especially someone like my father." Asha grimaced. "He's very outgoing, the life of the party. Mum's exactly the opposite."

"Do you—? Are you like your father?"

Asha couldn't hold back her laugh. "Hardly. The strange thing is I'm more like Mum. My stepmother, that is. I don't remember much about my real mother. She died when I was four years old."

"Oh. I'm sorry."

Asha nodded. "But my stepmother has been wonderful to me. I love her dearly. What about your parents?"

"Dad retired last year and they, Mum and Dad, have joined the Gray Nomads. They're touring Australia in a motor home. Last we heard they were in Broome, having a wonderful time. My grandmother Grace is spending a few months with them, too."

"And do you have a large family?"

"Just three of us. I have two older brothers, both lawyers. David's in Sydney at the moment, married with two kids. Jack's here in Brisbane. He's something of a best friend as well as a brother." A gentle, affectionate smile lit her face.

That same rush of temptation rippled through Asha and settled in the pit of her stomach. She had the sudden yearning for that smile to be for her. Asha's gaze settled on the soft curve of

41

Peri's mouth, and her breath caught in her throat. She desperately wanted to feel its softness, the sweetness within.

"My young sister is like that," Asha said, forcing those distracting thoughts aside.

"Michelle?"

"Yes." Asha nodded. "She's the family beauty. She's really bright, kind-hearted and so self-confident for her age she blows me away." Asha took her wallet out of the drawer and flipped it open to the photographs she had inside. She handed it to Peri. "That's Michelle there."

"She looks familiar, so she must be a little like you," Peri said, examining the photo. "How old is she?"

"She's seventeen, just started university, plans on getting her degree and then marrying her soccer-playing boyfriend, Danny." Asha smiled. "She'll probably succeed at all of the above."

"So she has her life all mapped out for her?" Peri remarked without expression as she handed the wallet back to Asha.

Asha hesitated, sensing the change in Peri's tone. Was she comparing her own plans for her life and how those plans had changed? "So it would seem."

Peri seemed to gather herself. "What about you? Have you mapped out your life, too? Job? Marriage?"

Asha shook her head, setting her wallet on the desk. "Not really. I wasn't sure what I wanted to do. I sort of slotted into librarianship. I mean, I didn't see being a librarian as my lifelong goal, but I guess you could say I've found my niche. And this"— Asha indicated the piles of certificates—"my research, is just the icing on the cake for me. I love it." Asha leaned forward, her elbows on the desk, chin resting on her hand. "So how did you come to own a temp agency?"

"Something similar to you," Peri said. "It just kind of happened. After I finished my business degree I wanted to take a break to decide what I wanted to do with my qualifications. I took a job with the Mitchell Agency and found myself really

42

enjoying it. So when the owner decided to retire, I bought the business. That was three years ago."

"So you own the agency? Now, that's impressive."

"Well, the bank and I own it." Peri gave a quick smile. "Although I, too, can't say I saw myself doing this when I was younger."

"All those many years ago," Asha teased and was rewarded with one of Peri Moyland's rare husky laughs.

"I'm twenty-eight, and please don't say I don't look it, because at the moment I know I do. Every year of it."

"I cannot tell a lie." Asha grinned. "You really don't look your age. I thought you were more my age."

Peri raised an eyebrow.

"I'm twenty-five. Nearly twenty-six."

Peri regarded Asha. "You look about eighteen," she said softly, and her clear gray eyes met Asha's.

CHAPTER THREE

They regarded each other for immeasurable moments, and Asha was the first to look away. She coughed slightly to cover the way her breath caught in her throat. When she looked up, Peri was again studying the glass paperweight.

Asha tried for a light laugh. "So when I'm forty I should get away with early thirties? I'll live in hope about that."

Peri also laughed softly and then an uncomfortable silence fell between them. As Asha sought a comment that might lighten the heavy tension that began to grow, a noise in the doorway had Asha looking up and Peri turning around.

"Oh, Vivienne. Hi!" Asha said brightly as Vivienne entered the study.

"So how are you two girls getting along with my project?"

Peri gave a slight wry grin. "Asha's getting along fine, without my help it seems." She stood up. "All I'm doing is holding her up."

Asha started to protest, but Peri help up her hand.

"I have to go anyway. I have a few things to catch up on at work so I'll leave you both to get on with it."

"You seem to be doing a lot of work lately," Vivienne said with a frown of concern. "Are you sure you're not overdoing it? You know the doctor said—"

"I'm sure I'm not, Viv. And I have to get back into it sooner rather than later. Oh, and don't forget," Peri paused as she went to leave, "I'm having dinner with Jack tonight. He's picking me up after work. We thought we'd share a meal, so I won't be home for dinner." She glanced at Asha. "I enjoyed chatting," she said quickly, and then she was gone.

Vivienne Chaseley sat slowly in the chair Peri had vacated. "My old bones are tired this morning."

"I'm more than happy to work on this alone if you want to rest," Asha said quickly.

"No. I wouldn't miss it for the world. It's far too interesting." She smiled conspiratorially. "And I knew Peri would be intrigued as well if she got involved."

Asha wasn't sure she'd stretch it that far, but Peri's obvious mistrust had abated somewhat.

"Although I'm still concerned that Peri might be returning to work too soon, I'm so pleased she's going out with Jack. He'll cheer her up. She needs to get out and start mixing with people again. And Jack's such a tonic, such fun to have around. I must introduce you to him. I'm sure you'll like him."

Asha murmured noncommittally and Vivienne sighed.

"I always thought Lance, that's Peri's ex-fiancé, was overly possessive of Peri," she said sadly. "You know, he wanted her to drop all her friends and only mix with his circle. I don't understand why some men feel the need to do that, do you? Some bizarre form of control, I suppose."

Asha knew she shouldn't be discussing Peri behind her back,

but curiosity overcame her reticence. "How long were they engaged?" she asked.

"Oh, about a year or so. But they knew each other for a while before that. In the beginning, Grace and I liked Lance, but oh, I don't know, it wasn't long before we decided we had reservations about him. Too smooth, if you know what I mean."

Asha nodded.

"He was a good-looking man, I'll give him that," Vivienne went on. "And he came from a wealthy and well-known family." She shook her head. "I know I shouldn't gossip," she said, voicing Asha's thoughts, "but I don't do it maliciously. I just love people. They're so interesting, aren't they?"

Asha laughed. "Some of them. Others not so much."

"Now! Now!" Vivienne wagged her finger. "As I'm always telling Peri, you shouldn't be cynical at your age. Cynicism is supposed to be reserved for those of us who have been regarding the world about us for a lot longer. To stay un-cynical at my age is a definite achievement."

"I can't argue with that," Asha said.

"So, what about you, dear?"

"Oh, I guess I'm just intermittently cynical."

Vivienne chuckled. "No, I mean boyfriends. Do you have a young man?"

"Oh. No. I—" Asha flushed. "No, I don't," she finished, not sure her relationship with Vivienne Chaseley warranted a 'tell all.' As much as Asha admired her, she had no way of knowing how Vivienne would feel if Asha admitted she preferred women.

Vivienne frowned. "You look so sad, my dear. Now, don't tell me you've had a bad experience like Peri," she said, concerned.

"Not exactly," Asha replied vaguely. "But something like that."

"Oh, my dear. I'm so sorry. When was this?"

"Last year. But anyway, it's over and done with." Asha gave a derogatory half smile. "Time to move on, as they say."

Vivienne nodded sympathetically. "That's right. It doesn't pay to dwell on it, which was exactly what I told Peri. But she, I don't know, she's just not back to her old self."

Would Peri ever be? Asha wondered, thinking of the cool, in-command-of-herself Peri Moyland. And knowing how devastated she herself had been when her relationship with Tessa failed, Asha could empathize with Peri. "Maybe Peri just needs more time to put it all behind her," Asha suggested softly.

"I suppose so." Vivienne nodded and sighed. "And betrayal of any kind is the unkindest cut of all. It's so deeply wounding."

Thoughts of Tessa surfaced in Asha's mind, and a wave of sadness washed over her.

"Especially when you love someone," Vivienne said.

"Even if love gets such bad press these days?"

"Oh, I believe in true love," Vivienne said with conviction. "Everyone should experience true love at least once in their life. Even if it doesn't work out."

"You don't think we have just one soul mate then?" Asha asked. "That we can love more than once?"

Vivienne shrugged. "There are so many different kinds of love. Your first love, of course, is special, but sometimes . . ." She sighed again. "My husband Dickie was a wonderful man, and as I said, we were comfortable together." She looked across at the portrait on the wall. "Dickie and I were always friends and we learned to love each other.

"You see, when we were young we were part of a group of friends. There was my best friend, Grace." She looked at Asha and explained. "That's Peri's grandmother. And there was Grace's future husband Joe Moyland, and Grace's bother, Bobby, and I, and Dickie and his first wife, Vera. We did everything together. Then the Second World War broke out, and all our lives were changed forever.

"All the young men went off to fight in various corners of the world. Dickie and Bobby both came home wounded. Dickie had shrapnel in his leg until the day he died. He came home first, and not long after he returned, Dickie and Vera became engaged. Bobby also had shrapnel wounds that became infected, so he came home, too, in time for Dickie and Vera's wedding." Her expression softened at the memory. "It was a lovely wedding."

"You were there?" Asha asked, surprised.

"Oh, yes." Vivienne smiled. "Bobby was Dickie's best man, and I was Vera's bridesmaid. That night Bobby danced me onto the veranda and asked me to marry him." Her expression softened. "I was so in love with Bobby. He was so handsome, so dashing. And such fun to be with.

"Then Dickie and Bobby had orders to report back for duty. They went to New Guinea, and Bobby was one of the brave boys who were lost on the Kokoda Trail. He died in Dickie's arms, and I don't think Dickie ever got over it. So many young lives lost." She took out a lace-edged handkerchief and dabbed her eyes. "War is horrific enough when considered as a whole, but when you bring it down to the loss of one fine young man who had his life before him, and who was so loved by his family and friends, then it's unconscionable. Every single young person lost in war leaves behind a toll of pain and lives torn apart.

"When Bobby was killed I lost my fiancé, but Bobby's mother lost her son just as she'd lost her husband, Bobby's father, in the Great War, and Grace lost her twin brother. It was a dark time for us all. For years, I just went on living, feeling as though part of me had died with Bobby. I needed to get away, so I went down to Sydney with my mother and stayed there. I couldn't seem to face the places I'd been with Bobby. My mother and I came back to Brisbane a year or so after Dickie's wife, Vera, died. I could see a matching loss in Dickie and, I guess we each sought comfort in someone who could empathize. We'd both lost our first loves, but we built a good life together. We were friends and came to genuinely love each other. We had Dickie's son, Richard, and then Nicolas and Rosemary came along." Vivienne shrugged again. "Life went on. And it was a good life."

"I think there's a photo here." Asha carefully moved some of the old photographs and picked out one of a handsome young man, looking little more than a boy, in his army uniform. She realized with a shock that he bore a strong resemblance to Peri. "He looks—"

"Like Peri's brother Jack," Vivienne finished and smiled sadly. "And Peri and Jack are very much alike. They take after their grandmother, Grace. Grace and Bobby were twins, born after their father was killed in World War One."

Asha turned the photo over, and on the back someone had written, "Robert George Gaines 1917–1942." She passed it to Vivienne and Vivienne nodded.

"That's dear Bobby. Taken before he left for Europe. Such a waste."

"He is really handsome," Asha said inanely, knowing nothing she said could make up for Vivienne's loss.

"But let's not wallow anymore." As Vivienne put the sepia photo on the desk, she accidentally knocked Asha's wallet to the floor. Asha stood up and retrieved it and Vivienne apologized.

"That's okay," Asha said. "I shouldn't have left it there. I was showing Peri a photograph of my young sister." She held it out for Vivienne to see.

Vivienne took the wallet and turned slightly, holding it to the light, studying the smallish photograph. She stilled, and her other hand fluttered to her throat.

Asha frowned. "It's Michelle. She's my half sister actually. And the other photo is of my stepmother."

Vivienne seemed to gather herself as she handed the wallet back to Asha. "Your sister's a very attractive young woman," she said.

Asha looked at the photograph. "Yes. She's so like my stepmother, and she has a great personality."

"You obviously have a very nice family," Vivienne said as Asha sat down again, then returned her wallet to the drawer. "How are you progressing?" Vivienne indicated the work on the desk in front of Asha.

"Actually, I've just found some papers referring to Richard's passage out of Australia in eighteen seventy," Asha said, showing Vivienne a copy of some paperwork. "It seems his younger brother came out here with him."

"Good gracious. I'd forgotten about that. Georgie Chaseley. We called him Uncle Georgie. That's how Grace's family and the Chaseleys became involved. Georgie married Bobby's widowed grandmother, Margaret Gaines. Margaret's son, Robert, was Bobby and Grace's father. And as I said, Grace is Peri's grandmother. It's such a pity Grace is away with Peri's parents just now, or you could have met her, too." Vivienne chuckled. "A little complicated, isn't it? Our lives, our families, the Chaseleys and the Moylands, are all intertwined."

"So I'm finding out." Asha grinned. "I'm not surprised, though. It happened fairly often in those days. My mother's great-grandparents lived in Victoria Street, Kelvin Grove, and they had six daughters who married young men living in Victoria and nearby streets. Then one of their granddaughters married the grandson of another family living in Victoria Street. So I consider Victoria Street to be the living center of that branch of my family."

Asha then shifted the subject back to the Chaseley family in general, encouraging Vivienne to reminisce while Asha took notes.

Asha had just walked down the stairs to join Vivienne for dinner when the front door opened. She stopped and turned as Peri entered, followed by a tall, fair-haired man.

The man said something Asha didn't catch, and Peri laughed, the unexpected sound of her laughter making Asha still. The light in the foyer shone on Peri's face, and Asha could only stare at her. Peri's face glowed with amusement, making her look much younger than her twenty-eight years. She looked carefree, vibrant and so very attractive she took Asha's breath away.

"If you don't stop making me laugh, I'll be far too exhausted to go out to dinner with you," Peri warned, giving the man a playful shove.

"Can't remember any sad stories, so you're stuck with the plain old happy me," replied the man.

Asha drew her gaze from Peri's face to look at her companion. He was slightly taller than Peri, but the resemblance between the two was striking. This would have to be Peri's brother.

"Is that you, Jackson?" Vivienne called from the dining room, and Jack Moyland's smile widened.

"The one and only, Viv," he called back. As he looked across the foyer he noticed Asha standing there.

Peri saw Asha at the same time as her brother did, but unlike her brother, Peri's smile faded.

"Hello there," Jack said easily.

"Oh. Asha. Hello. I didn't see you there," Peri said and moved forward with her brother, her expression closed. "This is my brother, Jack. Jack, meet Asha West." She made the introductions with obvious reluctance.

Jack Moyland glanced sideways at his sister before shaking Asha's hand. "You can't be the genealogist Peri told me about. I had a picture of gray hair, a bun, glasses and an *Olde Worlde* air."

A bubbly laugh escaped from Asha. "Sorry to disappoint you."

"Oh, you are not disappointing, believe me. Quite the contrary." Jack grinned wickedly. "I have the burning need to have my family history researched immediately."

Asha laughed with him while Peri managed a chilly smile.

"Come on through to the dining room." Vivienne's voice had them moving down the hallway. "Good. I see you've met Asha,"

Vivienne said after Jack had kissed her on the cheek. "Did Peri tell you Jack's a lawyer?" she asked Asha, and Jack held up his hands in mock surrender.

"And none of those disparaging lawyer jokes apply to me, I assure you."

Asha decided she liked Peri's brother. "So lawyers just get bad press, do they?"

"Oh, they do. They surely do."

"Just like all genealogists are gray-haired and wear glasses?"

Jack chuckled. "Touché. Shall we agree we're both exceptions to the rules?"

"It's a deal." Asha glanced at Peri, and it was obvious she wasn't as amused as her brother.

Peri checked her watch. "It's getting late, Jack. Shouldn't we be going?"

"I thought you wanted to change," remarked her brother. "Although why you want to beats me. You look perfectly fine as you are."

Asha's gaze automatically ran over Peri, taking in her neat, dark, figure-hugging suit, her long legs, her high heels, and she decided she totally agreed with Jack. Peri looked perfectly stunning as she was.

Peri slid a glance at Asha and flushed. "Oh. Yes. I do want to change. I won't be long." She left them, and Asha looked back to find Jack Moyland's eyes studying her, and she felt her face grow warm.

"I'm so pleased you're taking Peri to dinner, Jack." Vivienne broke in on Asha's sudden confusion. "It does her good to get out. You'll have to introduce her to some of your single young friends."

Jack looked askance and held up his hands. "No way, Viv. I don't want to be responsible again. I was the one who introduced her to Lance, remember? So my track record as a matchmaker is pretty ordinary."

"Now, that can't be helped. No one knew how badly Lance was going to behave." Vivienne patted his arm. "But Peri does need to get out more, and I won't worry about her if she's with you."

Jack turned to Asha with a beseeching expression. "I don't suppose you have a brother who's available, do you, Asha? To get me off the hook, so to speak."

"I've got five brothers, actually."

"Five?" he repeated incredulously.

Asha grinned at his surprise. "Yes. Five," she said. "Although the age difference might be a slight problem. Andrew, the eldest, is eight."

"Is he as cute as his sister?"

Asha wrinkled her nose. "I don't know about that. But he is pretty cute."

"Peri told me your father is Sean West, and I seem to remember reading somewhere he'd remarried. I'm something of a fan of his. He was a great cricketer. He's still involved in the game, isn't he? On the coaching side."

Asha nodded. "He's on the Queensland Bulls's coaching team, and he also does some junior coaching." She turned as Peri reentered the room.

She was wearing dark slacks now and a silvery, shimmery blouse that hugged her breasts, and for earth-shattering seconds, Asha couldn't take her eyes off her.

"And are your young brothers interested in the game?"

Jack's words drew Asha's reluctant attention and she nodded again. "Dad says Andrew and Brendan are naturals, so that pleases him no end. The others are a little young."

"You look lovely, Peri," Vivienne said and Asha slid another surreptitious glance at Peri before making herself study the pattern on the hand-embroidered tablecloth.

"Thanks, Viv. Shall we go?" Peri said to her brother.

Jack stood up. "Right. Nice to meet you, Asha. We must have

a chat about cricket sometime."

"Yes. Good to meet you, too, Jack. Have a nice night," Asha added with as much conviction as she could muster, and she could only watch as Peri walked out the door.

After lunch the next day Asha picked up the phone and dialed her mother's number. It rang a couple of times before Michelle murmured hello.

"Chelle. Hi! It's Asha. I didn't expect you to be home."

Michelle laughed. "I got sick of delving into the social sciences, so I decided to catch up on some rest. I've had too many late nights. I'm starting to look like I've got bags on the bags under my eyes and I needed some beauty sleep."

"Rubbish. You look fantastic."

"So now you've got a video phone? That must be one rich family you're working for."

"I guess they are pretty well off, but they're really nice, too."

"That'll make Mum feel better. You know, she really overreacted about you staying over there, didn't you think? I mean, you are twenty-five."

"You know how she worries."

"She sure does. And she even cross-examined me because she forgot to ask you who the people you're doing the research for are. It didn't help that I couldn't remember their names."

"It's Chaseley," Asha filled her sister in. "Let me talk to her and I'll set her mind at rest."

"She's gone down to visit her friend Meg from the choir, I think. Remember she broke her arm last week? Meg, I mean."

"Oh. I just wanted to give her the phone number here. The number's unlisted."

"Sure. Let me just find a pen."

Asha heard her sister rattling in the phone stand drawer.

"Okay. I'll write it in the front of Mum's phone directory. And what's their name again?" she asked after she'd copied the number Asha gave her.

"Chaseley. Mrs. Vivienne Chaseley."

"Got it. So how's the research going?"

Asha told Michelle all about the photographs and certificates uncovered in the small family chest that was sitting on the desk in front of her. They chatted for a while, and when her sister rang off, Asha sat back in her chair and ran her hand lightly over the beautifully smooth wood of the box.

Apart from the wealth of information stored inside the chest, it was a beautiful piece. The tooled pattern on the lid featured the smooth petals of frangipani flowers, intricately carved by a master craftsman, and the hinges and catch on the box were genuinely antique.

Asha ran her fingers lightly over the polished wood. At some time the small chest may have been lined with felt or silk, but if it had, the material had long gone. The rim of the box was a little rough where the material may have been attached.

She made sure the clasp was closed and carefully lifted the box, turning it over onto its back so she could examine the bottom. Maybe the craftsman had carved his or the owner's name or initials into the bottom of the box. She felt around, pausing when her fingers encountered a small indentation. What could it be? Asha could insert the tip of her little finger into the hole.

Rolling the box onto its lid, she switched on the desk lamp and drew it closer. There was definitely a small round hole, regular edges indicating it was put there on purpose rather than accidentally.

Asha frowned. Why would the box have a hole in the bottom? She hadn't noticed it when she'd looked inside the box. She carefully inserted the blunt end of her pencil and found the hole was about an inch and a half deep. She righted the box, opened the lid again and checked the bottom of the inside of the box.

Nothing.

Then she remembered a gift her father and stepmother had given her for her seventh or eighth birthday. It was a music box. You wound a key in the base and tinkling music played. Had this been a music box at some stage? Surely it was too big?

Looking in the top drawer of the desk, she found a ruler and measured the inside and outside dimensions of the box. There was a discrepancy of a couple of inches. It must have been a music box, she thought excitedly, and the mechanism might still be beneath the false bottom.

Perhaps if she pushed her pencil through the hole in the bottom she could prize the false bottom from the sides of the box. She lifted the box over onto its lid again, but this time the pencil barely went into the hole. Something must be obstructing it. If the music playing mechanism had come loose, surely it would rattle?

Asha lifted the box off the desk, and then gingerly gave it a shake. No, there was nothing metallic rattling inside the box. Her arms protested at the weight of the box, and she set it on its side. Whatever was in the false bottom had moved back again, and this time her pencil went right into the cavity.

Half an hour later, after careful tapping and manipulation the false bottom of the box popped out. Asha set the box right side up and excitedly opened the lid and removed the now loosened false bottom. The exposed cavity didn't hold a music cylinder, but it did contain a couple of old photographs, papers and two leather-bound books.

With a thrill of excitement, Asha slipped on her cotton gloves and looked at one of the photos. It was a cabinet photo, about four and a half inches by six and a half inches, making it larger than the more common carte-de-visite, and it was mounted on fairly thick card that was showing signs of deterioration caused by the acid in the paper. Even though it was faded and the edges damaged, Asha could see the faces of what appeared to be a wedding group. The bride and groom stood stiffly center stage. Around them stood a younger girl, a smaller boy, two young men and an older man. On the back of the photo was the name and address of the photographers in Newcastle-upon-Tyne. Someone had written in ink, now faded, "Elm Street, Benwell. Our Mary's marriage to Enoch Bolam. 1867."

Excitement grabbed at Asha again. She knew from the research she'd done so far that Richard Chaseley was from Northumberland. Was this his family? She peered at the young men in the photo. She was almost sure the taller one was Richard Chaseley. She compared it to the portrait of Richard and his family taken in Brisbane in 1885. Yes, the taller young man was definitely Richard Chaseley. If he was born in 1850, then he was seventeen years old in the faded photograph.

She picked up the other photo. Another wedding shot, this time of just the bride and groom, the fashions and condition of the photo indicating it had been taken later than the other one. The photographers this time were in Charters Towers, Queensland, and on the back of the photo, in what appeared to be the same handwriting, was written, "Margaret and Georgie. 29 September 1896."

Georgie Chaseley. This must be Richard's younger brother who had sailed with him for the colonies. Asha picked up her magnifying glass and peered at the other older photo again, but she couldn't be sure the other young man, or the boy, was George Chaseley.

Setting the photos aside, Asha unfolded the first piece of paper to find a marriage certificate for George Chaseley and Margaret Ann Gaines. George was a bachelor, aged 44 years, a storekeeper, son of Michael Chaseley, coal miner, and Mary Nolan. George's birthplace was given as Sacriston, Durham, and he had been in Queensland for twenty-six years. Margaret was a widow, aged 30 years, daughter of Robert Leston, a miner, and Alice Jefferies. She was born in Portsmouth, Hampshire, and had been in Queensland for twenty years.

The second certificate was a death certificate for William John Gaines, aged 33 yrs. Cause of death was a broken neck. There was also a birth certificate for Margaret and William Gaines's son, Robert, in 1892.

Asha then turned her attention to the books. There was no pattern on the cover of the first one, but the initials G. C. had been tooled on the second book. This book was slightly larger than the other one, and the flyleaf was inscribed with the same handwriting as the photographs. Georgie Chaseley. She put it aside and picked up the other, older book.

Setting it carefully on the desk, Asha sat down to examine it. She slowly opened the cover. On the flyleaf, the paper blotched and browning, was written, "Georgie Chaseley, 1870." Asha turned the page feeling excitement well inside her as she slowly and carefully began to read the neat, sloping script.

6th of September, 1870. This day begins the journal of Georgie Chaseley, aged eighteen years . . .

CHAPTER FOUR

6th of September, 1870. This day begins the journal of Georgie Chaseley, aged eighteen years, born in Sacriston, County Durham, and late of Benwell, Newcastle-upon-Tyne, now residing in Petrie Terrace, Brisbane, Australia.

My older brother, Richard, and I sailed from London aboard the ship, Star of the South. *With all our family gone, we sold our worldly goods to pay for our train fare to London. Richard took a job with a coal merchant to keep us until the ship sailed. I assisted performing errands for a grocer.*

We were neither of us sorry when our day of departure arrived to take us to our new land, for we found the city of London most crowded and unclean. We set sail and our journey was long.

It is not possible to describe the immensity and the changing colors of the oceans. I was convinced many times our ship remained still, for I thought we might never reach the far horizon. Other times the ship rolled *about so much we could not remain upright, and many were so ill. One man's leg was broke by a rolling water barrel, and we lost a poor sailor at sea when he was thrown from the mast to disappear beneath the tossing waves. Richard and I never could have thought to see such enormous waves, as tall as our ship and more. It was monstrous frightening. Many times we feared we would never lay eyes upon our new land.*

One day of good and calm weather Richard and I saw dolphins playing in the waves. The sailors told us that was what the big fish were named. On another day we saw a huge fish we perceived to be a dolphin, but the sailors were quick to correct us that it was a shark. One of the crew told of a sailor unfortunate to fall overboard, and before his mates could haul him in, a shark had taken his legs. Richard and I were unsure regarding the truth of this tale, but we have heard similar stories since arriving in Queensland.

At night there were times we watched the sea shining. It was such a pretty sight. The Captain told us the cause was phosphorus, a substance I admit to knowing not at all.

I must relate that I so enjoyed the evenings Richard and I sat with some of the sailors spinning yarns that told about their times at sea and in foreign ports. I can say I have never felt such freedom, and I enjoy it so. At such times I am much convinced Richard and I have made the best choice.

One of the seamen had lived for some years in the colony in the north, and he told many a tale of it. Not but three years past, gold was discovered in the north of Queensland, and diggers flock to the area. Another seaman said he had heard tell of a large nugget of gold named the Welcome Stranger, found in Victoria that weighed over 2,000 ounces. I became much excited about this, but Richard bade me not to think on it until we arrive at our destination and can acquire knowledge of such things for ourselves, which we have done.

One night the Captain learnt Richard and I the compass. He assures us it is very serviceable in the new land. If we should lose our way in the unsettled land, referred to as the bush, we can read a compass and find our course. Richard is set on having one when we reach our new home.

The sunrises, more especially as we neared the tropics, were a beauty to behold. I am not able to describe the colors, as I have not the words to do so.

During the voyage, there was sadness. Two small children and a woman died, the latter in childbirth, she leaving behind three other small children in the care of her bereaved husband. All who died were buried at sea, a solemn and lonely resting place in Davy Jones' Locker and a sad sight. Thanks be to Providence, fortune shone upon my brother and me, for we kept good health. There were no outbreaks of the fearsome diseases we heard could befall us aboard the ships.

The heat below decks was intolerable and maked Richard and I feel so very weak. I began to think fondly of the snow, which used to cause us such a trial. This also caused me to think of those we have left behind us. Richard misses his friends from the mine, and I much miss my good sweet friend Jane Robson, who by this time will have wed our brother-in-law, Enoch Bolam, he being a widower since our Mary died.

The most worst times were when we were becalmed. This time seemed to give way to much mean-spiritedness among the passengers. To lift our spirits at such times Richard and I spoke of the reason for which we set out: To make a new life in a new land.

8th of September, 1870. Our first view of Brisbane rendered Richard and I without speech. It could not be more different from the rows of miner's cottages we have left behind us. The river is wide and most beautiful, and ferries ply the banks.

We straight away found lodgings in a boarding house with rooms most small, and so unbearable was the heat we thought we might be back aboard the Star of the South.

With great haste, we sought work and found laborers were much needed. Richard thought to work alone to pay our keep, but I remained firm that I, too, should be able to work to pay my way. In the first week he but drove me insane keeping watch over me, but at last he is able to see I am come to no harm by hard labors.

We then set out to find more agreeable lodgings and now have a room in Wellington Street in the most appealing house of the Widow Carson, a jolly woman who is a more than passable cook. We have consented that I will also teach the three Carson boys their letters and numbers in exchange for a smaller rent.

After much quiet discussion, Richard had finally come to see that it was best to keep up our story. I was thus able to move freely about the city with Richard or alone, although Richard remonstrated with me many times over the latter, and I was made to promise not to do so after nightfall. I am wont to say I have almost forgotten my life before we left for the new land. I am mightily convinced that I am living the life I was meant to live.

The town where we make our home boasts a very fine parliament house, which adjoins the most pleasing botanical gardens. We learned the poor state of the city's funds were greatly improved by the discovery of gold in Gympie, some way north of Brisbane. The new hospital has been existent for three years to tend the needs of the growing population. Epidemics of tropical diseases are the plague of the town. Richard and I are mightily concerned to hear malaria, typhoid, smallpox, dysentery and dengue fever have killed many.

The town is most busy but much spread out, and the trees are greatly different from those Richard and I know from home. Mrs. Carson's oldest son, David, a quite pleasant-natured young man of fifteen years, told us many immigrants have journeyed to Queensland with the intention of searching for gold. Davie talks of going in search of his own fortune, but his mother soundly boxes his ears.

The very wealthy in this town have built on the hills around the settlement while workers have cottages in the valleys. I am sure Richard has eyes only for the hilltops.

Within the month of arriving, Richard found us both much more agreeable work, and I have instructed him not to worry so about me, for I am full of health and I grow strong from the heavy work. Our new positions are with the Smith Brothers, wealthy import and export merchants, who own a most beautiful house on the slopes of Bowen Hills. Richard said immediately he would have as grand a home for us as well. I have no doubt he will do so, for he is so dedicated.

9th of December, 1870. This morn James Smith learned Richard and I could read and write and well knew our numbers. We are now kept in the office, and I am more than agreeable to have left the hard work of the yard behind me, for it is so uncomfortable, most especially in the suffocating heat.

18th of June, 1871. Richard this day has made his own business. He has decided I am to keep his office. The Smith Brothers were unhappy to hear we were leaving but have wished us well and promised Richard some work. Richard and I were made humble they think so highly of us. One of the laborers in the yard came up to relate to me a story of a Chinese miner who had found a gold nugget in Victoria weighing 1,621 ounces. He leaves to seek his fortune next week. I repeated this to Richard, but he believes we will be better served remaining here in Brisbane.

20th of July, 1871. Richard is greatly pleased. He has taken an agreement with the well-known John Petrie's construction company and has hopes of this for the good future of his business. John Petrie was the first mayor of Brisbane.

I had for some time been trying to convince Richard we might try our luck in the goldfields in Gympie, as Davie Carson wants to do, but Richard says he wants to remain in Brisbane. I sense the very comely young woman, Miss Susannah Makepeace, who resides down the street with her family, has more to do with Richard's refusal. I espied him looking in the window of the jeweler just two doors from this office and believe he might ask for the young lady's hand in marriage. She is a *sweet girl, and he would do well to make a life with her.*

I voiced my intention to go to the goldfields alone, but Richard will not hear of it. I must continue to try to convince him I would be quite safe. The physical work I have done has made me hardy, and I can well handle myself. I have thoughts of my own concerning my own life. Perhaps when Richard is settled into marriage he might be prevailed upon to change his mind.

15th of September, 1872. This day Richard married his fiancée, Miss Susannah Makepeace. It was a very pretty wedding and Richard looked so handsome in his new suit. Susannah was equally beautiful in her white dress. Richard will live with the Makepeaces until he can make his own house. He has agreed that I should stay with Mrs. Carson.

There are many tales being told concerning the new goldfields in the North in a township called Charters Towers. Davie Carson is full of stories about gold being found lying upon the streets. Men have also set out for the new goldfields in Gulgong in New South Wales. Richard will hear none of this.

20th of December, 1872. It has been a strange day. Richard came to the office full of smiles. Susannah is to have a child, and Richard's chest is much puffed out. On my return to Mrs. Carson's cottage, she handed me a letter from home. It was writ by Reverend McNay and full of news. I was happy to read all about the comings and goings of the village. I then read the saddest of news. My sweet friend Jane had died in childbirth this twelve months past. My heart weighs heavy, for I did so love Jane and had done since we were young. I can but imagine Enoch's sadness to lose first our Mary and then dear Jane in this dreadful manner. All Enoch's family wealth could not save him from these losses.

≈≫≈

21st of December, 1872. Last night I barely slept. I cried so for Jane. Near morning, I had come to the decision it was time to make my own life. Richard's time will be well filled with his wife and child, and I fear he will scarce miss me. I have made my mind up, and I will journey to the goldfields of Charters Towers. There are fortunes being made there. I have decided I am not strong enough to stake a claim, but I am full of understanding of the ways of business, thanks to this time with Richard. I recall Richard relating to me dire warnings concerning the goldfields. He stated that a severe lack of provisions and inadequate transport to the Charters Towers fields cause much hardship and lawlessness. The miners will need provisions, and I shall set up a store to provide them with their needs. Now I must find a way to make Richard see that I am more than able to live my own life.

3rd of January, 1873. Times in the town have been monstrous hard. An outbreak of typhoid took many lives, including that of Susannah's younger sister, but ten years old, and the wife of James Smith, who leaves six young children. Richard was mightily worried about Susannah, as she has been poorly as she grows with child. Not a person felt at all like celebrating the arrival of the New Year.

8th of January, 1873. I fear Richard will make himself ill he works so hard. When I spoke of this, he paid me no heed but told me he has chosen to purchase land and a cottage atop a hill past Breakfast Creek. The land was part of an estate that must be sold since the owner has fallen on hard times. It is a cracking price, but Richard's mind is set.

3rd of February, 1873. Today Richard, Susannah, Mrs. Carson's son, Davie, and I took out the horse and carriage and ventured out to observe Richard's land. I have to say it is impressive. The view over the wide reach of the river is magnificent. Susannah was made quite speechless. Richard was excited like a small boy and ran around with his drawings of the house he has the need to build. He has made a bargain with a fellow for blocks of sandstone from a quarry near Ipswich. He told Susannah he had hopes of finishing the house before their baby is born, but he fears that will not come to pass. This does not seem to bother his young wife, whose eyes shine when she gazes upon my brother, who I admit has grown into a fine looking man. But most of all, Richard is a kind and generous man.

10th of April, 1873. Work has been started on Richard's house, and he fusses between that and Susannah's health, which the doctor assures him is exceedingly good. It is my decision to not raise the subject of the northern goldfields until after the child is safely born, but it greatly saddens me and I find it excessively difficult to sit at my work. To add to my dissatisfaction and his mother's sorrow, Davie Carson left this week to seek his fortune there. I so much wished to leave with him, but must find my patience.

26th of June, 1873. There is much joy. This day Susannah was delivered of a fine baby girl. She is a beauty like her mother and has a lusty cry. Richard has named her Susannah for her mother. Susannah has come through her ordeal with great fortitude. I am filled with admiration for all that she endured. It had Richard near out of his mind.

28th of August, 1873. The home Richard is building is a fine place. Although there is much still to be done, Richard and Susannah and the baby have moved into the section that is built.

Last evening I asked for time with him alone and informed him of my intention to make my way north. He was monstrous angry and loudly forbade me to go. I have not before seen my brother so angry. He stated most forcefully that he has the responsibility of me. I too became angry and told him he thought of me as a child but that I had reached my twenty-first year. We argued something fierce. I have to wonder what Susannah thought of this.

Then Richard sat down and spoke slow and quiet. He demanded I recall an incident these four years past. I had stayed too late when visiting Jane and was hurrying toward home in the growing dusk, my coat pulled tight about me against the biting cold. Suddenly rough hands were upon me, and I smelled the bitter odor of stale drink. There were three of them, the uncouth Dempsey boys, and against them I had no chance to free myself. Their disgusting hands pawed at my clothes, and had not Richard come in search of me, I do not doubt I would have suffered the worst fate imaginable. It was wicked of Richard to remind me of this, but I remained firm concerning my desire to travel north.

At the last, I conveyed my intention to leave with or without Richard's blessing. I fear he is most displeased with me, but I must stand firm. I reminded him his life is with his wife and his daughter now, and I must make my own life, for better or worse.

6th of September, 1873. On the tide tomorrow I sail for the north of the state. Richard has agreed that I go with the company of Mrs. Carson's second son, John. He is a strong lad of seventeen years, and his mother wishes that he journeys to inquire about his older brother, Davie, and how he fares. Truth be told, young John has a desire to try his luck at prospecting as well as his brother.

19th of October, 1873. I have been three weeks in the city of Charters Towers. It swarms with men from all over our world come to try to make their fortunes. It is a motley mix of humanity. There are many Chinese as well as local Aboriginal tribes. Germans, Swedes, Irish and English. More people stream in day by day.

I have acquired a suitable building for beginning my store. It is small, but there is space to add extra rooms in the back, and there are rooms atop for me to sleep. While in the port of Townsville, I set up my agents, no matter that John was fidgeting to get to the goldfields.

When we arrived we found Townsville to be a busy port. We ventured into Flinders Street to espy a great many bullock-drawn wagons, at least fifty or more, moving in procession for the goldfields. There were also coaches and men on horseback and on foot. I am told here in the north, bullock drays are able to carry two tons of goods, but they are now disappearing as the high tabletop wagons, with wide, steel-rimmed wheels, can carry ten tons or more.

John and I left Townsville by coach to the Haughton River and then on to Charters Towers. It was a rough and most uncomfortable journey, but the coach driver was most colorful and sang songs as he drove the eighty-two miles.

The Charters Towers goldfields were proclaimed on the 31st of August last year, and the town grows daily. I am impatient to begin my business. John has vowed to give me every assistance before he joins his brother. After the incident in Rockhampton, he is desperate to get back into my favors. Still, I know a goodly part of the fault was mine.

On our journey north, our ship put in to Rockhampton to load cargo. We lingered aboard, cooling our heels for some days while John begged to be able to go ashore to explore. I am unable to understand how Richard could believe that John would protect me. He is but a burly boy. I felt every inch the protector of that young man. Yet in that unexceptional port both John and I were derelict in our duties. From the safety of hindsight, we were both the victims of boredom, and a short walk around the wharf in the gathering dusk seemed just the ticket.

We came upon a hotel of sorts, not a place Richard and I were wont to frequent. It was the singing that gave me pause. I recall the evenings when I was a child when neighbors would gather. Old Mr. Reays would play his squeezebox, and we all would sing. That sound of singing spilling out onto the dusty path brought back the past with a wave of sudden melancholy. When John started inside, I am afraid to say I followed him.

The clientele was a mixed group made up of sailors and farmers and the occasional suited gentleman. I was mightily surprised to find some women, flashily dressed, laughing loudly and partaking of drink. It came to me that this might well be a house of ill repute. I was repulsed and much curious.

By this time John had overcome his surprise and had purchased drinks. I began to tell him I did not imbibe, when I saw a young woman regarding me with undisguised interest. I confess to being somewhat disconcerted, and I had swallowed half the drink before I had so much as tasted the vile brew.

The young woman smiled prettily and strolled across the room. She stood before me inquiring if I had visited the establishment on a previous occasion. This, or perchance the unaccustomed drink, caused me to laugh out loud. The young woman, who told me she was called Arabella, thought this most amusing. I barely recall how many drinks I took that evening, but I staggered and almost fell as Arabella led me up a narrow staircase almost unseen in the dark corner of the tavern.

The lamps were lit low and cast shadows in Arabella's room. The colors were rich red, and there was a high bed with a mound of inviting pillows. I scarce had time to gaze around me when Arabella came close to me, and I was aware of the sweet smell of her perfume, like flowers. I believe I inquired and was told it was lavender. It caused me to be as light-headed as the drink.

I was made aware of the curves of the young woman, the full bosom, the creamy white skin of her shoulders. I became faint and would have fallen had Arabella not moved me so that my back rested on the closed door.

My next memory was of her lips on mine. I barely breathed. I have never known such a feeling. No one had held me in such a way. Not even our Mam when I was a child. My body was filled with a wondrous joy.

Arabella soon led me to the bed, removed my coat, and I lay down before I should fall. My breath caught in my chest as she disrobed before me. I sat up and buried my face between her large breasts. She was undoing the button at my waist when I became quite sober. I could *never allow such intimacy.*

The young woman relaxed against me, murmuring in a soothing tone. I was overcome with a sadness for what I had lost, and I felt tears fill my eyes. I found myself confessing to Arabella my secret, the secret Richard and I had guarded for so long. I explained I could never be a man for her in the way she wanted.

She held me close again, undressed me with a fine gentleness. She ran her lips over my chest, her tongue licking my nipples. My blood ran hotly through my body and an ache swelled between my legs. I let Arabella remove my boots and then my trousers, and I was naked before her. Yet I felt no shame. She ran her fingers over me, and I was caught by a rapture that left me weak and shaking.

That night Arabella showed me a wondrous side of life I could not have imagined in my wildest dreams. We scarce slept, and in the light of dawn, I was much reluctant to don my clothes.

As I walked toward our ship, I am ashamed to say I only then gave a thought to young John Carson. I made haste along the wharf and was filled with relief when I espied him sitting on an upturned barrel. His clothes were rumpled and stained, and below his right eye his cheek was swollen and discolored. I called his name and he slowly peered up at me. He was unsure about where he had been or what had happened to him. What was obvious was that he had been in a fight. How much his sore head was the result of the fight and how much to the drink, we would never know.

I helped him aboard and to his cabin. He spent most of the remainder of the voyage there. I am ashamed to say I was much relieved to be left to my own devices, for I had much to think on and consider.

I have sent word to Richard that I am safely arrived so he may rest easy.

28th of September, 1876. It has been three years since I wrote in my journal. This time has passed so swiftly, for I have worked long and hard hours to build my business. Today Chaseley's General Store thrives. When I arrived in The Towers, I was much surprised by the size of the town. Miners continued to pour into the town like rats to a sewer, and I have heard it said ninety percent of the population is adult men.

They were, for the most part, a rough, unlawful bunch, and to walk the streets on a Friday night was the height of foolishness. A person would be held shoulder to shoulder with nary a move in any direction.

There is much money here, and as soon as I opened my doors I had a goodly number of customers. However, I get before myself. This past year I found new premises, newly erected, much larger than I had envisaged having the need of when I arrived. I am greatly pleased now, as my business has expanded so. The store is in the top end of town and has a most pleasing outlook.

The town thrives, and halls have been built by various lodges and churches where we are treated to wonderful entertainments.

I eagerly await the mail to hear news of my family, for I admit to being most lonely. John Carson found his brother Davie and cast in his lot with him. They do well on their claim and are able to send money home to their dear mother. I see them when they have need of supplies. We share news of home.

Just this week I received a letter from Richard with the joyous news Susannah has been delivered of a son. Richard has named him Michael for our father. I am so thankful all went well. Richard and Susannah were so distraught when they lost their baby, Susannah, at barely twelve months. Two months after this great loss, Susannah bore a daughter, who they named Georgina for me, then another daughter named Eliza, for Susannah's mother. Now Richard has the son he so desired.

Last year, John Petrie won the contract to build the Supreme Court, and as Richard works with him, Richard too had a most successful year.

Richard also tells me he attended the first Exhibition to be held in the city on the 22nd of August. Susannah was too heavy with child to attend, but Richard tells me a speech was made by the Governor declaring the Exhibition open, and a band played "God Save the Queen." In

71

Victoria Park an artillery salute made the ground tremble, steam engines whistled, and the crowd of some 15,000 cheered. Richard related it has been unseasonably hot and this heat caused much fainting at the spectacle.

Another memorable moment, he relates, was the completion of the Albert Railway Bridge at Indooroopilly. It is built of steel to ensure it is flood proof, and Richard tells me it will open up new suburbs along the rail line which now links Brisbane with Ipswich.

I read in the newspaper of a discovery in the center of this great land some three years past. An explorer, Mr. William Grosse, came upon a great mass of rock reaching 1,000 feet high and two miles long. He has named it Ayers Rock. This must be a magnificent sight to see. I must ask Richard if he knows of this.

28th of December, 1876. It was a lonely Christmas for me. My thoughts went to my brother and his family. I have such a yearning to see the babies, but my work is here. I read Richard's latest letter many times till I all but could recite it by heart. He tells me all children in the state are required now by law to attend school and that they are to receive their tuition free of charge. It is a most welcome law to be passed, for all of us have need of reading and writing.

On Boxing Day the Carson boys came into town and we ventured to McKinly's Hotel to drink to family and friends who are far from us. With memories from Rockhampton still so fresh in my mind, I was careful not to over-imbibe. I must be much aware of my position in the town. Not so John and Davie. They spent the night on my back veranda and awoke nursing sore heads.

On the Eve of the New Year, I have been invited to attend a party at the Phillips home.

Mr. Phillips owns the most successful bakery in town. He and his wife have been only just married, and I greatly enjoy being in their company. They are good friends to me. I am wont to wonder what the year of 1877 will bring.

8th of October, 1879. I have been remiss with my journal once again. My business continues to grow. I can say with all honesty that it is most successful. As is Richard's business in Brisbane. Our Mam and Pa would surely have been monstrous proud of us. I am ever thankful our Mam sent us to The Hall so we could learn our letters and numbers with Enoch and his sisters when the Bolams kindly offered this to our family. All this came about when Pa saved the youngest Bolam girl from drowning in the brook.

Charters Towers was declared a Municipality in 1877, and Mr. John McDonald was made the town's first mayor. There was much concern in the town with the tin rush in Herberton, but most of the miners hereabouts have set their hearts on finding the mother lode. It would seem everyone journeys to town on Friday nights still, and Gill Street is but a sea of people. Even the buses are made to go around other streets.

The Fire Brigade Band was established this past year, and on a Sunday afternoon it is most pleasant to hear the music as the bands play in Lissner Park. This is quite a social occasion for families. The last time I ventured there to hear the band, they played the popular patriotic song, "Advance Australia Fair," accompanied by the ladies' choir from the church. It was most delightful.

I am most partial to the social gatherings in the homes of my friends where we partake of games of cards.

This past month St. Columba's Church in Gill Street, just a short distance from my store, was torn down by a violent storm, but work has already begun on a new building. My own building, by some divine good providence, escaped damage.

News of this example of Nature's fury reached Brisbane, and Richard's letter, filled with concern, came to enquire how I had fared in this occurrence. I hastily informed him of my safety.

There is more to be read in the newspapers concerning a notorious gang of bushrangers in the south, named the Kelly Gang. This gang has robbed banks and shot and killed policemen. The Government has increased the reward to 2,000 pounds per head for these scoundrels.

I read also of the wreck of the clipper ship, Loch Ard, in Victoria, and the heroics of a young seaman who rescued a young girl floating on a piece of wreckage. They were the sole survivors of this terrible tragedy, of which there have been many in the waters surrounding this land. I recall a brave young girl, but sixteen years, who rode her horse into the raging waters so survivors could cling to her saddle and stirrups as the horse dragged them to safety. The young girl spent four hours of hardship in doing this and then rode homeward to raise the alarm. There are many stories of courage in this new land.

21st of January, 1880. I am most pleased with my business investments. At my instigation, Richard and I were fortunate enough to invest in Victory Company, and our outlay was repaid within three months. The Day Dawn Mining Company, Ltd. has paid a dividend much higher than was expected. The town has changed since reef gold was discovered, although many men still seek to dig their fortune on their own.

3rd of September,1880. Early this year, Richard was deeply concerned for Susannah's health, for she suffered so much with an infection in her lungs. She was most poorly, and Richard feared she would not survive, but his letter this week tells me Susannah is much improved. The children continue to grow and I treasure the photograph he has sent to me of his most comely family. Young Georgina puts me in mind of our Mam and our sister Mary, and Michael is the image of his father. Eliza is a sweet child with fair curls like her mother. She is a frail and tiny child, and I know Richard and Susannah despair of raising her. Maryann, the baby, born this past year, is as dark as Eliza is fair, but shares her features.

Richard tells me wide verandas are being added to Parliament House at last. The many complaints by the members about the stifling *heat during the summer months have finally encouraged some action.*

News is come concerning the notorious bushrangers, the Kelly Gang, who many think to be innocent. Their leader, Ned Kelly, who protected himself in a steel armor, was wounded, and the rest of the gang killed after a three-day siege at Glenrowan. Ned Kelly is to be hanged.

3rd of January, 1883. More years have passed, and our town continues to grow. Richard's letters have been full of his purchase of land about the city. My brother has become a successful businessman. He has added large verandas on all sides of his home, and he tells me the view is magnificent displaying the wide Brisbane River to the city and around to the mountains. One day I hope to see it. Work is beginning on the extensions Richard plans. He feels the need to add a residence for the servants.

I am much amazed by his latest story. It was such an unusual occurrence that Richard related it to me. He believes it almost started a war in Brisbane. The Captain of the SS Gayundah, a gun boat, perceived he had been unfairly treated and brought the ship up river and trained the ship's guns on Parliament House. Battles, verbal and physical, broke out between the crew and some townspeople and continued until the Captain was persuaded to abandon his intentions.

This last year Mr. Phillips purchased a piano, and it was brought into town on the back of a wagon. I am unable to believe he has paid one hundred guineas for the instrument, and it has caused him much worry as it was conveyed here. Since this event, we enjoy much singing together at the Phillips's home, as Mrs. Phillips is a most passable pianist. It was unfortunate he did not wait but three months, for the railway has now opened, linking Townsville and Charters Towers. The Premier of Queensland and seventy invited guests arrived in the Towers on the 4th of December last for the official opening of the Great Northern Railway link between Townsville and our town.

Tomorrow on the train I expect a load of tinned food that has become most popular with my customers.

8th of March, 1883. Sad news I have received this morn. Richard's dear, sweet Eliza passed this life of the whooping cough. She was just turned eight years, and Richard is sorely hurt. I suspect sweet little Eliza was a favorite, although he would not admit to this. He was so brokenhearted he was unable to put his pen to paper, and the sad news was conveyed by Susannah.

12th of November, 1884. The heat is becoming most disagreeable and I fear we will have a most uncomfortable summer. Drought continues to plague the country.

Some most comely buildings in the Victorian style have been erected, which surely is a sign of the town's continuing wealth. St. Paul's Church of England Church was erected last year, and the sound of hammers and saws is only just drowned out by the sound of the ore batteries. The town continues to grow. The School of Arts has a Lending Library boasting some two thousand and five hundred volumes. I am so pleased to spend some of my leisure time reading books on many and knowledgeable subjects.

A story as interesting as that found in a book was told to me just recently. A woman who calls herself Mrs. Kingsley came into the store to purchase provisions. I had made her acquaintance on previous occasions. She and her husband and family had traveled in a covered cart over twelve hundred miles from a town by the name of Cobar in New South Wales. They suffered many privations and on one occasion they were attacked by hostile aborigines. Another time, when her husband was taken ill, this stoic lady went in search of their horse, only to become quite lost. Friendly aborigines showed her back to her camp and found her horse. Her husband has been working in the mines and has the desire to move on to the Woolgar goldfields. It is most obvious the woman is again with child, and I must have great admiration for her courage to attempt such an undertaking in her delicate condition.

30th of December, 1886. This year the Miners' Union was established amid mixed feelings. I am in agreement that the miners need to improve working conditions and fight to raise their poor wages.

After a period of ten months in the construction, the courthouse is now open. The cost for the building was 4,565 pounds.

Richard relates that this past August, horse-drawn trams began operation between Woolloongabba and Breakfast Creek. He finds them most convenient.

There is often talk for North Queensland to become a separate colony. Many feel the north more than earns its way, more so than the south.

28th of February, 1887. The news we received from Brisbane is not good. It appears the rains have caused much tragedy. Floods have swamped families in the low areas. Many have lost jobs, Richard's letter relates, and are being weighed down by debt. Richard knows of families who are becoming destitute. There is much illness and misery. He considered bringing Susannah and the children north, but the weather has been so dreadful, even though we expect it this season, that he could not trust his family to such inclement seas. It is a great pity, as I still yearn to see the children.

We had here a storm of great magnitude this past Friday night. There was no drop of rain, only fierce lightning and thunder like to render one deaf. A stockman on Kilarney Downs was struck by lightning and did not recover. A large tree fell on the cottage of my delivery boy, and the family barely escaped with their lives.

10th of October, 1888. This year, this past January saw scenes of great celebration in the town, for it was the 100th Anniversary of the arrival of the First Fleet. Thus, our new land is 100 years old. Richard told me also of parades in Brisbane and fireworks, which they all watched from the safety of their veranda.

11th of October, 1888. I was much tired last evening, so I continue my journal tonight. A letter from home arrived this day full of news. Richard recounts to me his business has been so busy such is the need for new buildings in the city. He fears I will scarce recognize Brisbane when I return. All vacant sites in Queen Street have been taken up, and the street is very much a showpiece. New immigrants may stay free of charge in the Government Store and in the Kangaroo Point Immigrant Barracks. Richard has sent to me Mr. William Clarson's magnificent panorama view of the city which has appeared in the Illustrated Sydney News, *and it shows a fine and expanding city.*

Susannah and the children keep well, thanks to Providence. I became most desperately homesick when Richard told me they all thought of me last night when they were fortunate enough to partake of a rosella pie the new cook baked. Knowing how much I was partial to these native fruits, they spoke of me and my photograph was fetched for all to look at me. Richard promises when I return Susannah intends to have Cook bake a rosella pie for me at the first opportunity.

Our town continues to grow and change. The Royal Arcade on the corner of Mossman and Gill streets is most agreeable and many people stroll through the shops. We had news that a test bore in Winton gushed artesian water. This water from beneath the ground was much welcomed, for the country is ever in the grip of terrible drought.

6th of February, 1889. The weather continues to be monstrous hot. We must pity the poor souls in Cloncurry where the temperature last month recorded 127°. This is the highest temperature since such measurements began in this land.

Richard posted me a collection of the newspaper The Bulletin, *which has given me much reading pleasure. I am taken with the two young poets Andrew Barton Paterson, who writes as "The Banjo," and Henry Lawson.*

※

29th of October, 1889. Richard relates that the capital city continues to rapidly expand with increased shipping. The new Customs House is now completed after three years. The copper-clad dome is especially pleasing. He tells me he has business in Townsville and will journey north within the month. He will make the trip out here to the Towers to assure himself of my welfare. It fills me with great joy that I am to see him at last, and I scarce can settle.

10th of December, 1889. What a week of emotions. Richard has made the journey north to visit at last. He brought with him young Georgina. She is turned fifteen now and so like our Mam I almost cried. She is a beauty to be sure and has much sense like our Mam. She set to and helped me in the store, and when it came time for them to return to Brisbane, she begged her father to be allowed to stay behind. Richard would hear none of it, which reduced Georgina to tears. Richard appealed to me for assistance, much upset by his daughter's distress. I quickly assured Georgina I would visit the family as soon as I was able. I have made a promise to Georgina I will attend her sixteenth birthday party the next year.

12th of April, 1890. There has been another tragedy at sea. The Royal Mail steamer Quetta was lost in Torres Strait, drowning nearly half of those on board. Men have lost their whole families. A young girl floated for thirty-six hours in waters frequented by sharks. Another young girl swam to Aconeih Isle and by some miracle was saved. Survivors recount horrible tales of the incident.

I cannot say I am a comfortable traveler when on the seas, and I was much pleased to read of the report that the steamer, Arawatta, made a record of twenty-five and a half hours to journey between Rockhampton and Brisbane. My memories of the much longer journey these seventeen *years past stay with me, along with our long and difficult journey out to this land.*

6th of June, 1890. I am returned from my visit to Richard and Susannah. It was as Richard said. I did not recognize the town I left behind seventeen years ago. It is a bustling place with much to recommend it. And when I speak of that I must include Richard's magnificent house he has named Tyneholme. The house has many outstanding appointments, and Susannah is rightly proud of it. As Richard has told me, the views from the wide verandas sweep along the magnificent river to the town and out to the mountains. Richard has surely made a success of himself.

However, by far the most pleasure I had was in making the acquaintance of the children. Of course, I had made the acquaintance of Georgina last year, and I was filled with amazement at the change in her. At sixteen, she is quite a little lady and a favorite of the young men who flock around her. This causes my brother to frown so, which in turn, amuses Susannah. Michael is fourteen years old and a serious boy who has begun to work with his father when he is not studying at the prestigious Brisbane Grammar School. Maryann is twelve and Susannah worries so about her. She is a pretty little minx without a deal of sense. Susannah hopes she will settle as she grows older.

Susannah showed to me the musical box that Richard purchased for her birthday from one of the Chinese hawkers when he visited the Towers. She is much taken with it, and it has pride of place in the drawing room. Her delight in this gift turns her eyes lovingly toward my brother. Richard is surely a fortunate man.

Now I am home in the north, and my rooms over the store seem empty after the fullness of Tyneholme. I feel the need to think seriously of selling up my business and joining my family. Richard has agreed to assist me to find another business in Brisbane as soon as I need to do so.

I have carried back with me as much reading matter as I could find. This last evening I was entertained by a wonderful poem entitled, "The

Man From Snowy River," written by "The Banjo." I found it to be such a rollicking yarn.

10th of August, 1890. Today I felt as though my heart was filled to bursting. I was arranging an order of senna tea and blue bottles of castor oil behind my counter when I heard a step on the floor. I turned to see a young woman of such beauty I was totally robbed of speech. I had thought my heartbeats would be heard, and I felt my face grow excessive hot. She was gazing at a new bonnet I had placed on a stand. It was festooned with trails of ribbons, and I had the great need to place it upon her fine dark curls.

I was so put off my self-possession that when the uncharitable Mrs. Charles marched up demanding to be served at the instant, I handed her Dr. Beecham's Liver Pills instead of her customary Perry Davis's Painkillers. The irony of my choice had me stifling a laugh.

When Mrs. Charles left with a hoity sniff, I drew myself quickly together and approached the young woman who had taken my breath away. When I addressed her, asking if I may be of some assistance to her, my voice sounded quite unlike my own. She turned and smiled so prettily at me. Her sweet lips were most inviting, and I thought that I might faint. She shyly asked for candles, and as I placed them on the counter, she looked with interest at my jars of spices. I asked her what she had need of, and a sadness touched her face. She told me ruefully that she had not the finances for more than the candles.

Before we could talk more, heavy footsteps drew our attention, and we looked around to see a tall handsome fellow striding toward us. As he came nearer, I was taken by the hardness of his expression, the dissatisfied glowering of his brows. When I turned back to the young woman, an awful change had overcome her. I am convinced she was in fear of the man, and my hand strayed to the length of wood I kept beneath the counter for my protection. The man threw a few coins on the counter and bade the woman bring the purchase and leave. She would not meet my gaze and hurried after the man.

As chance would have it, Mrs. Phillips was entering the store, and the rude man scarce gave her room to step inside. Mrs. Phillips, a woman made of stern strength, sent him a frown that would have surely withered a more mannered man. When I inquired as to who the couple were, Mrs. Phillips related that they were newly arrived to work a claim out at Mining Camp No. 2. The man, Will Gaines, was acquainted with a family who lived by the railway and his new young wife, Margaret by name, was of good family from Townsville. Her parents had been tragically lost in a buggy accident before her marriage. Mrs. Phillips made no bones about the fact that the young Mrs. Gaines had married beneath her. I could observe no reason to disagree with her sentiments.

Margaret. I perceived her beautiful face each way I turned, and I was filled with joy, and then a great despair.

CHAPTER FIVE

Asha was thrilled by the description of the voyage from London after Georgie and his brother, Richard, boarded the *Star of the South* bound for their new life in Australia. It seemed that George Chaseley had begun his journal some time after landing in Moreton Bay.

She read on, enthralled, until the shadows made her realize, she should be heading downstairs to dinner. She replaced the books and papers in the chest, suddenly guilty she hadn't told Vivienne of her find straight away. But she hadn't been able to stop reading Georgie's story.

However, she ate alone as Margo informed her Peri had taken Vivienne to see a friend, a member of the Women's Guild who had taken suddenly ill, so Asha's news would have to wait until the next morning.

After her solitary dinner, Asha returned to the study and the old journals, her curiosity piqued by Georgie's first sight of Margaret. She checked the marriage certificate. This must be Margaret Gaines, who was Peri's great-great-grandmother. Peri would want to see this, too. And Vivienne would be so excited.

The first entry in the second book was dated 1st September, 1890. It seemed that George Chaseley had just extended his store. George Chaseley didn't make daily entries in his journal. In fact, sometimes there was a gap of months before he added his thoughts and the happenings and news from home. She was totally absorbed as she followed the growing love story between Vivienne's husband's great-uncle and the married Margaret Gaines.

Taking great care Asha turned the pages.

1st of September, 1890. Today I left Mrs. Phillips's niece in charge of the store and rode out to Mining Camp No. 2. I could not contain myself a moment longer. I had to see sweet Margaret once more. Good sense bade me take caution, for the young lady was a married woman, but my heart's yearning dispatched my good reasoning with ease and swiftness.

My pretext for my journey was to take some printed notices out to the camp to announce the dance that was to be held to help raise funds for the hospital. The women were each to bring a plate of food, and these celebrations were well known in the district for the suppers, which were magnificent feasts.

The day was excessively hot and still, with nary a breath to move the leaves or grasses. We have all prayed for rain to settle the dust, but I suspect our prayers will go unanswered, for the sky is naught but blue.

By the time I reached the camp, I could scarce catch my breath my heart was racing so. I stopped to nail my notices to trees, my eyes searching for Will Gaines's stake. Finally, I saw him working with a pick. He was shirtless, his broad shoulders gleaming, and I could believe to an innocent young girl he would be most comely. I called down to him about the dance, but he made no comment and set back to his work.

I moved on, and when I caught sight of his camp, my heart began to ache. Sweet Margaret came to the opening of the rough dwelling that defied description. Old galvanized iron formed a roof, and the walls were made of canvas and some bark. Outside beneath more rusted iron was set the kitchen, open to the elements.

"Mrs. Gaines," I said her name politely and removed my hat. I could hear my voice again was not my own.

"Mr. Chaseley," she acknowledged me, her poor sunburned cheeks flushing.

Her dark curls were gathered on top of her head with a piece of ribbon, and a few fine tendrils had escaped to rest on the curve of her neck. I had the great desire to place my lips to those sweet tendrils, and my heart raced at a delirious pace.

I hurriedly explained about the dance and handed her the notice. She made a show of reading it and then remarked that a dance would be an enjoyable occasion. When I inquired about whether she would join in the frivolity, she looked most melancholy and told me her husband did not care for dancing. It would seem I am to be disappointed, for I will not see her there. With a reluctant sense of propriety, I left her then and I knew she watched as I rode away.

29th of December, 1890. This Christmastime has been most rushed. I had many customers to the store and fell into my bed each night exhausted, to toss and turn in the wretched heat. Most of us feel tired and disinclined to move about, but there is much to do.

Mrs. Phillips was delivered of a bouncing baby boy this last night, the Phillips's sixth child. It is fortunate Mr. Phillips is such a fine baker, for it is a large family to feed and clothe.

Richard sent news that the family is well and that his business continues to increase. He bade me to celebrate a joyous festive season and they all send their love to me.

My sweet Margaret came to the store this afternoon. She appears so tired, and I worry so much for her. She purchased a small amount of supplies and bade me a soft Happy New Year as she hurried out to join her husband.

The residents of the town will without doubt be most rollicking with there being over one hundred hotels in the town to entertain their revelries.

This past year was opened the Stock Exchange, which has been established to raise funds for the deep reef mines.

Mr. Daley took possession of a number of safety bicycles with the new pneumatic tires and some of the young men delight in riding out to Ravenswood and back for an outing. These bicycles, having two wheels, have been called man's most efficient machine. I have added to my stock some superior shovels come from England, which have proved most popular. There is much competition for my store these times. Aridas Store, which was opened by two Sudanese brothers some four years ago, sells many exotic wares.

The noise of the large iron breakers smashing boulders is colossal, and ninety percent of the gold comes from mines in or nearby the town. Many miners are dying from Miner's Phthisis caused by dust on the lungs. Rock falls in the shafts have also claimed many men.

We must look to the next year with hope for good health.

27th of September, 1891. I have read that the Premier of New South Wales, Sir Henry Parkes, has given a rousing address on the Federation of the Australian States. This was greeted with unprompted cheering. By all accounts, most are in agreement and now speak of "one people, with one destiny." I am sure it is the most convenient thing to rule this great land under one government.

8th of November, 1891. This day Margaret journeyed into town with her husband and Jim Jones on his wagon. She appeared so drawn and tired that I bade her to sit down by the window to catch any breeze there might be. It is obvious she is with child, and my heart aches with dread for her. We have lost so many women in childbirth in the family, I fear for her.

When I brought her a glass of cool water, she thanked me for my kindness and I saw tears fill her eyes. I then fetched a fan and attempted to make a breeze for her. She said I was so kind and her sweet voice trembled and her tears fell even more. I passed her my handkerchief and she dried her eyes. She professed to feel most foolish, and that her tears did fall most of the time these days. I then assured her it was quite natural for women in her delicate condition to feel that way. When I inquired if she had visited the doctor, she shook her head and told me they could scarce afford the doctor's fee.

I had seen her husband drive on down Gill Street with Jim Jones, and I was reassured that I would perceive his wagon returning, so I took it upon myself to suggest she call in on Mrs. Phillips at the bakery. Mrs. Phillips is much experienced in the matters of women's troubles and is the most well thought of midwife in the town. Margaret shyly shook her head and told me she could not be so bold as to speak to Mrs. Phillips. I smiled at this and bade my young assistant watch the store while I escorted Mrs. Gaines to the bakery. I left the young woman in Mrs. Phillips's care and I was sure the midwife would have much good advice to impart.

19th of December, 1891. This morning at sunrise, before the heat had time to settle upon us, I rode out to Mining Camp No. 2 to satisfy myself on the health of Margaret. I had not set eyes on her sweet face since her visit many weeks ago. I was most pleased to have news of her from Mrs. Phillips who had kindly visited her on two occasions. Mrs. Phillips expressed dismay that the young woman was to deliver her baby in such crude surroundings. Mrs. Phillips spoke on this to Will Gaines, but he would have none of his wife moving into town with Mrs. Phillips until the babe was born.

This day Will Gaines was again at work on his claim and failed to notice me as I passed by. I suspect he has a duffer there, as he fails to scratch a bare living.

I have to admit to a little secrecy when I approach, for I feel Margaret has a fear of her husband's anger. I am aware I must take the utmost care not to displease *Will Gaines* for fear sweet *Margaret* would be made to suffer the consequences. He has often been to town in the company of other miners and was monstrous belligerent when the drink was in him.

Margaret's tired smile melted my heart, and I was able to see how difficult it was for her in the heat in her condition. I took a box from my saddlebag and gave her the wrapped piece of *Turkish* delight I had brought her for a *Christmas* offering.

At first, she was reluctant to accept the tidbit, but at last, I convinced her to keep it. She nibbled the corner and her smile of enjoyment meant so much to me.

We conversed about the weather, and she shyly bade me notice the sprig of wattle she had hung upon the doorway of her humpy as a *Christmas* decoration. I barely saved myself from putting my arms about her poor tired body and professing my deepest feelings for her. I took my leave with the heaviest of hearts, and when I turned back, she had continued to stand with her little hand waving to me.

My next stop was the *Jones's* claim. Here I sought the aid of Mrs. *Jones*, a rough but kindly woman. I made her a payment and obtained her promise that she would dispatch her eldest son to ride to town for Mrs. *Phillips* when young Mrs. *Gaines's* time was come. I professed this was to be the secret wish of a relative of *Margaret's* and silently asked a Higher Being to forgive my falsehood. Mrs. *Jones*, I had come to note, had no love of *Will Gaines*, what with his encouragement of her husband to over-imbibe. The good lady made an exclamation of disgust in the direction of *Will Gaines* and made me that promise. Since the *Towers Brewery* served its first brew in *January* past, *Will* and his cronies are wont to be observed as excellent customers.

On my way back to town, although satisfied with my discussion with Mrs. *Jones*, I still suffered from the fear of what was to come. I am mindful of our dear mother, who was taken giving birth to our sister, *Kate*, who lived but a week. Our sister, *Mary*, barely of eleven years, then took on the responsibility of the house for Pa. As I grew older, I helped where I could. Nine years later, our *Mary* herself had succumbed when her own child was stillborn, and my dear friend *Jane* from my *childhood, was lost this way. All this death weighed heavily upon me, and my fear for that sweet, gentle girl increased threefold.*

3rd of January, 1892. There has been much news concerning the shearers' strike, and Richard and I have had much discussion on this. The shearers have set up camps and are armed with rifles. They say shearing wet animals is making them unwell and they are asking more than the pay of ten shillings for one hundred sheep shorn.

Richard was most amazed when I related to him that the Brilliant Mine yielded 36,605 ounces of gold this past year, and the total of exports from North Queensland was 923,969 pounds, a wealth indeed. More than two million shares were traded in the Stock Exchange, which had been struggling to maintain itself for over six months after commencing operations. The discovery of the Brilliant Reef brought a rush these past six months. Our town is the largest city in the State outside Brisbane, and the population of fifteen thousand is said to likely double within the next ten years. The four hundred stampers make a frightful noise.

In Townsville there is much concern regarding crocodiles. A white lad and a kanaka were taken by one of these fearsome beasts, right in the township. Phillips related to me that stray horses have been mauled and parts of them eaten. It is a truly awful thought.

A Chinese hawker came by this past week, and I was so taken with the beauty of his exotic wares that I was wont to purchase a length of silk for Margaret. I have hopes of gathering the boldness to give this to her, but I fear my courage will fail me.

3rd of March, 1892. This morn, as day was breaking, Margaret gave birth to a healthy son who will be named Robert. As I requested, young Jones rode to fetch Mrs. Phillips, and that dear lady returned not an hour ago with the wonderful news. She reports that Margaret is in great spirits and Mrs. Jones was to be of assistance to her. Will Gaines is now here in town to buy drinks for his cronies. It is to be hoped he will be in a stupor before heading back to the camp this night.

1st of May, 1892. This morn, Margaret journeyed into town with Mrs. Jones. I have no knowledge of how she convinced Will Gaines to allow her to do so, but I am so grateful to see her with my own eyes. She carried the babe into the store for me to admire. He is truly a handsome child, and Margaret's face was all aglow as she gazed at the tiny cherub. What I would give to have this sweet woman gaze at me with such love.

Mrs. Jones went about her business, leaving Margaret with me. I sat her in a comfortable chair and hurried upstairs to brew her some tea. I set it all on a lace-covered tray and added some fresh made cake from Phillips' Bakery. Margaret gazed at it with such delight. She smiled up at me, and I was sure the whole world around me stopped. I so wanted to take her in my arms and keep her safe. Some of my feelings may have been conveyed to her, and a pretty flush colored her cheeks. I was suddenly filled with remorse, fearing she would leave, but she showed nary a sign of horror. If I was as other men, I would surely relate the feelings in my heart. But I dare not speak of this.

9th of July, 1892. Word arrived from Richard, and his letter contained much concern. He tells me the south of the country is gripped by financial crisis and that banks are closing every day. The State of Victoria is worst hit. He has hopes it will not reach the north but begs I take every precaution to protect my assets.

18th of August, 1892. I was wont to take some supplies out to the Mining Camp No. 2 due to the sudden illness of my cart boy. Will Gaines was working at his sluice and barely gave me time of day. I continued on to the pitiful tent he provided as home for his wife Margaret and their child. That sweet girl tried to keep her face hidden from me, but her wee babe set to crying and when she turned, I saw her poor face. The bruises were fresh and fierce and I became weak with the need to take her into the comfort of my arms. All at once, I experienced a burning anger and I yearned to kill that cowardly, awful man who was her husband.

Indeed I believe I turned and would have rushed right down and taken great pleasure in squeezing his throat until he drew no breath and lay dead. Margaret put her hand upon my arm, made me pause, then bade me to calm myself. Her whispered words stay with me. "I could not bear to lose you, too, my brave Georgie." Her sweet, small hand that rested on my arm was rough and work-worn, fingers red and raw with chilblains from the cold. If only there was some way I could free this sweet woman from this dreadful life.

21st of December, 1892. Today came news from Richard. All is well there, although Richard is concerned for Maryann. She is leading them a merry dance with her coquettish ways. He is ever wishful she will gain half the sense of her sister, Georgina.

Richard also says there has been much talk about the Government House. Many considered it was far too small for entertaining guests of the governor. Richard thinks John Petrie desires to build a new one, but Richard fears there may not be the finances.

I was this last week given a young goat. I have told Mrs. Phillips she can have the milk for the children, and in return she can feed the animal with her scraps. When the goat is fattened up, we will have fresh meat for Christmastime.

Mrs. Phillips related to me that she has heard from Mrs. Jones that Margaret has taken in sewing. The miners who are alone need their shirts mended, and she makes some extra pocket money. I fear she would not see much of this, as Will Gaines is not a generous man.

శ్రీౄ

91

8th of March, 1893. I have much news from Richard. On the 5th of February, a huge amount of rain fell in a day, and near dawn the next day a wall of water swept down the river, bearing houses and trees before it. The northern end of Victoria Bridge was swept away. The economy on the other side of the river will surely suffer greatly. The capital is crippled. Almost all of the Brisbane River Valley is under water. Richard tells me the Brisbane River rose 70 inches before registration became impossible. This catastrophe appears to be the result of three cyclones, which have hit the coast in the past month. Flooding stretches from Rockhampton to Grafton in the south.

It was amazing to hear the Indooroopilly Railway Bridge also failed when hit by a wave of boiling floodwaters that battered the structure with felled trees, houses and river barges. Passengers now must cross the river to the outlying western settlements aboard ferries, and there is much unrest concerning the inflated cost of fares.

Another tale Richard told to me concerns a gunboat, which broke its moorings and ended up high and dry near Government House before being washed back again. Three other ships were washed into the Botanic Garden and left stranded until another flood two weeks later floated them free.

Richard tells me these are the worst floods of the nineteenth century, and he fears the results of the financial crash will be far-reaching through the State. He fortunately has ensured the safety of his own businesses, but many self-made men will lose everything. His concern was for my own business, but I was able to assure him I have followed his dictates and spread my investments. However, I feel sure my store will survive and this town is far richer than most.

The force of nature is a thing of disbelief, and we are all sick at heart for this doomed city. While the floods bring such despair to our Capital there are stories here of swagmen dying of thirst out past Hughenden.

8th of June, 1893. Richard tells me he has heard the great flood reached a height of ten feet and ten inches. He was most correct when he envisaged financial crashes. The first bank here to collapse was the Australian Joint Stock Bank this past April. This was followed by the London Chartered Bank and the Bank of North Queensland within the month. The collapse of the Queensland National Bank has been most devastating for many prominent mines and mills.

With hindsight, many are of the opinion that those souls who left the town and set out for the great gold rushes in Coolgardie in the west of this land are much better placed. This, of course, only the passage of time will disclose.

I have taken some losses, but they are not so extreme that I am unable to weather them. I am ever most indebted to my brother for his most sound advice.

5th of August, 1893. This morn was almost balmy, and I was much aware of the beauty of the day. I decided to make the most of it and partake of some fresh air. I set out and was not able to steer away from the direction my heart bade me take. Will Gaines was not at his claim, so I rode carefully toward his camp.

Margaret was tending the fire and turned to smile as I approached. Once again, that smile filled my heart. She told me her husband was over at the Jones's claim helping with a derrick.

The baby lay in his box cradle waving his tiny fists. I remarked on his growth, and that seemed to greatly please Margaret. She offered to me tea and fresh-made damper. In the making of damper, flour is kneaded with water and cooked in the coals. It can be almost unpalatable. However, Margaret can make a fine and tasty damper, which she spread with the syrup I sent out with Mrs. Jones.

I made heartfelt compliments to her, for it is difficult to cook out here in the camp. I had once become bold enough to suggest to Will Gaines that, with the babe, Margaret might be better placed in the town, but the difficult man became incensed. He stated to me that a wife's place was with her husband to do for him. So Margaret makes the best of it. She has planted out a vegetable garden, but water is scarce and the searing heat makes it all but impossible.

When we had eaten the damper, I commented on the pleasant smell of her cooking pot. She told me with some excitement that the miner, Cousins, had shot a kangaroo and Will had traded a cake Margaret had baked for some kangaroo meat. She dipped her ladle in the pot and offered it to me to taste. The stew was particularly delicious.

I remained with her as long as I dared, and even though I had no knowledge of when I might see her sweet face again, I rode home with my thoughts singing.

10th of November, 1893. The city of Brisbane has begun to rebuild and Richard is even more busy. Michael is a wonderful help to him. This year HRH Prince Albert Victor and HRH Prince George Edward visited Brisbane Grammar School on Gregory Terrace, which is Michael's old school. Richard related that they are all well.

23rd of December, 1893. Some of the miners don't even stop for Christmas, and Will Gaines is one of them. My sweet Margaret made festive decorations from paper chains, which she hung upon a small, spindly bush by their humpy. Young Robbie took hold of my hand and led me to regard their Christmas tree, his eyes, Margaret's eyes, round with wonder, his tiny finger pointing at the display. He is a child of great beauty, like his sweet mother, and I have the deepest of longings that he was my own son.

I managed to pass Margaret some sweets for her and the boy, who continues to grow. He keeps his mother busy chasing after him. Margaret is so afraid he will injure himself on discarded pieces of equipment, or that he may fall down a rocky slope to the almost dry creek bed.

I wish I could take her away from this dreadful life. At least in the township there is some semblance of civilization. Out here in the bush with these rough miners is no place for a woman like Margaret.

The weather is so hot we keep forever vigilant in case a spark sets off the dry, dead grass. Bushfires, I fear, are unstoppable in this harsh land. In the heat our lives are made more miserable by clouds of insects, most especially flies, that cover a man's back like a cloak. They gather around nostrils and mouths until you fear you might go mad with brushing them away.

5th of April, 1894. Will Gaines has been quick with his fists again. My poor Margaret could barely open her eye. I found her alone at the tent camp with just young Robbie for company. The mine workings were idle, and according to Margaret, the miners were over the hill to a meeting. There has been more unrest concerning claim jumping and the price of gold. The Good Lord knows what these unfortunate men can do about it. There certainly are not enough police in the area, it has grown so large.

At least I am thankful for the miners' meeting. It allowed for me to spend time alone with my sweet girl. I can barely stand to see her suffer so at the hands of that scoundrel husband. I overcame my timidity to urgently voice these words to her as we watched over Robbie playing in the dirt. For once, she did not bade me cease, but her small hand clutched my arm and tears ran down her sunburned cheeks. With no thought for prying eyes, I clasped her to me and held her safe. For joyous moments her sweet soft lips touched mine before she pulled away, horrified at her indiscretion. I begged her to let me take her and the baby away, but she became exceedingly agitated. She is convinced Will Gaines would hunt us down and kill us all. I came away with a feeling of such hopelessness, and I am taken by such powerlessness that I have scarce slept since. There must be something that can be done.

14th of June, 1894. There is such commotion at Mining Camp No.2 this day. It would seem Will Gaines has gone missing. Margaret sent Jim Jones's boy to ride into town for the Constable. There has been no sighting of Will Gaines for two days past.

He was in the Excelsior Hotel on Friday night with a group of other miners, for I saw him there myself. It set me to worrying about Margaret and the boy out there at the camp alone at night. I also saw him stagger out of the hotel with Cousins and Jones as I took a late-night walk with Phillips. The three were so drunk they could barely climb into Jones's wagon. I commented on this to Phillips as we stood and watched the spectacle. Phillips laughed and said it was to be hoped the horse knew its way home.

When poor Margaret awoke next morning, Cousins and Jones were sleeping off the drink, but Will Gaines was nowhere to be found.

21st of June, 1894. Still there is no sighting of Will Gaines. The troopers have called in a black tracker, but no trail has been found. Yesterday some of the women persuaded Margaret and the boy to come into the town to await the outcome of the searches. As the days pass, the likelihood of good news passes too. Mr. and Mrs. Phillips have kindly taken in Margaret and the boy, and I took extra supplies for them this evening.

25th of June, 1894. Will Gaines is missing still, and I try not to feel a small amount of gladness. He was such a brute of a man. Although Margaret says it is the drink that makes him that way. When he is sober he can be quite fine, she tells me. It is my belief the disappointment Will Gaines feels because his claim has not paid off only sets him to drinking all the more.

I have taken to visiting my sweet Margaret each evening after dinner. Of course, Mrs. Phillips is our chaperone, and I make some small excuse to talk to Phillips himself. The boy delights in running to me to be hoisted high, and this day I saw the first small smile on my Margaret's sweet mouth.

❧

30th of June, 1894. All the town is abuzz with the news. A body was found down an abandoned mineshaft not half a mile from Mining Camp No. 2. The shaft was covered with a branch and grasses, and but for a station outrider's dog, it would surely not ever have been discovered.

The dog became agitated and set to barking and could not be drawn away. The shaft was but a dozen feet deep, and upon investigation, the horseman thought he saw a man's body down at the bottom. He fetched help and the remains were brought to the surface. My poor Margaret was asked to view the clothes and boots, and she recognized these as belonging to her husband, Will Gaines.

Dr. Robertson declared the cause of death to be a broken neck, which must have occurred when Gaines fell into the shaft. A blow to the back of the neck was deemed to have been caused when Gaines toppled backward into the hole.

The police decided the branch had fallen over part of the shaft and wind had blown the grasses, which caught upon the branch.

The death appears not to be suspicious, for many citizens, besides Phillips and myself, were witness to the drunken state of Will Gaines when he left the Excelsior Hotel that Friday night. Truth be told, Will Gaines had made himself many enemies and few friends. He was far too ready with his fists, and I was not the only witness to poor Margaret's bruises. If Will Gaines met with foul play out in that dark night, not a body seemed ready to question Dr. Robertson's diagnosis of the incident.

18th of July, 1894. The funeral of Will Gaines was a small affair. Only Jones and Cousins took time from their labors to attend. Mrs. Phillips has made herself a great support for the widow and the Phillips have agreed for Margaret and the boy to stay in their house as long as she has wish to. Phillips and I arranged for Jones's eldest son to work Will Gaines's claim until any relatives can be found.

With Mrs. Phillips happy to watch young Robbie with her own brood, my sweet Margaret has agreed to come and help me in the shop in the morning when trade is brisk. The amount I will pay her will keep her and the boy.

23rd of October, 1894. Margaret begins to look a little better. Good food provided by Mrs. Phillips has taken the thinness from her body, and her cheeks now display an amount of color. I am watchful that she does not overtax herself, and my rewards are to see her sweet lips lift into a smile.

There has been another shearers' strike and we have heard of shearing sheds and homesteads having been set alight. There is talk of a shootout between police and rebel shearers on a sheep station northwest of Winton. The Queensland Mounted Infantry rode west from Charters Towers to take charge of the militants. The Queensland strikers have been unable to prevent the hiring of scab labor from the south, and the deadlock between the shearers and the pastoralists has not been resolved. News came of a river steamer on the Darling that was bringing shearers to the region that was burned to the waterline.

I am ashamed to say it is difficult for me to take so many goings-on to heart, as my heart's space is so full of my sweet girl.

18th of March, 1895. Margaret has become indispensable to me at the store and the customers are most fond of her. She continues to reside with the Phillips family, and even in her widow's dress, she blooms. The harshness of her life out at the mining camp is behind her, and she converses brightly with everyone. Young Robbie has had his second birthday and is a strong and loving little boy.

A letter from Richard arrived to announce that Maryann had married William Reid. The couple eloped to Sydney. Richard and Susannah are sorely tried by her. The young man is not of a type her parents would have chosen, but the deed is now done. Georgina has become betrothed to Alexa Santino, a master coach maker, who was born in the Victoria goldfields. His father was an Italian and his mother an English governess. Richard thinks highly of him and plans to offer the young man a position in his business.

16th of July, 1895. I sorely miss my sweet Margaret. Although I am much pleased to see my family and to observe the city of Brisbane again, I greatly need to have Margaret near me. Tomorrow I sail for home and am filled with much anticipation.

Georgina's wedding was a sight to behold. She was so beautiful. Richard was so overcome he could barely speak. I am much taken with her new husband. He has kindly eyes and I am sure they will deal well together.

Maryann and her husband arrived from Sydney for the wedding festivities, and I feel Richard and Susannah's disquiet about her husband, William Reid. He looks well enough, but his conversation is most boastful. Maryann is with child and wants to remain near her mother until the birth.

While I visited the city, the new Indooroopilly Bridge was opened, and the railway operates again after the great flood washed the bridge away. This bridge is impressive, a two-span steel bridge supported by abutments and concrete piers. Surely it will endure.

1st of October, 1895. I have made some inquiries with the owners of the building adjacent to my store, and I am hopeful that they will allow me to purchase the property. Margaret agrees with me that it would be most beneficial to add more space to the store.

I have begun to take Robbie with me to the lending library, and he is most captivated by the stories we read together. We have only finished the reading of The Adventures of Tom Sawyer, and I see in the newspaper that the author of this wonderful book, Mr. Samuel L. Clemens, who writes as Mark Twain, has arrived in Sydney. How wonderful it must be for those who have spoken with him.

A traveler passing through the town related to me that the poem of "Waltzing Matilda," penned by "The Banjo," was put to music and sung at a gathering in Winton earlier in this year, and is quickly becoming a favorite tune.

15th of October, 1895. This day I purchased the premises beside the store and soon work will begin to combine the buildings and extend the store. I am much pleased with this property, as my stock has outgrown this building. I obtained from McKinly's Hotel a bottle of their best wine for Margaret and I to celebrate. We made a toast to the success of the new venture. I had thought to light two candles and, in the flickering light, Margaret had never looked so beautiful to me.

I took her hand and raised it to my lips. Perhaps it was the unaccustomed wine that loosed my tongue, but I was unable to prevent myself from professing my great regard for her. She took her hand away and her soft lips trembled. I do declare my heartbeats stopped and I thought my life was lost. Then she raised her eyes, brimming with tears, and she clutched my hand again. My sweet Margaret told me I was the kindest person she had ever met.

I had a burning desire to carry her up to my room, but there was much to tell her, things I feared would cause her love to turn from me. I will savor this time for as long as I am able. I walked her home to the Phillips's house, and beneath the tamarind tree, by their gate, her wondrous lips met mine.

22nd of January, 1896. News arrived that my niece Maryann was delivered of a baby girl in the New Year. She is a bonny babe who is to be named Susannah after her grandmother. To think of Richard and Susannah as grandparents has caused me to feel my age. I am now in my forty-fourth year, and my mirror tells me my hair begins to turn to gray. I feel concern that I am far too old for my Margaret, who is but thirty years.

No relatives of Will Gaines have been found to this date, so the claim, such as it is, will go to young Robbie. An argument broke out at the mining camp where Jones's eldest boy works Will Gaines's claim and there was need for the police to be called. During the disagreement it appeared an inebriated Jones fell down a rock-strewn slope and was injured about his head. The poor fellow was pronounced dead by Dr. Robertson. I feel for Mrs. Jones, who I have always seen as a good and kind woman. Fortunately, she has three other just grown boys to work Jones's claim. The funeral is to be held tomorrow.

Last weekend past I harnessed up the cart and drove Margaret and young Robbie out to the river to partake of a picnic. The Burdekin River is only sand with a few shallow pools at the present. We put the billy on to boil and enjoyed cups of tea. The milk we wrapped in damp cloths to keep it from turning stale. With this we partook of one of Mrs. Phillips's fresh cakes.

Robbie took much pleasure in tossing small pebbles and sticks into the water, and Margaret went to him to ensure he did not tumble over the bank. I sat back in the shade and seized the opportunity to observe my Margaret. Her beauty never fails to cause my heart to swell with love. Our closeness fills me with a bittersweet joy. I am desperate to ask for her hand in marriage but fear what I must tell her. I greatly need to be honest with her, and my heart knows she deserves this from me. I long to make her mine, but to do this I must speak to her about so much that has been kept a secret for so long. My greatest fear is that she would turn from me in hate, for this would surely break my heart.

17th of May, 1896. I have read with much optimism of women in South Australia, who have, for the first time, exercised their right to vote. This is as it should be, for women are as much capable as men. It is to be hoped our State will follow this sensible landmark. The changes are a long time in the making since the first Australian Women's Suffrage was formed in Melbourne over ten years past.

๛

28th of July, 1896. With great joy, I have learnt that Georgina was safely delivered of twin baby girls on the 8th of July. They have been named Rose and Maria for Alexa's mother and grandmother. Susannah tells me Georgina is a fine mother and deliriously happy. Alexa bursts with pride.

Maryann's husband, William Reid, has lost his job again and seems disinclined to take a position with Richard. Next week they leave for Sydney where William hopes to get work. Maryann is to leave her baby daughter with Susannah and Richard until they are settled in Sydney.

29th of July, 1896. Last evening when I walked Margaret home after the store was closed, we stopped beneath the tamarind tree and I lifted her hand to my lips. She leaned against me, her hands on my chest, and she kissed me sweetly on the lips. In a trembling voice she asked me what she might do without me. I assured her there was no need for her to do so. She then asked me why I was, why I had always been, so good to her.

Because I love you, I had the burning need to say. The words trembled upon my lips as she gazed up at me with her clear, gentle eyes. Before I could prevent myself, I told her, my voice filled with much agitation and not my own, that I loved her with all my heart and my life. I professed to have loved her from the moment I had set my eyes upon her and that I would love her forever.

She gave a soft sigh, slid her arms around me and placed her head upon my heart. It was at this time she uttered the words I thought not to hear. She told me she loved me with all her own heart. Our kisses were urgent and I allowed my hand to rest upon her soft breast, felt her nipple harden against my hand. We both breathed so fastly, and I took her hand, drew her down the garden to the wooden seat behind some bushes, away from prying eyes.

Once there, I kissed her again and pulled her upon my lap. She murmured softly as I stroked her fine hair, her soft throat, my fingers finding her nipple again. She buried her face in my neck, nibbled soft kisses against my skin, made wondrous mewling sounds that further stirred my blood. I pushed aside her bodice and my lips suckled at her breast. Bold now, and consumed by great desire, I ran my hand shakily on her thigh, found her center through her underclothing. I was filled with love for her, and I made good use of the wondrous secrets I had been taught in that house of ill repute in Rockhampton years ago.

My own darling clutched me fiercely and whispered my name as tremors took hold of her body. She sobbed into my shoulder and I put small kisses on her earlobe, her hot face, and then her sweet, soft lips. I was much aware that she was overcome by shyness, and at last she haltingly told me that she had not before felt that way. I asked if not even with her late husband, but she shook her head, making her curls bounce softly against my skin. With tears upon her cheeks, she hesitantly related to me the horror and pain she had experienced when Will Gaines sated his husbandly desires. Had that cruel man been alive still, I fear I would have killed him again.

I soothed her tears and promised there would be no pain for her from me. This caused me to recall my vow to confess my secret, and I was held more by a monstrous fear. With much reluctance, I bade her take my arm and walk with me down the wide path to the Phillips's back fence, lest we be overheard. After a time, I explained to her that I could never be a man for her. I explained the reason why this was so and assured her that I would understand if she wished not to marry me. She cried then and clutched my hand to her cheek. Likewise, tears flowed down my face as she professed to love me all the more. My sweet Margaret is a woman of Great Exception.

This morning Mrs. Phillips was the first to be told of our betrothal. I must now write a letter to Richard and find a way to explain to him my love for this most wonderful of women. I fear it will not be easy.

20th of August, 1896. Richard's long-awaited letter arrived this day. His handwriting becomes spider-like, and I fear he ages now. He sends best wishes on my coming marriage and makes no recriminations.

I was much surprised, and this leads me to fear his memory may be fading. I was saddened to hear my suspicions were not unfounded for, in the same post, arrived a note from Susannah. She tells me Richard's health is not good, and he has given over much of the business to Michael. He tires quickly and his hands begin to tremble.

Georgina and the twins continue to thrive, and young Susannah grows quickly. Richard gets much joy from his grandbabies. They have not heard from Maryann and William Reid these past six months. When last Susannah heard, they planned to journey to England and had no desire to be reunited with their child. I admit to being much amazed by Maryann's behavior. Susannah also sent her best wishes for my marriage and bade me consider bringing Margaret down to Brisbane so they may make her acquaintance. She fears Richard will not again be well enough to make the journey north.

1st of October, 1896. At last, my Margaret is finally mine. Each night I hold her close to my heart and pray to God I am worthy of her. Robbie sleeps now in the small room beside our own. Margaret has told him I am now his father and he hugged me tightly and asked if he could be allowed to call me Papa, as the young Phillips children call their father. The word is so sweet to my ears, and I am so thankful for the blessings that have become mine. Although I thought it impossible, I believe I love my Margaret more since we became wed. The pleasure we bring each other in our room is so much more than I have ever dreamed of. My life is now so fulfilled.

29th of December, 1896. Christmastime shared with Margaret and young Robbie was a thing to behold. After the boy retired to bed, Margaret and I quickly decorated a small tree the eldest Phillips boy had cut for me. We then placed gaily-wrapped gifts beneath it. We laughed softly like children and then kissed beneath a sprig of wattle. My Margaret's kisses fired my blood, and I carried her quickly up to our room and lay her upon our bed. I took my place beside her and found her sweet, secret places. I am scarce able to believe my great fortune that this wondrous life is now mine.

In the morning Robbie's eyes were wide with surprise when he saw the tree and gifts. He has implored me each evening to read to him from his book, Seven Little Australians by the author Ethel Turner. During the day he has sorely tried his mother's patience with the tin whistle he received. I have suspicion that that instrument may be hidden away.

I am much blessed.

I read in the newspaper that the first moving pictures were played at the Tivoli Theatre in Sydney this past September. There were moving pictures that showed traffic crossing Westminster Bridge in London and a crowd of people in the Strand. I would much like to have seen this, though I fear I would not recognize the old country now after being gone these twenty-six years. I must ask Richard if he read of this amazing invention.

16th of August, 1897. On Sunday afternoon last, Margaret and I drove Robbie up to the summit of Towers Hill where we were able to gaze out over the town. It was a most inspiring view. To the west of the town is the Great Dividing Range, and then begins the boundless plains that stretch toward the Gulf of Carpentaria.

A shining report has been tendered concerning the town, which informs us that twenty thousand souls now live within four square miles of where the first prospectors made their camps twenty-five years ago. The town boasts many fine businesses—to which I humbly add Chaseley's Store—many elegant residences, and many conveniences, such as electric light in the streets. The Post Office is to have a magnificent clock tower, with the clock being imported from England. This will be most pleasing to the eye. There is now a high-level railway bridge over the Burdekin River, which will serve the town in all weathers.

I have seen much change here in the town and find no regrets con-

cerning my decision to venture north to make my life. For into that life has come to me my most treasured possession, my dear sweet Margaret.

30th of August, 1897. An urgent letter arrived this day from Susannah. Richard entertained a great desire to see His Excellency the Governor open the final stage of the New Victoria Bridge in Brisbane. He enlisted the family's aid to carry him to the ceremony. This was also the sixtieth birthday of Queen Victoria, and Richard so wished to be there.

However, Susannah feels the ordeal was too much for Richard and his health declines so rapidly. She begs me come with all haste that I might look upon him one last time. Margaret can see how despairing I am over this news and agrees with Susannah that I should go. I cannot bear to be without Margaret, so I have made plans with Mrs. Phillips to have care of the store and I will set out at first light with Margaret and Robbie by my side. It is a journey I have so much wished to make with my sweet Margaret. But not for reasons so sad as this.

6th of May, 1898. This will be the last night Margaret and I and young Robbie will spend in our store. Tomorrow the new owners, a pleasant enough couple, will begin their new lives as the owners of Chaseley's Store. We journey south once again, this time to our new life in Brisbane.

I am much thankful that I arrived in the city last year in time to behold my dear brother before he was taken from us. How he had changed, grown so thin, but his eyes brightened when they rested upon me. At first, he inquired with much cheer about my health, and the appearance of the weather, and I was moved to wonder if he had confused me with an acquaintance.

When we had been left alone, he then clutched at my hand and asked me if I was happy. I assured him I had never been more happy in my life. He admitted to not understanding how I could marry and he

106

became agitated. I gently set him back against his pillows and bade him not to worry so. He was quiet for some time and then his hand in mine tightened. He asked if he had harmed me by his decision before we set out from London. I reminded him that the decision had been taken by the both of us and I prevailed upon him, in all honesty, that I had not suffered a moment of regret. He begged to be told if I felt unnatural. I assured him I did not.

He then said he was concerned for my wife, who he declared to be a most likeable woman. I sat down beside my dear brother and related the life, the awfulness, that my Margaret had suffered during her marriage with her first husband, Will Gaines. I told of how Will Gaines had left this world with nary a friend but a great number of enemies. Will Gaines was nothing but a cruel, cowardly drunkard. When I had finished, I swore to Richard that Margaret and I loved each other deeply, that I had every intention of keeping her safe and assisting her to raise her boy. Richard nodded and fell into a doze. I gently disengaged our hands, but he stirred again.

He began to talk of England, his eyes most melancholy. We spoke of the hardships of our old life in the mining villages, and of our dear Mam and baby Kate, taken when we were but children, of our Pa, killed with our older brother, Michael, in that dreadful mine explosion nearly thirty years ago, of our young brother Benjamin, crushed by a coal truck when he was but twelve years old, and of our sweet sister, Mary, who was lost with her wee babe. We were both of us then moved to tears for that which we had lost, and for what we had since found.

We buried my brother but ten days later. Susannah was inconsolable, but in a few days she had rallied, for she had the house to run and young Susannah to care for.

When it came the time for Margaret and me to return north, my sister-in-law tearfully begged us to stay, even though she knew we were unable to do so. I arranged for Georgina and the twins to remain with her mother for a few weeks and, after a discussion with Margaret, I made Susannah a promise we would somehow return to Brisbane and the family.

And so another journey begins. Tomorrow we make our way south to keep that promise.

Asha read well into the night, unable to stop until she had finished the second journal. As she carefully closed the cover, she realized tears were streaming down her face.

CHAPTER SIX

With her new printer cartridge in her hand, Asha started toward the house. Vivienne had been as thrilled as Asha had been when Asha showed her what she'd found in the box. Asha had suggested she transcribe the diaries for Vivienne to read so they didn't damage the old books, and she agreed wholeheartedly. So Asha had spent the morning doing just that. She'd given Vivienne the beginning of Georgie Chaseley's first journal she'd printed out and she'd barely begun printing out the next section when the light on the printer began to flash. As she had forgotten to bring an extra cartridge with her, she drove down to the nearest office supply store for a replacement.

Asha strode around the garden beds, and something moved in her peripheral vision. She turned to see Joe Deneen sitting on the edge of the veranda, elbows on his knees, chin resting on one hand. His whole mien suggested he was feeling down. Hesitating for only a moment, Asha changed her direction slightly, her feet crunching on the gravel pathway. Joe looked up at her approach.

"Afternoon, Joe," Asha said. "You look like you've lost a dollar and found ten cents."

He looked at her and sighed. "That about covers it."

This close, Asha could see his incredibly long dark eyelashes and the sad curve of his perfect lips. Couple that with his wonderful physique and, Asha thought, Whoa! Even a committed lesbian could see what a knockout he was. "What's up?" she asked and he grimaced.

"Guess I'm a bit down."

Asha paused. He looked much the same as Michelle had the last time she'd had an argument with her boyfriend, Danny. "Let me guess. Woman trouble?"

He looked up at her in surprise. "How did you know?"

"Maybe I'm just psychic." She laughed. "Want to talk about it?"

"Nah!" He sighed again.

"Okay." Asha went to continue on her way.

"I don't understand women," he said, frowning.

Asha hid her amusement and sat down beside him.

After a moment he turned to face her. "A guy just never knows where he is with women."

"What happened?"

"I just don't understand them," he repeated with another long-suffering sigh.

"I'm starting to believe you." Asha gave him a friendly nudge. "So, is it too painful to talk about?"

"It's my girlfriend. Tammy. You might have seen her here helping me with the garden the other day."

Asha had seen a petite curvaceous brunette shadowing Joe, but she hadn't noticed the girl doing anything more than feeling Joe's flexed muscles. "I believe I did see her."

"She's absolutely hot, you know." His eyes fell to Asha's chest and quickly away. "Fantastic figure. A real, um, she's great look-ing. Other guys just drool. But, anyway, she makes me nuts."

"What do you do?"

"Me?" He looked indignant. "Absolutely zilch. Well, nothing that bad. I just had a couple of drinks with the guys the other night after the game. We won, you know. It was just a couple. I mean, I'm not stupid, you know. I know if I have any more I get as silly as a cut snake. Apart from that, I take care of my body. I have to. It's my job to stay fit."

"Very sensible." Asha couldn't prevent herself from a quick glance at his physical attributes. "And you're doing a great job, by the way."

Joe flexed his biceps. "You think?"

Asha laughed and he grinned.

"But I'm not just a body, you know," he said, sobering. "And I want Tammy to realize that. I know I've only got a certain number of years in the game, all that barring injury, so I know I have to plan for my future. I mean, look at your father." He stopped and looked a little sheepish. "Mrs. C. told me you were Sean West's daughter. He's tops, by the way. But, anyway, your father knew he could only play rep cricket for so long, so he started his sports store. That was using his head." Joe tapped his forehead.

"Mmm," Asha murmured.

"And I'm planning for my future, too. That's one of the rea-sons I stayed so long after the game. There were lots of media people there as well, and I managed to get the chance to do a stint on Channel Nine's Footy Show. It was a dream come true. You see, I'm aiming to do sports presenting when I retire from playing, and this could be my chance for a bit of exposure, to show what I can do."

Asha knew with his good looks he had every chance of realiz-ing that dream. "We all need a goal."

"Right. And that's what I told Tammy." He bit off an excla-mation. "But she wants me to go to some work thing of hers the night I'm booked to do the Footy Show."

"Ah. A little shortsighted of her," Asha said, wondering why Tammy wouldn't be thrilled to be able to tell everyone her boyfriend was on television.

"Shortsighted? That's exactly it."

"You can't suggest you go to the next of Tammy's work dos?"

"I didn't get that far. We both did some yelling and she . . ." He kicked at the pebble garden edge with his work boot. "She just walked off. That was two days ago."

"You could try ringing her."

"I know. The point is, I'm not sure I want to. I mean, she's sexy as hell, but . . ." He stopped and sighed again. "I think she's a bit immature."

"How old is she?"

"Seventeen. Nearly eighteen. I think I might go for older women in the future." He gave that a moment's reflection and turned back to Asha. "Do you have a boyfriend, Asha?"

"No," Asha replied carefully.

"Sorry." Joe looked a little embarrassed. "That was a bit transparent. But you're a foxy lady. How come you don't have a boyfriend?"

Asha shrugged. "Guess I'm not what guys are looking for."

Joe snorted in disbelief. "Yeah, right! You're great looking, easy to talk to. Why wouldn't you be?"

"Thanks for the vote of confidence." Asha shrugged again. "I'm quite happy to be between dances, so to speak."

"How long since you've been in a relationship?"

"About six months. Should have been a year," she added ruefully.

"What did he do? Another woman?"

"Something like that." It would be easy to be honest, but Asha always hesitated. You never really knew how other people would react, and because Joe moved in the epitome of blokey circles of football, she was doubly cautious. "I suppose you could say it was more like other women."

"Bummer! He must have been nuts." Joe paused. "Don't suppose you'd care to, um, go for dinner or something sometime?"

"You mean, be your first older woman?" Asha asked lightly, noticing he'd gone a little pink about his ears again.

Joe laughed softly. "I guess something like that."

"I, uh," Asha tried to choose her words carefully.

"Thanks, but no thanks?" Joe suggested flatly.

"Joe, you're a really nice person, and if I was looking for a guy—"

"You'd pick me. I know," Joe finished self-derisively.

Asha smiled. "That's it. But seriously, Joe, as I said, I don't think I'm ready for another relationship. Breathing space is always good, I think. Maybe for you, too."

"Yeah. I suppose you're right," Joe acknowledged. "Pity, though. I really like you, Asha. I can, you know, talk to you."

"Thank you, Joe. Just give it time with Tammy. Who knows? She might not be the lost cause you seem to think she is."

"Yeah, I'm pretty sure she is somehow. I know Aunt Margo wasn't keen on her. Guess I'd better get back to it. My uncle'll have my hide if I don't keep this place up to his standards while he's off work." He stood up, held out his hand to Asha and pulled her to her feet. Keeping hold of her hand, he leaned forward and kissed her lightly.

Asha stilled, suddenly aware they were out in the open, that anyone could see them. "Joe, I—"

He winked at her and gave her a grin. "If you change your mind, decide you want to try a younger bloke, promise you'll let me know."

Asha couldn't help laughing at him. "As in, if I want a toy boy I know where to come?"

Joe gave a throaty chuckle. "Exactly." He sobered. "Thanks, Asha. For being so nice, you know, for listening."

"Anytime," she said and Joe walked off toward the garage. As

113

Asha turned to continue around to the front of the house, she thought she heard a footfall on the veranda above. Pausing, she looked up. Had someone been eavesdropping? Not that it mattered. What could they have heard? An amateur counseling session? She shrugged it off and followed the path to the main entrance.

Asha was crossing the vestibule, heading toward the staircase, when she looked up to see Peri at the top of the stairs. Asha smiled. She jogged up the steps, joining the other woman. "Hello. I thought you were at work."

"And that's where I thought I'd find you," Peri said, her voice devoid of expression, and Asha hesitated slightly.

Was Peri being critical of her work schedule? Asha knew her hours were her own, and Vivienne was fine with that arrangement. "I needed a new printer cartridge." She held up her package. "And I was feeling a little square-eyed from the computer screen, so I took the opportunity to get out for some fresh air and a change of scene. Did you want to see me for anything special?"

A dull flush touched Peri's cheeks. "No. Not really. I was just wondering how things were going. With the research."

"Oh. It's going magnificently. Did Vivienne tell you I found some old journals in the bottom of the chest?"

"I haven't seen her since I got back. What sort of journals?" Peri asked, and Asha could see she was intrigued now.

Asha grinned. "Absolutely fabulous ones. Come on and I'll show you."

Turning and heading along the hallway to the study, Asha was very aware of Peri so close behind her. By the time she reached the desk, she felt as though her mouth was totally dry and her skin was damp and clammy. Not meeting Peri's eyes, she handed her a pair of soft gloves and then donned a pair herself. "These will ensure we don't damage the books. They're over a hundred years old, although they're in remarkable condition considering their age."

She handed the first journal to Peri, and she carefully opened it, reading the first entry. "I remember my grandmother talking about her Grandpa Georgie. This is his account of his arrival in Australia?"

Asha nodded and grinned. "His firsthand account. And it continues through his time in Brisbane, then in Charters Towers, and it finishes when they return to Brisbane in 1897. It's amazing."

"Can I read it? Without damaging it, I mean," Peri asked.

"I'm transcribing it. Vivienne has the first part I've printed, so you can read it when she's finished. I was about to finish printing out the rest of the first section, which I would have done if my printer hadn't gone on strike. Hence the new cartridge. If you like I can print you out your own copy. Vivienne also wants me to do a copy to send to your grandmother."

Reluctantly Peri handed the book back to Asha, who returned it to the desk. She then passed Peri the photograph of Georgie and Margaret and their wedding day.

Peri read the inscription on the back. "This is Georgie and Margaret? I've never seen this. And I don't recall Vivienne ever showing it to us."

"She hadn't seen it either. It was hidden under a false bottom in the box, along with the journals and some certificates." Asha showed Peri where she'd found the books. "It's just fantastic."

Peri studied the photo. "They look nice. And in love."

"They were, according to the journal. Vivienne remembers them. Georgie was ninety-eight when he died in 1950, and Margaret, who was younger, died a few months later."

"You're right. It's amazing." Peri returned the photo. "Who do think would have hidden the books and photos in the box, and why would they have done that? I mean, is there a family secret in the journals?"

"Not that I can tell." Asha frowned. "Although Georgie hints at something that happened before they left London. I'll get onto some more research as soon as I've finished the transcription. And as for who hid it all in the box, we don't know that either. Vivienne and I were trying to piece together a timeline for the box, and as far as I can tell, it was a music box Richard Chaseley gave to his wife, Susannah. After his death, Vivienne says Susannah eventually moved in with one of her daughters. We surmise Georgie would have kept his own journals, so maybe Susannah gave the box to Georgie and Margaret. Either he put them in the box before he died, or Margaret did after his death." Asha shrugged. "Or one of the family hid them after Margaret died. There are lots of possibilities."

"I guess so." Peri frowned. "But for them to be hidden you'd think there would be something in them someone didn't want the family to know about, wouldn't you?"

"Maybe originally it was just for safekeeping." Asha grinned. "But a family secret is far more exciting, don't you think?"

Peri smiled, too. "I think that might depend on the secret."

Asha swallowed, wondering if Peri felt the change in the atmosphere around them. Or was she simply imagining it? Wanting something to be there when it wasn't. "I think most family historians hope for an interesting secret or two," she said as evenly as she could.

"And you have no idea what our family secret might be?"

"Not at this stage. And we might never know why the journals were hidden. But, as Vivienne said, we'll be doing our darnedest to unravel the mystery."

"Yes. I can imagine how excited Viv is about it. Thanks for showing it to me." Peri indicated the books on the desk. She looked as though she'd say more, but she gave a soft cough and turned away. "My curiosity's definitely sparked, so I think I'll go and see how much of the journal Viv's read and what she thinks about it. But I'd like my own copy, too." With that, she left Asha alone in the study, gazing at the empty doorway.

"Asha? It's Dad."

Asha was surprised. Her father usually left phone calls to Karen. "Hi, Dad. How are you?"

"Fine, love."

"And Karen and the boys?"

"Fighting fit. Quite literally sometimes." He chuckled. "But I'm ringing up about Wednesday night."

"Wednesday night?" Asha tried to sort out her obviously failing memory.

"Yes. The Awards Dinner. Karen said she told you about it a couple of months ago."

"Oh. Yes. I vaguely remember that." Asha frowned.

"So? You've kept it free, haven't you?"

"Well, I guess I am free."

"Fantastic, because you're going with your old dad. So get out your best bib and tucker, maybe that little black dress you wore the night we went out for my birthday. Now, that looked great."

"What's it all about, Dad? Where are we going?" Asha asked, prepared to cry off.

"I've got tickets to the Sports Awards dinner at the Sheraton for all of us."

"All of us?"

"Karen and I, Michelle and Danny and you and your boyfriend."

Boyfriend? Asha's heart sank. "Oh, Dad, I don't know. I'm not all that into sports."

"Rubbish. You came to all my matches when I was playing."

Asha made a face at the telephone. Only when he wanted the three of them there. Asha knew her stepmother hadn't enjoyed it any more than Asha and Michelle had.

"Now, no excuses," her father continued. "Michelle and

117

Danny are coming. And, Asha, Laura's okay about you both coming along. I know how loyal you are and that's fine, but this is a special night because it seems your good old dad has been nominated for an award this year. I haven't had a nomination in years." He laughed, obviously very pleased. "It'll be like old times."

"What sort of award have you been nominated for?" Asha asked, curious, too.

"No idea. But they want me there and I have tickets for family and friends. So Karen and I, Michelle and Danny and you and your boyfriend will be sitting at a table with some other sporting greats." He reeled off names that included another cricketer and a well-known swimmer.

Asha sighed. "Okay. But I'll come on my own."

"Don't be silly, love. It'll give me a chance to look over your latest boyfriend."

Asha almost laughed. The only time she'd ever brought a boy home, she was thirteen years old, and Neil was a friend who had begged her to introduce him to her famous father. It had cost Neil the best hamburger on the menu at the local café, and she'd made him pay up, too. "What makes you think I have a boyfriend, Dad?"

"What? My beautiful daughter! If you don't then guys these days aren't up to scratch."

"I'd feel better coming on my own," Asha said, but her father continued.

"Anyway, I thought Karen said you told her you had a boyfriend down the coast."

That had been ages ago and only after Karen had cross-examined her mercilessly. In a weak moment Asha had hinted at a special friend simply to appease Karen at the time. "That was last year and we're not together anymore."

"Oh. The guy's a fool and you're well rid of him. But look, love, if you come alone it'll make the table look lopsided."

"Lopsided?" Asha burst out laughing. "Since when have you been into balance and related stuff, Dad?"

Sean West laughed, too. "You know me so well, don't you, love. No, it's orders from Karen. She said to tell you if you haven't got anyone to come with you she knows this nice guy who cleans her sister's pool."

"A pool boy?"

"Nothing wrong with a pool boy, love," her father said with mock seriousness. "It's an honest job. And I can tell you, in the looks department even I can see he's a ten. Now, intellectually, I'm not sure, but how bad can he be for one night? What do you say, Asha?"

"I say thanks, but no thanks to the pool boy. I'll find someone for myself." Asha thought of Peri. Peri said she didn't mind cricket as a sport, and she knew who Sean West was. Maybe she'd like to go. Would she accept Asha's invitation? Would Asha have the nerve to ask her? "I'll see what I can do, Dad," she said finally. "What time?"

"We're all meeting at six. Here at our place. They're sending a stretch limo, apparently."

"Dad, what about Mum? Are you sure?"

"You know Laura never liked these dos." There was a commotion in the background. "Look, love, I've got to go. I'm taking the boys down to the park for a game of soccer. I'll see you on Wednesday night. Oh, and Asha, please come along. I feel like I never see you these days."

After murmuring good-bye Asha sat for a while trying to decide what to do. She loved her father, but she recognized he had a new life and had for nine years. But being nominated for this award obviously meant a lot to him. He'd phoned himself instead of deputizing Karen. Then she thought about her stepmother and picked up the phone.

"Hi, Mum. It's Asha."

"Hello, love. You just caught me. I'm off to dinner with some friends."

"That's great. Um, how are you?"

"I'm fine, and before you get all maternal, I know about your father's award and the dinner and no, I really don't want to go."

Asha laughed ruefully. "Am I that transparent?"

"On the odd occasion. But this time your father rang and told me all about it. It's very prestigious apparently, and I think it would be lovely if you two girls went with him."

"That's pretty generous, Mum," Asha said and her mother chuckled.

"No, it's not. You have to admit having his wife and his ex-wife at the same table would be way too avant-garde, even for your father."

"I guess it would." Asha laughed with her stepmother. "How does Michelle feel about going?"

"She's fine. She rang Danny and they're both going. Do you want to speak to her?"

"No. It's okay, Mum. If you're okay with it."

"I am. And I'm sure you should go too. Apart from that, Wednesday is my choir night. Now, I really have to go, Asha, or I'll be late."

"Okay. Tell Chelle I'll see her tomorrow night. Bye, Mum."

Asha had barely hung up when Vivienne joined her.

"How's the typing on the second journal going?" she asked. "I've just finished reading the first one for the second time, and I can scarcely contain myself thinking about the next episode in Uncle Georgie's life, especially now that he's met Margaret."

"I know. I keep stopping and thinking about all their lives. It's the most exciting thing I've ever seen." Asha picked up the typed pages. "This is it, the end of the first one and all of Georgie's second journal."

"Oh, my dear. That's wonderful," Vivienne said, and then smiled broadly. "It's all far too exciting for words."

Asha took a spring clip from the desk drawer and clipped the pile of typed pages together. "Ah, Vivienne, before you go," she said quickly as Vivienne stood up to leave. "I was wondering if Peri was home?"

"She was, dear, but she's gone off up to Townsville to address some conference or other. She was anxious to read Uncle Georgie's journal too, so she's taken the first part with her because she wasn't sure when she'd be back. Probably not until Thursday she seemed to think."

"Oh. I see."

"Can I help you with anything?"

"No, not really. Unless you'd like to go to a very dressy awards dinner at the Sheraton tomorrow night?" Asha explained her father's invitation. "And as I haven't caught up with many people here in Brisbane, apart from my family, since I came home. I was going to ask Peri if she'd like to go with me."

"Now that's disappointing. I'm sure Peri would have loved to have gone along. And I'd go with you myself except I find going out at night a little too much for me these days. What about young Joe?"

Asha hadn't thought about Joe Deneen, but she was sure he would be attending the sporting night of nights anyway. The Broncos were leading the rugby league competition, so Joe and his teammates would have been invited as a matter of course. Apart from that, the elusive Tammy may be back in the picture. "I think Joe has a girlfriend, so I wouldn't feel right about asking him."

"Mmm." Vivienne nodded. "That would be the little brunette I see hanging around him. No, it wouldn't be right to ask him in that case. Such a pity. Joe would look magnificent in a tuxedo."

Asha laughed. "I can't dispute that."

"Now, let me see." Vivienne put her finger to her cheek. "Who else could we get to accompany you?"

"It's no big deal. I'll think of someone." Asha stopped at the sound of footsteps in the hallway.

Jack Moyland appeared in the doorway and cheerfully tapped on the open door. "Afternoon, ladies. May I join you?" He crossed to kiss Vivienne on the cheek. "Margo told me you were up here. I called in to drop off this book for Peri." He indicated the book in his hand. "But it seems she's jetted off again."

"Yes. Townsville, this time. I worry she'll overdo it."

"She'll be fine, Viv. She knows she can't push herself the way she was doing. I'm pretty sure she's learned a lesson where that's concerned." Jack sat on the corner of the desk. "And how are you, Asha? Finished transcribing great-great-grandfather Georgie's journals? Peri told me all about them, and I'm dying to read them."

"Just printed out the second one for Vivienne." She picked up Georgie's first journal and opened it to show Jack. He came around the desk and looked at the open page without touching it. She was amazed again by his resemblance to Peri. Yet on Peri the effect of fair hair, gray eyes, high cheekbones and firm jaw were so very feminine, while Jack, although taller and broader and with slightly darker hair, was the epitome of the handsome male.

"That's incredible," Jack said. "And Peri said the journals were in a hidden compartment in an old box. Any idea how they got there?"

"Not yet, and we may never know, but it's a wonderful story," she said and Vivienne agreed with her.

She retold the story of how Asha had come to find the journals. "And I couldn't wait to tell your grandmother. Grace was as amazed as I was, even though we knew our families are woven together."

"I've heard Mum and Gran talk about Margaret and Georgie Chaseley, of course," Jack said. "They owned a store in Ipswich I seem to remember." Jack turned to Asha. "And you're going to put it in the book for Richard?"

"Oh, yes," Vivienne replied for Asha. "It's so exciting."

Jack chuckled and then quirked his eyebrows. "Lucky we didn't uncover any family secrets. Although I've always fancied having a bushranger on the family tree."

Asha shrugged ruefully. "I haven't found any to date. What about the Moylands?"

"All lawyers." He stopped and grimaced. "Whoa! Say no more."

Asha laughed and caught Vivienne looking speculatively from Jack to herself.

"I don't suppose you're free tomorrow evening, are you, Jackson?" Vivienne asked and Asha almost groaned.

CHAPTER SEVEN

"Tomorrow night? Sure. What's on?" Jack asked easily.

"Um. No. It's okay, Vivienne," Asha said.

"Asha has some tickets to a sporting night." Vivienne turned back to Asha. "What was it again, my dear?"

Asha felt herself flushing. "It's a Sporting Awards Dinner, but it doesn't matter. Honestly," she assured Jack.

"You mean the Sporting Awards night at the Sheraton? You have tickets?" Jack's eyebrows rose again, and Asha was again reminded of Peri. "I'm impressed."

"Asha's father's getting an award," Vivienne added.

"Actually he may not even get the award. He's just been nominated for one. It's a black-tie dinner and probably with loads of boring speeches."

"And you need a partner?" Jack stood up and bowed. "I'd be honored to escort you, fair maiden."

Asha didn't know what to say.

"She was going to ask Peri," Vivienne said. "But she's in Townsville."

"Peri?" He raised the famous Moyland eyebrows again. "Ah! Then it's your lucky day, Asha. I'm known as the next best thing. If you can't get Peri, then I'm next in line."

"Oh, I didn't mean—" Asha started to apologize, and Jack laughed good-naturedly.

"I know. It's okay. But I have to say my sister's misfortune is my good luck in this case."

"Well, Dad did say to bring a friend and—" Asha smiled. "I'd be happy for you to come along, but are you sure you want to put yourself through it?"

"Will I get to meet your famous father?"

"Yes."

Jack grinned. "Then it's a done deal. What time shall I pick you up?"

"We have to meet at Dad's at six. He suggested a drink before we all, that's Dad and Karen and my sister, Michelle, and her boyfriend, go together in the stretch limo he's arranged." Asha wrinkled her nose.

"Stretch limo? Impressive. That can only mean a red carpet."

Asha blanched. "Oh, no. I hadn't thought of that. Tell me you're joking?"

"It stands to reason," Jack said with mock seriousness. "This is the night of nights for Queensland sport."

"I think I may have to call it off," Asha said and groaned.

Jack feigned horror. "Can I still go on my own?"

"Are you sure you want to go at all? Black tie and boring speeches, remember?"

"I think I can cope." He grinned. "I'd really like to go, Asha, if you don't mind my company instead of Peri's."

"Of course she doesn't mind," said Vivienne, giving him a tap on his arm. "You'll be the most handsome man in the room."

Jack rolled his eyes. "Not that she's biased."

"Not that biased." Asha laughed. At least Jack had a sense of humor. And he was the next best thing to Peri, she reminded herself wryly. Jack had said so himself.

"Okay, I'd best be off," he said. "I have some work to finish tonight and I have to dust off my tux." He kissed Vivienne on the cheek and paused by the door. "I'll pick you up tomorrow evening, Asha?"

She nodded, and with a smile, he was gone.

"Such a nice young man," Vivienne said, looking speculatively at Asha.

Asha chose to ignore Vivienne's so-obvious matchmaking. "Do you remember if Georgie and Margaret lived here in Brisbane?" she asked, hoping to distract her.

Vivienne frowned. "I believe they did, although I'm not too sure of the time frame. Mind you, I didn't see them all that often, only when I went with Grace to visit them. And Jack was right. They did have a small shop in Ipswich. They ran that until Georgie was in his eighties." Vivienne hesitated, thinking back. "You know, I do believe they must have been in Ipswich for quite a time, because I remember Susannah and her second husband bought them out of their large store."

"Susannah?" Asha frowned. "Was that Maryann and William Reid's daughter who lived with her grandparents?"

"That's right. Maryann and her husband came back from England and took Susannah off with them. Grace told me her grandmother, Susannah, died within the year. Everyone said she died of a broken heart, losing the granddaughter she'd raised from a baby."

Asha consulted her notes. "That would have been 1904."

Vivienne nodded. "Then Maryann brought Susannah back. I'm not sure why. Susannah then lived with Uncle Georgie and Aunt Margaret. She married Robert Gaines, Margaret's son, before he went off to the Great War. He was killed before

Susannah had the twins, Bobby and Grace."

"That's so sad."

"Yes. Grace has always regretted not knowing her father, but Uncle Georgie and Aunt Margaret told her so much about him. It was a terrible loss. Susannah remarried when Grace and Bobby were, oh, about eight years old. That's when I met Grace, when they moved to Brisbane. We've been friends ever since that first day she came to school." Vivienne smiled. "I'd love you to meet Grace. She's a wonderful person. Peri's so much like her."

Asha pushed thoughts of Peri out of her mind. It was way too distracting.

"Now, let me see." Vivienne frowned again. "Susannah and Grace's stepfather, Edward Ward, that was his name. That's right. I remember now. When Susannah and Edward bought the store, Grace was working here in Brisbane, and so she stayed with my family. Bobby boarded with Richard's family. So Susannah and Edward must have gone to Ipswich about 1935. They bought the store from Uncle Georgie and Aunt Margaret. It was a large general store and the building still exists to this day. Now, Uncle Georgie and Aunt Margaret must have bought the smaller shop at that time, do you think?"

"Probably. I can do some research into that. But they would have been quite elderly by then. Georgie would have been nearing seventy."

Vivienne laughed. "Quite elderly? My dear, at seventy, Uncle Georgie would have been a spring chicken."

Asha laughed too.

"I remember they were at Grace and Joe's wedding in 1942. Uncle Georgie was a very handsome man, I thought. Clean-shaven, thick dark hair, not overly tall, but a fine stamp of a man. He would have been ninety then, but he was very fit and healthy. Aunt Margaret was a good bit younger than he was, late seventies I'd say, but the nicest woman. Such a kind face.

"I know they came to Vera's funeral, and they were at our

wedding, too, in 1950. Uncle Georgie had aged by then, and I do believe he died that same year. Aunt Margaret died not long after Uncle Georgie. They were such a close couple." Vivienne's face softened at the memory.

Asha passed her the wedding photo of Georgie Chaseley and Margaret Gaines.

"Yes, that's such a good likeness of them. To think I've never seen this photo. And it was in the music box all this time."

"Yes."

Asha indicated the stack of typed pages she'd passed to Vivienne. "Now that I've finished typing up the second journal I want to do more work on the actual book. Then I'll start researching the Chaseleys in England. I was going to get onto that as soon as I'd finished compiling the family records here in Australia."

"Will they be easy to find?" Vivienne asked.

"If the records exist, and they may not, they should be easy because of all the information in Georgie's journal. There are relative dates and places. It's wonderful."

"I was astounded at the amount of history of the period in Georgie's journals," Vivienne said. "So much interesting information."

"Absolutely," said Asha. "And I was thinking about that. Living in different cities, Richard and Georgie would have exchanged news about everything going on around them. There's little doubt they both worked hard, worked long hours, and they wouldn't have had much time for socializing. At least, they wouldn't have had the spare time we enjoy today. So everything that happened would have been food for Georgie's journals."

"I'm sure you're right. From what I've already read, both boys seemed to show a thirst for knowledge and an awareness of the world around them. Dickie would have so enjoyed the journals, too, Asha. And it's such a heritage for Richard and the children. How will you go about finding the family in England?"

"I'll begin with the census returns. Richard and Georgie left England before the 1871 census, but hopefully I'll find them on the 1861 census."

Vivienne smiled. "This is so exciting. Grace wanted to come home immediately, but I told her I'd send her a copy by express post. I'll get Peri to do that for me."

"That's right. I was going to print out a copy for her, wasn't I?"

"Whenever you get a moment. That would be wonderful. And Rosemary wants to read it, too. I was talking to her last night and told her about the journals. She was amazed they had been hidden away for so long. Oh, and the most exciting news of all is that my daughter's coming home soon."

"That's great. How long is it since you saw her?"

"A month or so. She hinted then that she might retire, but I don't dare hope she might come home for good. I miss her so much. But she's such a busy lawyer. Her father and I were so proud of her." Vivienne sighed. "She had dinner with Richard, Timothy and Megan last week, and when I spoke to Richard he said she looked tired. So this is especially good news for me, that she's coming home." She smiled. "As I think I mentioned to you, it was Rosemary who first suggested I get our family history done. She was home for the weekend when I showed her Betty's book you'd written. When I told her you had written it, she said she thought she'd heard of you."

Asha was surprised "She had?"

"Yes. She was thinking about getting someone to research the family and coincidently, there I was with Betty's book. Anyway, Rosemary's looking forward to meeting you."

Asha grimaced. "I hope she won't be disappointed with what I've done. I mean, the journals sell themselves, but—"

"I couldn't be happier with what you're doing, Asha. You're far too modest, my dear."

"It's just that I know how much this project means to you."

"Now, you just stop worrying. Without you we'd never have discovered the journals in the old chest. Now, I *must* go and read the rest of the journals."

She left Asha then, and Asha went back to working on Vivienne's book.

Jack Moyland collected Asha the next evening and, much to her surprise, Asha had a most enjoyable night. Jack was an amusing companion and her father seemed to like him. Of course, she knew she'd have to reiterate that Jack was just a friend, in case the family got the wrong idea.

Asha relaxed back into the comfortable seat of Jack's Subaru as he drove her home. There was only a minimum of traffic, as the evening had gone on longer than Asha had anticipated. "Thanks again, Jack, for stepping into the breach, so to speak," she said.

Jack flicked on his indicator and changed lanes. "No worries. I had a ball. Your father's a great bloke. Thank you for letting me substitute for Peri."

Into Asha's mind flashed a picture of Peri in a tux, all long legs and lithe grace, and her mouth went dry. But then, Asha conceded, Peri would look great in anything. And out of it. Desire caught at her and she shifted in her seat, making a show of adjusting her seat belt.

". . . and your father really deserved that award."

With a flash of guilt, Asha realized she'd missed part of Jack's conversation and she drew herself together. "He was pretty overcome," she said, feeling bad.

"I like your family, too," Jack continued. "Michelle told me she's your half sister."

"Yes, and the boys are our half brothers." Asha gave a derisive grin. "The Wests are a very modern family."

130

Jack chuckled. "And your father's a very brave man to take on a second family at his age."

Asha smiled. "Michelle gives him heaps about that. He seems to thrive on it though." She stifled a yawn.

"I saw that yawn," Jack said teasingly and Asha laughed.

"Sorry. Nothing to do with the company. It's just past my bedtime."

Jack checked his watch. "What? The night is young, or the morning is early." He grinned crookedly. "Whichever way you choose to look at it."

"Well, unfortunately for me, it's aging as we speak."

Jack yawned, too. "Oh, no." He apologized. "Now I've spoiled my high-living, hard-playing image." He shrugged ruefully. "So I guess there'll be no partying on till dawn at a string of nightclubs for us?"

"I'm afraid not. For me, anyway," Asha told him. "But there's always time for you after you drop me off."

Jack laughed. "The spirit's willing, but the body is, unfortunately, weak."

He continued to make easy conversation about various aspects of the evening, and soon they were turning in through the gates and pulling up in front of Tyneholme. Jack switched off the engine and turned to Asha, his face illuminated by the exterior lights on the veranda. He smiled Peri's smile.

"I've had a great night, Asha, and I really am grateful to have had the chance to go."

"I'm just glad it wasn't too boring or too traumatic."

"Even the red carpet?" he asked with a grin, and Asha bit off a giggle.

"Now that part was traumatic."

"You looked pretty spectacular."

Asha stiffened. "Thank you," she said carefully as she unclipped her seat belt.

Jack took her hand and raised it to his lips, kissing it lightly.

"Maybe we can do this again sometime, hmm?"

"I think the Awards Night is a yearly event." She tried for lightness and he laughed softly.

"Then, please pencil my name in. No, I meant perhaps dinner one evening."

"Um. Thank you." Life would be so easy if she could simply say yes, she told herself. "I like you very much, Jack, but—"

"But your heart belongs to another?"

Asha stilled. "I—I do care about someone else," she said carefully.

"And does this someone care about you?"

"I don't know." Asha looked away from him.

Jack sighed. "Peri does look better in a tux than I do," he said softly.

Startled, Asha snatched her hand from his. "What? I don't know what you mean."

"I could be wrong, but I just had the impression you batted for the other team."

Asha swallowed again. "Jack, I—"

"It's okay, Asha. You don't have to tell me. It's your business. But we can be friends, can't we?"

"Of course. Friends." She drew a steadying breath. "I, uh, this isn't something I talk about. It's difficult."

Jack nodded. "I can imagine it would be. Have you known you were all your life?"

Asha paused and then found herself replying. "Pretty much. Since my teens at least," she said, and felt suddenly light, free.

"And since your father asked me my intentions, I take it your family doesn't know."

"My father asked you about our relationship?" Asha said, amazed that her father would do that.

"Very subtly. I think he inferred he'd take a cricket bat to me if I upset you in any way."

Asha was appalled, and then Jack laughed.

"I was having you on. Sorry, Asha, I couldn't resist. He didn't say anything, but he gave me a pretty fair third degree."

"I'm sorry. He shouldn't have done that."

"He seems to think some guy broke your heart, and fairly recently, too."

Asha shook her head.

"Too painful to talk about?" he asked gently and Asha felt like crying. She'd never discussed her breakup with Tessa with anyone. She hadn't thought about her in ages, but the betrayal still hurt.

"It was a woman," she said. "Last year."

Jack took her hand again and squeezed it. "No doubt about these women. Break your heart every time." He grinned crookedly. "Happens to the best of us."

"I suppose it does. Did you . . . ? Did someone break your heart?"

"Years ago now." He gave a shrug. "Water under the bridge now, but I still remember how bad it made me feel."

"Yes, as you say, it is water under the bridge. But I am sorry my father embarrassed you, and I also apologize if I gave you any mixed messages or anything."

"You didn't. I suspected you were a lesbian when I first met you."

"You did? But how?"

"Oh, let's just say I watched you watching Peri."

Asha was horrified. "There's nothing between your sister and me."

"But you want there to be. Am I right?"

"Jack, please don't say anything about this to Peri. She'd be mortified."

Jack gave her hand a little shake. "Are you so sure about that?"

"Of course I'm sure. Peri's straight. She was engaged."

Jack swore softly. "Lance was an ass. Sorry, but none of us

133

liked him in the end. So, have you asked Peri if she leans the same way?"

"I can't ask her that."

"I suppose not." Jack laughed. "I can imagine nothing would freak out straight women more than unwanted lesbian attention. But you were going to ask Peri to go to the Awards night with you tonight, weren't you?"

"That's different."

Jack raised his eyebrows. "If you say so. Would she have gone with you, do you think?"

Asha paused. "I don't know."

"You know, for what it's worth, I think she'd have jumped at the chance." Asha looked at him and he sighed. "I worry about her, what she's doing to herself."

"What do you mean? She said she was feeling better," Asha said. "She is, isn't she?"

"Physically, yes. After she broke up with Lance, she threw herself into her work. Then she got this virus. She'd been working too hard for too long and she took ages to get over it. Mum and Dad only agreed to go away on their planned tour of the Outback if she promised to stay with Viv and take it slowly getting back to work full time.

"But to get back to the lesbian thing, quite honestly, Asha, I've wondered about Peri for years, about her sexual orientation, but like you, I haven't had the nerve to ask her. She's never been overly interested in guys, apart from Lance, and I think he did all the running, probably because Peri was so disinterested."

"That doesn't mean she's a lesbian," Asha said flatly.

"No. Not on it's own, but I also saw the way she looked at you. I've never seen her look at a guy that way."

Asha felt her breath swell in her chest. Could Jack be right? "What way?"

"You know exactly which way. So," he continued, "my advice, again for what it's worth, is to ask her."

"I can't do that. I have too much to lose."

Jack shrugged again. "It's your call, Asha, but there might be so much to gain."

Asha put her hand on the door handle. "I should go in. It's late. Thanks, Jack. For coming with me tonight, and for, well, being understanding."

"That's me. Mr. Understanding." He smiled derisively. "You know if I can't have you myself, I'll be pushing for Peri. I'd like to keep you in the family."

Asha shook her head and climbed out of the car. "Goodnight, Jack." She crossed the veranda and carefully unlocked the door. Turning back, she lifted her hand in a quick wave. He gave her the thumbs up and drove away.

She stood in the foyer for long minutes thinking about what Jack had said. Could he be right about Peri? If he was? It wouldn't change anything, she told herself. Peri had hardly given her any encouragement.

Asha quietly closed the front door, wincing when the lock clicked into place, the sound seeming to echo in the silence. She paused for a moment, listening. Vivienne always left a dim night-light burning over the staircase. In the glow, Asha took off her heels and padded over the parquetry floor. She then carefully climbed up to the next floor. Turning left at the top of the stairs, she swapped her shoes to her other hand and lightly felt the wall as she moved forward into the darker hallway toward her room.

She'd barely taken a couple of steps when the hall was flooded with light. Startled, Asha dropped her shoes and turned to see Peri standing by the light switch on the other side of the stairs.

CHAPTER EIGHT

"It's just me. Asha," she said quickly, quietly. "I'm sorry I'm so late. I didn't mean to wake you up. I thought you were still in Townsville."

"I was. I arrived back a couple of hours ago." Peri stood watching Asha, one hand still on the light switch. Her feet were bare and she wore dark silk boxer shorts and a thin shoestring strap chemise that stopped a couple of inches short of her waistband.

Asha felt her nerve endings go on alert, and she swallowed anxiously. Peri was displaying far too much smooth skin for Asha's peace of mind. She reminded herself to breathe, while part of her reflected self-derisively that the feelings she was experiencing had more to do with other parts of her body, and that those particular parts seemed to have minds of their own.

She remembered what Jack had said, that he'd wondered

about Peri's sexual orientation for years. And that he'd seen the way Peri looked at her. She felt her stomach quiver, and she hastily pushed the thought from her mind. She couldn't afford to think about that, not with Peri so close, looking so desirable.

Peri moved forward, apparently unaware of, or unconcerned about, her state of undress.

Asha dragged her gaze from the length of Peri's long, shapely legs.

"I thought—" Peri paused. "I heard a noise and I thought perhaps someone had broken in."

"No. It's just me. Luckily," Asha added, part of her horrified at the situation had she actually been an intruder. "I was trying to be quiet," she finished impotently. A heavy silence fell and the tension between them grew.

"I didn't expect to be this late," Asha felt compelled to add. "It was an awards dinner. My father was given an award for his contribution to cricket. He was really thrilled about it."

"I guess he must have been."

Had Peri moved a step closer? Asha could see her eyes now. She watched as Peri's gaze skittered quickly over her, and she grew hot. Asha moved and her thin shawl slipped off one shoulder, leaving it bare. She wanted to settle it protectively about her again, but she couldn't seem to make herself move. Her shoulderless top was suddenly far too revealing.

"You look—" The tip of Peri's tongue dampened her lips and a flash of fire grew in the pit of Asha's stomach, surging to burn with an ache between her legs. "You look fantastic," Peri said, her voice low and husky.

"Thank you. It was a black-tie affair. At the Sheraton. It was pretty swish. Everyone was dressed up." Asha's gaze moved over Peri. She wished she had the nerve to tell Peri no one at the Awards Night came close to the way Peri looked at the moment. Sensual. Inviting. Dangerous. And then Asha realized Peri had caught her out, had seen Asha's gaze travel the length of Peri's lean body. She flushed, hoping desperately that Peri couldn't read her thoughts. "I—I didn't mean to wake you," she repeated.

"That's okay. I couldn't sleep. I was about to switch on the light and try reading."

Asha was over-aware of the enticing shape of Peri's nipples outlined by the clinging material of her top, and she closed her eyes to regain her faltering control. She must have swayed slightly, for Peri started forward and put a cool hand on Asha's arm.

"Are you all right?"

"Yes. No. I think so." How would Peri react if Asha told her the truth? She was so attracted to this woman she was in danger of throwing her usual caution to the four winds and taking Peri in her arms. But if Jack were wrong, then that would create far more problems. What sort of turmoil would she throw the household into if she caused Peri to run screaming? Asha almost laughed and bit her lip to hold back the hysterical sound.

"Do you need help to your room?" Peri asked, her voice suddenly cool.

Asha stared at her. Did Peri think she was drunk? "I haven't been drinking. Honestly. I just—" Her eyes strayed to the outline of Peri's breasts, moved slowly upward, took in the erratic beat of the pulse at the base of her throat, settled on the full red lips, and then shakily met Peri's gaze. She desperately wanted to make love to her and, with a swell of panic, she knew she hadn't been able to disguise her emotions. She began to steel herself for Peri's revulsion, her rejection.

Peri's hand on Asha's arm loosened, and then her fingers slid lightly, slowly up Asha's arm, over the bare skin of her shoulder. She took her hand away and then gently brushed her knuckles over Asha's mouth, her touch feather soft, so enticing.

A tremor washed over Asha and she gave a breathy gasp, her eyes widening in surprise.

Peri pulled her hand away, and she seemed pale in the artificial light. She swallowed convulsively, her expression stricken. "I'm sorry," she said brokenly and went to turn away.

Asha reached out quickly, her hand resting on Peri's hip, feeling the silky material of her boxer shorts. "Wait! Peri! Don't—"

"I wasn't—I wouldn't have—"

"Don't go. Please. I want—" Asha stepped forward at the same moment Peri did, and their breasts brushed together.

For long moments they stood transfixed, while the world around them grew heavy with that same numbing tension. Then they moved together, their arms sliding around each other, and Asha at last felt Peri's soft, sensual lips on hers. Asha moaned, the sound low in her throat, and Peri sank against her, melting into her, deepening the kiss. Asha's hands moved downward, cupping Peri's silk-clad buttocks, holding Peri tightly against her.

They drew slightly apart, both breathless, both gasping air into their lungs.

Peri exhaled shakily and leaned forward, resting her forehead against Asha's as they both fought for control. Then Peri straightened and stepped back a little, her arms still around Asha. "I'm sorry," she said shakily. "I shouldn't have done that. I don't know what I was thinking." Her eyes met Asha's and Peri flushed, her gaze falling to settle on Asha's lips, and she drew another unsteady breath. "You kiss . . . That kiss . . . It was . . . I'm not sorry," she finished unevenly. "Not for a minute." She shook her head. "I just can't believe I . . . do you hate me?"

Asha put her finger gently on Peri's lips. "No. Of course not. I could never do that."

"I don't know why I—" Peri swallowed. "Yes, I do," she added softly. "I've wanted to do it for so long."

"And I want to do it again," Asha said and leaned forward until her lips met Peri's. Asha's hands inched up to the expanse of bare skin at Peri's waist, her fingers slipping beneath her light top, finding the indentation of her spine.

They kissed deeply, drew apart again, and then Peri moved

forward until her thighs rested against Asha's. "God, Asha! I want to touch you, but I don't know how. I have no idea what—"

Asha took hold of Peri's hand, led her down the hall and into her room. She switched on the light, turned down the dimmer and closed the door behind them. They dissolved into each other's arms again, kissing hungrily, bodies melting into each other. Asha's shawl fell to the floor. Her hands moved Peri's top higher, her fingers splayed over Peri's smooth midriff. Then her hands slid over Peri's firm breasts, her thumbs teasing the hardened nipples.

Peri moaned. "I can't stand. I think I need to sit down."

They moved together to the bed. Asha pulled back the bedspread and they sat side by side in silence.

"I don't know what's happening," Peri got out at last. "When you touch me, I melt."

"It's the same for me." Asha wrapped her arms around Peri and held her close. She nibbled soft kisses along her shoulder, then up the arch of her neck, to claim her lips again. Then she slowly lifted Peri's top, pulled it over her head, reached up to caress her bare breasts, and as she watched, Peri's eyes darkened with passion. She leaned forward and flicked one rosy, aroused nipple with her tongue.

Peri moaned, moved her fingers into Asha's hair and held her fiercely against her body.

"My God! That feels so good. I can't believe it feels so good." Her hands cupped Asha's face, and she leaned forward to kiss her deeply.

They fell back on the bed in a tangle of arms and legs. Peri's fingers fumbled at Asha's waist and undid her belt. Then she freed her top, pushed it up and pulled it off. Her mouth covered Asha's nipple through the lace of her strapless bra, and Asha arched against her. "I want to see you, too," she murmured, and Asha helped her unhook her bra then cast it aside. Peri drew a sharp breath then buried her face between Asha's breasts for interminable moments before she took one full peak in her mouth and sucked gently.

It was Asha's turn to moan. She slipped her hands between them to caress Peri's breasts.

"Asha, I can't. I need to—" Peri gasped.

"I know. So do I." Asha shimmied out of her slacks and struggled with her pantyhose. She gave a broken laugh as Peri reached to help her.

Then she lay naked and Peri ran her shaking hand lightly, wonderingly over the line of Asha's hip. Peri's fingertips, soft and arousing, traveled up from the curve of Asha's hip to the indentation of her waist, and over her firm midriff to slowly caress Asha's breast. Asha's nipples tightened, and she thrust to meet Peri's palm, sending waves of pure desire spiraling downward to center between her legs.

"Now you," Asha said thickly, slowly insinuating her fingers beneath the waistband of Peri's shorts, pulling them slowly down over her slim hips.

Peri kicked her shorts off, her gaze still moving wonderingly over Asha, her eyes deep pools of wanting, her lips soft and swollen from their kisses.

Asha reached out, drew Peri into her arms and they lay together, kissing, murmuring huskily.

"I want to touch you," Peri said against Asha's mouth.

"Me, too. I want you to. And I want to touch you, too," she said, her voice thick.

"I don't think I know how," Peri whispered, her lips now sliding soft, urgent kisses on Asha's breasts. "I mean, I sort of know. I don't know what you want, what you like."

Asha took her hand, kissed each finger, and then, holding Peri's gaze, she placed Peri's hand over the triangle of dark curls between her legs.

Peri's hand cupped Asha's mound and then her fingers were in the damp curls. She found Asha's center, and Asha caught her breath.

"Did I hurt you?" Peri pulled her hand away.

"No. Please." Asha quickly stayed Peri's hand, guided it back, and then she moved against her fingers. Peri matched her pace. She leaned over, took Asha's nipple in her mouth, and Asha cascaded into her orgasm, Peri's name trembling on her lips.

When she'd calmed, she kissed Peri tenderly, then slowly deepened the kiss, her fingers sliding over Peri's breasts. Peri's hips thrust against Asha's leg and Asha moved her hand down, her fingers slipping into the moistness. Almost instantly Peri collapsed against Asha, her body shuddering.

"My God!" Peri whispered and clutched Asha to her. "That was fantastic."

Asha moved over her, straddling her, lowering her breasts until they touched Peri's. Peri cupped Asha's breasts almost reverently and then her thumb tips teased Asha's nipples until Asha threw back her head as frissons of pleasure surged through her body. Peri replaced her thumbs with her mouth, her hand sliding down between their bodies.

Aroused again, they rolled slickly together, making love with a sensual fever that left them both gasping and breathless. They lay together, sated bodies still entwined, and Asha closed her eyes, her face nuzzling the soft indentation of Peri's neck, her arm holding Peri close. She dozed for moments or hours, and when she opened her eyes she found Peri watching her. She smiled sleepily. "I'm sorry, I must have dozed off."

"The little death, according to the French. Although I'm not entirely sure about the gender of the author or the recipient," Peri said softly and then flushed. "And don't be sorry. I've heard it's the best compliment. I take it that way, anyhow."

"It was just spectacular," Asha said honestly, running her finger gently over the line of Peri's jaw. "And so were you."

"And you. It was just about breathtaking, wasn't it?" Peri grinned crookedly. "Plus fantastic, earth-shattering, magnificent.

And more."

Asha chuckled. "I'd second all of that."

"I wouldn't have believed it could be so good. How you made me feel." Peri swallowed. "I mean, before . . . I never considered . . ." She shook her head slightly.

"You've never considered making love with a woman?" Asha finished.

"No. Yes. Not exactly." Color washed Peri's cheeks and she frowned slightly.

Asha smiled again. "Not exactly is a little ambiguous, don't you think?"

Peri flushed.

"It's okay," Asha said quickly and kissed her chin. "I understand what you mean."

"I guess I thought I never liked sex all that much." Peri's fingers plucked at the edge of the sheet she must have pulled over them. "I mean, I knew it was a part of life, but for me, well, it was never a big part of *my* life. When Lance and I got together, I think I hoped it would get better. It didn't much." She grimaced. "You asked me if I'd ever considered making love with a woman," she continued, "and I think I have. But I buried it deeply in my subconscious somewhere. It only surfaced in my dreams and I'd wake up not remembering them but being filled with a sense of loss, of reaching out for something just beyond my grasp. So the answer would have to be, not exactly. Not until I met you," she finished huskily.

"Ah." Asha murmured, self-satisfied. "So I walked into your life and resurrected your dreams?"

"Yes." Peri laughed softly and then sobered. "I never experienced"—she swallowed. "I never had an orgasm with Lance," she said, sliding a quick glance at Asha and away again. "It just never seemed real. I felt as though I was a bystander, not part of it." She made an agitated movement with her hand. "I can't explain it."

143

"I think you just did and really well," Asha said, taking Peri's hand and squeezing it reassuringly.

"I guess that was one of the reasons he wanted out. And part of me can't blame him for that. I just wished he could have been more honorable, about it. When I found out about him and Janet, things got a little heated, and he said, among other things, that I was totally unfeeling." She paused. "He said a lot of things, actually. Hurtful things. I tried to tell myself most of it stemmed from his guilt, but I think the guilt was as much mine." She sighed. "If I were totally honest, I'd have to say he had a point on that score. He also accused me of being frigid."

Asha exclaimed in disgust. "I think we've put that little misconception to rest, don't you agree?"

Peri laughed again. "I suppose we have."

Asha lifted the sheet, kissed the tip of Peri's breast and watched her nipple pucker to attention. "I suspect he didn't have the right touch, don't you think?" she asked lightly. She let her tongue tip tease the rosy peak again and Peri shuddered. "I don't think the jury would even have to retire to consider their verdict."

Peri grinned crookedly and then her lashes fell to shield the expression in her eyes. "Have you? Had any experience? With a woman, I mean? Are you?"

"Am I a lesbian? Yes, I am," she said.

Peri swallowed. "How long have you known?"

"Since I was in my teens."

"But how did you know?"

Asha shrugged. "At first I didn't really know what it meant. I just felt out of step. Then one of the guys made some stupid, derogatory comment about lesbians, and I remember feeling very strange. Sort of hot and then cold. I could see myself standing off from myself, with everything falling into place inside me. I slunk away to think about it, and I was terrified. I'd heard the word lesbian before I really knew what a lesbian was, but until that moment I hadn't thought about it in terms of myself."

"Were you attracted to anyone?" Peri asked and Asha shook her head.

"Not at the time." She gave a soft laugh. "Then we got this new English teacher. That was a different story. I decided it was time to do some serious research. And here I am over ten years later, a fully-fledged lesbian."

"Viv said you'd had a relationship breakup."

Asha nodded, her fingers absently rubbing at the smooth skin on Peri's arm. "Yes. And it was with a woman. We were together for over a year. I was in love with her and I thought she loved me. She didn't. End of story."

Peri bit her lip. "I thought I was in love with Lance. I told myself I was because I thought it was expected of me. I thought he loved me, too. He professed to. But for the last six months, he was having an affair with my best friend. I could understand that he had fallen out of love with me, but I couldn't cope with the betrayal."

Asha ran her hand sympathetically over Peri's arm. "It was the same with me, when I found out Tessa was lying to me."

"Do you still love her?" Peri asked evenly enough.

Asha hesitated. She'd thought she did. Before she left the coast to come home she'd thought she'd never stop loving Tessa. But she hadn't so much as thought about her for some time. Since she met Peri, a little voice inside her said, and Asha's heart constricted. What if Peri didn't feel the same? Asha had declared she'd never again let anyone as close to her as she'd let Tessa. She had to be wary.

"You don't have to answer that," Peri said and Asha shook her head.

"No, I want to answer you. I don't think I still love her. But I did love her and it hurt so much."

Peri nodded. "Me, too." Peri paused. "Thank you," she said lowly.

Asha glanced at her quickly. "For what, exactly?"

"For showing me there is an alternative."

"Oh, an alternative." Asha grinned. "Oh, yes, there's definitely an alternative." She leaned over and let her lips slide over Peri's chin until her lips found Peri's soft, so inviting mouth. And soon they were moving, murmuring together.

CHAPTER NINE

The sun was shining brightly through the lace curtains on the French doors when Asha stirred. She stretched her stiff muscles and smiled lazily as the events of the evening before came back to her. She rolled over, deliciously naked beneath the sheet, and caught sight of her shawl draped over the standard lamp. Her shoes were on the floor, so Peri must have retrieved them from where she'd dropped them outside in the hallway.

Asha sat up, pushed herself to her feet and pulled an oversized T-shirt over her head. She padded across to read the note that was taped to her shawl.

Asha. I have to fly to Sydney this morning, but I'll be back late tomorrow. Till then, thanks. For saving my life. Peri.

Asha kissed the paper and returned to sit on the edge of the bed with its tousled sheets. She lifted the pillow, drew in the faint lingering scent of Peri Moyland. How could she have imagined that Peri was cold? That impression couldn't be further from the truth. Peri was vibrant, so warm, incredibly sexy, and the thought of her made Asha's heart swell. The word love drifted, insinuated itself into her mind and she found herself shaking her head. No. Not love. She didn't want to be so vulnerable again. It couldn't be love. Could it?

Somewhere in the house was the faint sound of a phone ringing, and Asha glanced at her bedside clock. She was way too late for breakfast, and she needed to take a shower and get to work on Vivienne's book. She'd think about Peri later, convince herself she wasn't falling in love with her. Yet part of her suggested she was deluding herself, and when the warm water cascaded over her skin, her traitorous body's responses to memories of Peri only reinforced that sentiment.

After showering and dressing, Asha made herself a cup of tea and some toast, which she ate hungrily. She carried a second cup of tea into the study and sat down behind the desk. She wanted to check the English census returns for the Chaseley family. Switching on her notebook, she sipped her tea as she waited for it to boot up. The ringing of her mobile phone in the drawer of the desk made her jump. She placed her teacup on the desk and reached for the phone. Glancing at the caller ID, she put the phone to her ear with a smile. "Morning, Michelle."

"Hello yourself," said her sister. "How are you after your late night?"

Asha flushed. For one breathtaking second Asha thought her sister was referring to those amazing hours she'd spent with Peri. "Oh. Fine. I do admit I slept in a little later this morning though."

"Me, too. Luckily, I don't have classes today. It was pretty good, wasn't it? Last night, I mean. Dad was stoked over the award, wasn't he? He got choked up. I've never seen him get like that, have you?"

"No. But he rallied and made a pretty impressive acceptance

speech."

"I guess I sort of forget how famous he is. Danny reckons he's the best fast bowler Australia has ever produced."

"So it would seem." Asha recalled Jack had said that as well.

"Suppose it's because he's just our father." Michelle bit off a laugh. "Last night at the dinner, I kept looking at Dad in his suit and bow tie and thinking it was all so weird. I mean, I've never really seen him in that situation. Not that I remember, anyway." Michelle gave a little chuckle. "You know, when Dad left Mum, I had a hard time seeing what Karen saw in him. Apart from the money, that is. But last night I realized Dad was really pretty handsome in an old guy sort of way."

"I'm sure Dad would find that most reassuring."

"Do you think?" Michelle asked. "Anyway, Danny said it was a mega important honor and he was way impressed. Men are funny, aren't they?"

Asha laughed again. "I think it was a very prestigious award."

"Mmmm. I guess so. You didn't tell me you knew Joe Deneen. Danny nearly passed out when he came over to our table."

Michelle's change of subject took Asha unawares. "I thought I told you. He works here at Tyneholme."

"He works there? What does he do?"

"The gardens are really extensive and need a full-time gardener. That's Joe's uncle. Joe's standing in for him because he's had surgery."

"Oh. Joe's pretty cute, isn't he? In fact, the whole night was impressive all 'round. I felt like I should pinch myself in case I was dreaming. Didn't you, Ash?"

"Yes, I know what you mean. But it was all a little too public for me," Asha said with feeling.

"Too public!" Michelle chuckled. "Then you better get used to it, Asha, because I've just seen us all on TV."

"On TV? What on earth are you talking about, Chelle?"

"It was this morning. On *Sunrise*. Mum called me out of bed to watch it. They replayed some of Dad's speech and must have interviewed him sometime afterward because he was still in his suit. Karen looked good, too. You'd never know she'd had five kids, would you?"

"No. She did look really nice. The color of the dress suited her. They made a great looking couple."

"Mmm," agreed Michelle. "Then they showed Danny and me and said what a great soccer player he was. He is going to be just so blown away. And he looked so great, Ash. And really hot."

"And I'd say you looked pretty special, too," Asha put in before her sister could begin extolling Danny's virtues. And then she felt mean-spirited. "You both would have."

"Thanks. I guess I looked okay." Her sister paused for dramatic effect. "Then the camera swung around and panned over you and Jack."

Asha groaned. "They really showed us? Tell me they just skimmed over us."

"Yeah, right! You're Sean West's firstborn. He held you on his shoulder when he took six for twenty-one at the MCG. To bowl out six batsmen in one game for just twenty-one runs is still talked about in cricket circles. We're talking historical stuff. No wonder that was on page one of the paper."

"I was about seven years old, so that was eighteen years ago."

"And there was that photo in the paper where he was bowling to you in the backyard when he was first chosen to play for Australia. Face it, Ash, you are news."

"Okay, so what about that cute shot of you sitting on his knee clutching the cricket ball he used when he saved the Ashes for Australia?" Asha reminded her sister.

"My point exactly. I didn't really think about it before, but Ash, we are newsworthy. So, where was I? Oh, yes. The camera moved away from Danny and me and there you were. With Jack. It was so romantic."

"Oh, no."

"Oh, yes. You were smiling, oh, and nice cleavage by the way. So, you're smiling and Jack's looking at you as though you're the only woman in the room."

"Chelle! Tell me you're exaggerating," Asha appealed, and Michelle laughed.

"Only a little. But you did look sort of close. He's really nice. Jack, I mean."

"He is nice. And I only asked him because Vivienne suggested I should, and I thought he'd like to go because he admired Dad as a cricketer." And because I wanted to go with Peri, she added to herself and then pushed the thought hurriedly away.

"Ash!" Michelle exclaimed again. "You didn't tell him that, did you?"

"Not in so many words. I just said I had the tickets and would he like to go. He said he would. So we went."

"Sheez! Ash! You are hopeless. Jack is so great. Good-looking. Funny. Not too old. Smart. Has a job. A career even. And he drives a cool WRX. He's a keeper, Ash."

"Chelle, give me a break! I've only known him for five minutes." She hadn't known Peri for much longer, she thought, but it seemed like a lifetime.

"And your point is?" Michelle said sarcastically. "I knew Danny was the one in seconds. But anyway, I think Jack likes you. He was so, I don't know, nice with you. And it seems to me he's everything a girl could ask for in a guy. You can't deny that, Ash." She paused. "Unless he's gay."

"Of course he's not gay," Asha said quickly. "And I'm not denying he's a great bloke. Look, Chelle, I think we need to talk."

"Talk! I thought we were."

"Chelle!"

"Okay. What do you want to talk about? Not Jack Moyland, apparently."

151

"Yes and no." Asha sighed. "Just things."

"Serious things I take it?" Michelle asked softly. "Like you being a lesbian?"

Asha was shocked speechless.

"You can tell me I'm wrong, Ash," Michelle added, and Asha sensed her uncertainty.

"What if I didn't?" Asha swallowed. "Tell you you're wrong, I mean."

"Like that would change anything. You'd still be my favorite sister."

"I'm your only sister," Asha said, a knot of tears in her throat.

"My only lesbian sister. Right?"

Asha took a steadying breath. "I suppose I am," she admitted softly. "Would you be all right with that?"

"Sure. Are you all right with it?" Michelle asked.

"Yes." Asha got the word out, changed her phone to her other ear and flexed her knuckles. "So. How long have you known?"

"That's what I was going to ask you."

"Then, most of my life," Asha said.

"But what about that guy you liked at school? Neil something."

"He was gay, too."

"Really?" Michelle whistled softly. "Wow! No wonder he was so great looking. I had a huge crush on him when I was eight."

Asha laughed softly. "I had a crush on him, too."

"Oh. You just didn't want to do the kissy stuff, hey?"

"That about covers it."

"It must be hard, Ash, you know, to find someone, I mean. Another lesbian. How can you tell? That someone is or might be."

Asha shrugged and then realized her sister couldn't see her. "It can be difficult," she said carefully.

"Is there someone?"

152

Peri's face appeared in Asha's mind so vividly she felt her body grow hot. Then she saw them only hours ago, damp, naked, bodies moving together. "Maybe. It's early days."

"What's she like?"

"Beautiful." Asha paused and gave an embarrassed laugh.

"I'd like to meet her," Michelle said sincerely. "When you're ready, I mean."

"And I'd like her to meet you, too."

"Have there, you know, been other girlfriends? Before, I mean." Michelle drew a sharp breath. "Far out, Ash! Not Tessa. Tell me you weren't involved with her."

"I was. But not now."

"Thanks heavens! She was a piranha. Mum and I really didn't like her at all. As a matter of fact," Michelle continued, "Mum almost told you she didn't trust her, but she didn't want to upset you because you seemed such good friends."

"That's over," Asha said. "So there's no need to worry any more."

"I am *so* glad," Michelle said with feeling.

"So what made you twig about me?" Asha asked. "I thought I was pretty careful."

"I don't know. I guess it must have been hovering in the back of my mind and it just seemed to pop out. Weird, hey? I have to say, Ash, I often wondered why you didn't have a string of guys in tow. But this, I guess this answers a lot of questions."

"Realizing I was a lesbian answered a lot of questions for me, too," Asha said dryly.

"I guess." There was a moment of silence. "Oh! My! God! I've just thought about—Oh, my God!"

"What, Chelle? What is it?" Asha was alarmed.

"I've just thought about sex. Do you, you know, have sex?"

"It's not just about that, Chelle." Asha felt her face grow hot. "I just feel more in tune with a woman than I do with a man."

"Oh." Michelle paused again, and then made a strangled

153

sound. "Oh, no. Does that mean you were sleeping with Tessa? Like sexually? Now that is gross."

"Chelle," Asha admonished, glad she'd closed the door of the study behind her. It wouldn't do for Vivienne to walk in and overhear her conversation. "Sex with a woman, for me, is natural."

"No. I don't mean just sex. I meant sex with that Tessa. I didn't mean—" Michelle expelled a breath. "So the sex thing, Ash. What do you do?"

"Michelle! Can we wait until I get used to you knowing before we get down to specifics?"

"Sure," Michelle said lightly. "I mean, I've seen some porno movies and I've read stuff, but I've never had the chance to talk to a real lesbian about it. Ten percent of the population is supposed to be gay. You're part of a minority. And it's part of the human condition, you know, Ash."

"So it's said." Asha felt herself smile. "And when did you see porno movies?"

"My lips are sealed. But they were pretty tame I think."

"I hope so."

"Have I embarrassed you?" Michelle asked.

"Just a bit."

Michelle giggled. "Okay. I'll let you off the hook. For now."

"I'd appreciate that."

"Right. Anyway, what I'm actually ringing about," Michelle said matter-of-factly, "is because Mum wanted me to ring you."

"Is she there?"

"No. Relax, Ash. She's gone down to the supermarket. She wants you to come over for lunch today, just the three of us. I think she's feeling a bit fragile, what with Dad and the awards dinner."

"Is she all right?" Asha was concerned. "I rang her after I spoke with Dad and she told me she was all right about us going."

"She didn't mind. Not really. But it might be nice if we both have lunch with her, don't you think? We've scarcely seen you since you started that job."

"I know. My research has been pretty full on. But I think you're right. It would make Mum feel better. What time for lunch then?"

"Twelvish okay?"

"Sure. Will I bring a salad?"

"No, Mum said not to worry. She's getting some ham and salads herself." Michelle paused. "Ash, do you think you'll tell Mum? About the lesbian thing? I know you haven't told her because she absolutely cross-examined me about Jack after we saw the show this morning. I think she's hoping you and Jack might, you know, get together, be happy, have kids. The whole nine yards."

Asha groaned. "I don't want to upset her, Chelle."

"I'm sure she'll understand. She loves you, Ash."

"I know she does and I love her. That's why I don't want to take the chance on hurting her."

"But this is weird, Ash. Being a lesbian is part of you, a big part, I'd say. So why wouldn't you want to tell her?"

"People, sometimes the nicest people, can't cope with the thought of homosexuality. I'm scared, Chelle, because I couldn't bear it if Mum—" Asha swallowed convulsively.

"Ash, come on. Mum would be the first to tell you your life is yours to live as you choose. She just wants you to be happy. If that means you want to shack up with a woman, so be it."

"Shack up?" Asha blew a raspberry. "You young people are such absolute romantics, aren't you?"

Michelle laughed and then sobered. "Have you considered Mum might feel hurt you *haven't* shared something so important with her?"

Asha was silent as she gave her sister's point some thought. "Were you?"

"What? Hurt? No. Okay, maybe just a bit. But I can understand why you haven't told me." Michelle sighed loudly. "You sure know how to complicate life, Ash. But seriously, do you think you'll tell Mum?"

"I want to." Asha thought again of Peri. "When the time's right. So don't say anything, Chelle, please."

"As if. It's your story, as they say."

"Thanks. I guess I'd better go. I have some work I need to do on Vivienne's book before I come over for lunch."

"Right. It'll be good to see you. Especially as I want to satisfy myself you haven't grown two heads since you told me you were a lesbian. See ya."

Asha was left with the sound of her sister's teasing laughter.

After she'd piled the second copy of the transcript of the second journal on the desk, Asha sat and looked at it, experiencing again a wonder that she could be part of what was such a wonderful and interesting life. She felt so close to Georgie Chaseley, and the thought of his love for his Margaret and their life together brought a lump to her throat. Vivienne was fortunate to have such a colorful story to add to the history of the family.

Glancing at the time, she secured the second copy with a clip, found Vivienne and gave the pages to her for Grace Moyland. Of course, Vivienne was full of questions about Asha's evening with Jack, and Asha fielded her questions as best she could. Asha gave her a quick rundown on the night and then explained she was having lunch with her mother. Leaving Vivienne to put the copies of the journals into an envelope for Grace, Asha hurried to her room to change. She slipped on a pair of tailored shorts and a dress T-shirt and headed out to her car. A little over half an hour later she pulled into the drive of her stepmother's house.

"It's so good to see you, love," said Laura West, greeting Asha with a warm hug and a kiss. "You look wonderful."

"Thanks, Mum. So you do." And Asha knew it was true. Her stepmother was an attractive woman in her own right and certainly didn't look her forty-eight years. There was no gray in her fairish hair, and her daily walks kept her fit and healthy. Had she wanted to remarry in the nine years since her divorce, she wouldn't have had any difficulty finding a new husband.

It was strange, Asha reflected, how you never recognized your parents as sexual beings. Yet Asha could see that men would find her stepmother attractive.

"So, how is my other television star?" her stepmother said as she added some grape tomatoes to the tossed salad she was making.

Asha leaned on the table and grimaced. "I haven't had the pleasure of seeing it yet. I did see the camera crews last night, but I didn't realize they were trained on Michelle and me. Dad's supposed to be the famous one."

Laura laughed. "Maybe so, but when he has two beautiful daughters like you and Michelle, who can blame them? And you did look beautiful. Both my girls did."

"I thought I heard you drive in," said Michelle, joining them in the kitchen. "Both your girls did what, Mum?"

"I was telling Asha how great you both looked on TV this morning."

Michelle wrinkled her nose. "I guess I looked okay, but Asha's the photogenic one."

"Oh, sure." Asha chuckled. "The face that launched a thousand ships."

Michelle joined in her laughter and then gave her sister a piercing look. "And you look particularly, I don't know, sort of really happy or something."

Thoughts of Peri Moyland sent aftershocks of desire washing over Asha, and she felt herself flush.

Michelle pointed then wriggled her finger at Asha, and Asha's flush deepened as she thought about her earlier conversation with her sister. "And now you're blushing. What could that mean? Let's see. If we were in the middle of a trashy romance, we'd all be thinking it was l-o-o-v-e." She drew out the syllables.

Asha raised her hands and let them fall. "My sister the drama queen."

Laura smiled and picked up the salad, shooing them before her into the dining room, but not before she'd also given Asha a piercing look.

They sat down to eat, passing salads and laughing together as Michelle told their mother some outrageous anecdotes from the evening before. As they carried their cups back into the living room after clearing away the meal, a car gave two short beeps outside.

Michelle set her teacup aside. "That'll be Danny. He's taking me to the movies before he goes to training. I'll leave you and Asha to some quality time, Mum. See you, Ash," she said looking pointedly from her sister to her mother. And then she was gone.

Asha swallowed and made a show of stirring her tea.

"This is nice. It will give us some time together," her mother said as they heard the car drive away.

"Mmmm." Asha sipped her tea.

"I'm glad you both enjoyed the dinner last night. Your father rang me this morning to tell me about the award and to say how much it meant to him to have you both there."

"It was a good evening," Asha conceded. "Dad was a little overwhelmed I think."

"He deserved that award. He gave a lot of years to the game of cricket." Laura paused. "He was also quite taken with your young man."

"He's just a friend, Mum," Asha began, wishing she could change the direction of the conversation.

"Michelle says he's a lawyer. He's very handsome, too. Have you known him long?"

"Not long," Asha said carefully, wondering how she was going to handle what she wanted to say.

Her stepmother laughed softly. "I can hear Michelle saying, 'here comes the inquisition.'"

Asha laughed, too, if somewhat nervously. "I suppose we did look like a couple, but we're not. Actually, I've only just met him," she declared as casually as she could.

"I understand. There's no rush. It's sensible to get to know each other before you start getting serious," Laura said lightly.

"Yes. That's sensible." Asha could feel her heartbeats rising to choke her, and she swallowed again. "Mum. About that. Jack and me." She drew a calming breath.

Her stepmother set her teacup down on its saucer. "I don't mean to pry, love. I know you're more than old enough to make your own way in life, and I'd hate you to think I was interfering, but I'd just like to see you meet someone nice, fall in love, have someone special to share your life."

Asha thought about Peri, saw her eyes filled with passion, felt the softness of her lips. She looked down at her hands where they rested on her knees. "Actually, I think I have, Mum. I think I've fallen in love."

Laura beamed. "You have? Asha, that's wonderful. And he did look so nice."

Asha looked at her mother in surprise. She'd momentarily forgotten Jack Moyland. "Oh, not with Jack."

Laura looked at Asha in surprise.

"Although Jack's a really nice guy. I mean, I'm in love with someone else."

"And does he feel the same about you?" Laura asked.

"I don't know." Asha smiled crookedly. "I desperately hope so, but—"

"And he couldn't go with you to the dinner last night?" Her stepmother waited patiently for Asha to continue.

"Um, no." Asha took a steadying breath. "Mum, you know

I've always been, well, different. From everyone else, I mean. Growing up."

"You weren't different," Laura said. "You were perhaps a little shy."

"No. I mean I didn't go out much. With guys."

A dull flush colored Asha's stepmother's cheeks, and Asha rushed on before she lost her nerve.

"It never felt right to me, Mum. With guys. Not like it did with women." There! She'd said it. Allowed the words to be released after keeping them imprisoned for so long.

The silence in the room grew. Asha felt as though it was moving around her, pressing in on her. She glanced at her stepmother and took in the frozen expression on her face.

"What I'm trying to say, Mum, is that I'm a lesbian." The word echoed in the quiet room.

Laura's hand fluttered to her mouth. "A lesbian?" she whispered. "Oh, Asha, no. No." She shook her head.

"I haven't told you before because I didn't want to upset you." Asha swallowed again. "But I can't go on pretending."

There was silence again.

"Do you hate me?" Asha asked hollowly, standing up.

Her stepmother looked up and shook her head. "Hate you? No, Asha, I could never do that." She stood up then, held out her arms, and Asha dissolved into them. "I love you," Laura murmured soothingly into Asha's hair.

They both began to cry, clinging to each other. When they drew apart, Asha wiped her eyes with the back of her hand. Laura reached for tissues from the box on the coffee table and passed one to Asha.

"I thought, when you didn't say anything, that you were disgusted or something." Asha blew her nose.

"No. No. I just . . . I was just a little shocked. And concerned. Life can be so difficult under so-called accepted circumstances. To be different is so much harder. I could see all that before you."

"It's just that I couldn't let myself acknowledge it for such a long time. Then I met Tessa and, she made me see it was right for me."

"Tessa?" Laura repeated. "Oh, Asha."

"I was in love with her. Or I thought I was. I let myself confuse how I felt about her, all that she offered"—Asha flushed and looked away—"with love. I know now what a mistake I made. She said she loved me, too, but she, well, she didn't. That's partly why I came home," she finished thickly.

Laura took her hand and led her to sit beside her on the sofa. "I'm sorry, Asha. And you still love her?"

"No." Asha shook her head. "It was over a long time ago. I just wouldn't let it go. She was my—It was the first time." She sighed and looked at her stepmother. "I know you and Michelle didn't like her, but in the beginning, we did have some good times together."

"I did have reservations," Laura said carefully. "I thought she was a little superficial."

Asha gave a crooked smile. "That's diplomatic."

"All right, I thought she was *very* superficial."

Asha laughed then. "Michelle wasn't quite as restrained."

"Michelle knows? About all this?"

"Yes. I told her this morning." Asha shook her head. "She said she knew already."

"She did? She never breathed a word. Although when I'd say I wished you'd find a nice young man, she told me you'd sort yourself out when you were ready." Laura sighed. "Young people are so much more aware than we ever were at that age."

"So you knew all about lesbians when you were Chelle's age?" Asha asked lightly.

Her stepmother's face suffused with color, and she looked uncharacteristically flustered. "Of course we knew," she said quickly and Asha squeezed her hand.

"I was just teasing, Mum," Asha reassured her. "Would you prefer it if we didn't talk about it? I mean, it must be a shock and I'll understand if you want some time to get used to the idea."

"No, Asha. You know you can talk to me about anything. I'm just worried about you. Do you realize what it will be like having to hide away, not let the world know your feelings, be made to feel like a freak? And there are hurtful people, Asha. Bigoted, intolerant people who could physically harm you."

"Mum, it's not that bad. And try not to worry about me. I know what you're saying is true, but I don't want to live a life that's a lie. Can you understand that?"

Laura nodded reluctantly, lifted Asha's hand and kissed it before releasing it. "You always were a seriously courageous little girl." She smiled. "It appears you've not changed in that respect."

"I just don't want you to worry about me, Mum."

"It's my job to do that. But I'll try not to. You haven't told your father, have you?"

Asha shook her head. "No. But I guess I should. How do you think he'll react?"

"He'll get over it. He'll have to because he thinks you hung the stars and the moon."

"Oh, sure." Asha laughed.

"He does. But you should tell him soon. I think he's under the misapprehension you and that young man last night are a couple. He seemed very impressed by him."

Asha bit her lip again. "Jack is impressive. The truth is I wanted to ask someone else." Asha paused. "His sister."

"Oh, Asha. I hope this Jack knows that."

"Yes, he knows. About my being a lesbian. I told him last night." She shook her head. "And he knows about Peri. That's his sister. He was okay with it. I told you he was a nice guy. And besides, he all but hero-worships Dad," she added with a laugh.

Laura rolled her eyes. "Doesn't everybody do that?"

Asha looked at her mother, wondering if she was more upset about the breakup with her father than she was admitting to. She was trying to formulate the question when her stepmother sighed.

"It's all right, love. I don't begrudge your father his life with Karen. Karen's the sort of woman he always should have married."

"He still cheated on you," Asha exclaimed.

"I wasn't exactly the best wife." Laura shook her head. "I think I was more swayed by being your mother than by being a wife." She swallowed. "I so wanted a family. Your father made that possible, and I'll be forever grateful to him for you and Michelle. Anyway"—she patted Asha's knee—"tell me about Jack and his sister."

"Well, they're sort of relatives of the family where I'm staying."

"Sort of relatives?" Laura repeated in surprise.

"I guess you'd say relatives by marriage, according to my research. And I found these wonderful old journals about the family and Queensland from the 1870s to the late 1890s. It was so fascinating. Vivienne's ecstatic."

"Vivienne?" Laura said after a moment, and something in her voice made Asha pause before continuing.

"Yes. She's the woman who's commissioned me to do the history of her husband's family. Finding the journals has made my job so much easier. They were in a beautiful wooden box, quite large, and it used to be a music box. The books were in a false bottom."

"Hidden?"

Asha frowned. "Yes. Although I'm not sure why. You see, Jack and Peri's great-great-grandmother was a widow who married the writer of the journals. He was one of the two Chaseley brothers who came out to Australia from England in 1870."

"Chaseley?" Laura said thickly and Asha noticed her mother's face had suddenly paled.

"Yes. Richard and George Chaseley."

Laura was silent.

"Mum? What is it?"

"Nothing." She moved her hand agitatedly. Her fingers going to her throat, she began to worry the collar of her blouse. "I just didn't realize. We haven't spoken. I didn't know anything about your research."

"I did leave the Chaseley's phone number and address with Michelle."

"She must have forgotten to tell me."

"The house is magnificent, and I have a sort of self-contained room. I work in Vivienne's husband's study. Vivienne was married to Richard's grandson, also called Richard."

"Dickie," her stepmother said hoarsely.

Asha stared at her. "You know the Chaseleys?"

CHAPTER TEN

Laura's fingers fidgeted with her collar again and then finally she nodded. "Do they know?" She shook her head. "No. They wouldn't. The name West would mean nothing to them."

"Mum! What's going on?" Asha asked, unable to comprehend what her stepmother was saying.

"I can't—" She drew a steadying breath before continuing. "I worked for the Chaseleys a long time ago. Before I met your father. When I left—Asha, you haven't told them who you are, have you? Or who I am?"

Asha shook her head. "I don't understand. Vivienne knows I'm Sean West's daughter, that I have a stepmother and a sister."

"You mustn't tell them about me, Asha. I want your promise you'll never mention my name," Laura said urgently.

"But why? I mean why would I? And why wouldn't you want them to know I was connected to you?"

"I told you I left suddenly, and I don't want them to know where I am."

"Mum, you're scaring me." Asha frowned. "What could you possibly be hiding from the Chaseleys? Unless . . . My God! Did you steal from them?"

"Of course not. I just don't want to talk about it. Let's leave it, Asha."

"Mum, you can't leave it like this," Asha said. "How did you come to work for the Chaseleys in the first place?"

Laura sighed. "I was Viv's secretary. She did a lot of charity work and she needed an assistant, someone to do office work." Laura sank onto the edge of the lounge chair and Asha sat down, too. "My parents had just died within months of each other, and I'd given up my job to look after them when they were ill. When everything was settled and the debts paid, I was almost destitute. I needed work quickly, and the lawyer who handled my parents' estate suggested me to Viv for the job as her assistant. He was a relative of the Chaseleys. Joe Moyland."

"Moyland?" Asha was taken aback. "That's Peri's and Jack's name. It must have been their father."

Laura stood up again then walked over to the window. "I worked there, and lived there, for over a year."

"But you've never mentioned any of this to us," Asha said softly.

"It was the best and the worst time of my life. I was young, not yet twenty-one, and I fell in love. But it wasn't acceptable." She began to pace the floor while Asha mentally reviewed her research. Vivienne had two sons, Richard, her stepson, and her biological son, Nicolas. It would have been twenty-seven or so years ago. Richard would have been married. Nicolas, on the other hand, would be about her stepmother's age.

"You fell in love with Nicolas Chaseley?"

Laura stilled, her back to Asha. "I can't talk about this, Asha."

"The Chaseleys sent you away because you loved their son?"

Laura was silent.

"I can't understand that." Asha shook her head. "Why would they do that? It's cruel."

"I became pregnant."

Asha was speechless as she tried to process what her step-mother had said.

"Why didn't he marry you?"

"That was the very last thing I wanted," her stepmother said huskily.

Asha swallowed. "What happened to the baby?"

After a tense silence, Laura simply shook her head.

"Oh, Mum." Asha crossed to her stepmother, put her arms around her, and they cried together for the second time that day.

"I felt adoption was the right choice," Laura said at last.

"Why didn't you want to marry him? The baby's father, I mean," Asha asked when she'd passed her stepmother the tissues some time later.

"I don't think I can talk about it, Asha."

"He's divorced," Asha said. "Nicolas Chaseley was married, but he's divorced now."

"Asha, I don't want to hear about him."

"But, if you loved him . . . You must have loved him very much."

Laura shook her head. "Oh, no," she said vehemently. "No, I didn't. Quite the opposite. He was a spoilt playboy."

"Did he, well, take advantage of you?" Asha asked and her stepmother grimaced.

"Such an old-fashioned term these days. But I suppose it does cover it. He took advantage of me in the worst possible way. I thought he was, if not a friend, then an ally, if you like. He pro-fessed to be. I loved someone, and he found out about it. He told me he'd seen us together. I was terrified he'd tell his family, but he said he wouldn't."

"You mean he blackmailed you?" Asha was horrified.

167

"Not exactly. He did tell me everyone would be against us, that no one would understand. It fed my own insecurities, and I let what he said frighten me. It frightened us both, my"—she paused and flushed again—"lover and I. And so we argued and broke off our relationship. But we couldn't stay away from each other. We loved each other so. My lover wanted us to go away together. Interstate or overseas. But I was too much of a coward. We had one final argument." Laura shook her head sadly. "I was so upset that night. There was a party, just a small one, and I escaped outside, walked over to the garage where the new unit was being built for Richard and Sara. Nicolas followed me and offered his shoulder to cry on.

"I was distraught and naive." Laura worried at the tissue she held. "He'd brought a bottle of wine and glasses and convinced me one little drink would make me feel better. I was upset. And reckless. I allowed him to convince me to have another drink. I didn't remember much after that, but I woke up in the morning where he'd just left me. It was my lover who found me and thought I'd . . . I swore Nicolas had raped me, but—" She choked back a sob. "Everyone thought I'd willingly gone out there with him, especially since he told them just that."

Asha took her stepmother's hand and held it in her own.

"I still remember the disappointment I saw in Viv's eyes. In everyone's eyes. I wanted to leave, but Viv insisted I stay until she could find someone else. Nicolas had gone to visit friends in New Zealand and my lover had left for the States. I was devastated. There was only Richard and Sara at Tyneholme, so I agreed.

"Then I found out I was pregnant, and I knew I couldn't stay in my condition. Viv found me another job in Sydney and helped me with money until my baby was born. I decided adoption would be best for the baby because I wasn't in any fit state to look after myself, let alone a child. Afterward, I don't think I did more than exist from day to day."

"Oh, Mum. That's terrible."

"A couple of years later, I was sitting in a park in my lunch break, watching children playing, when your father appeared with you. He was playing cricket in Sydney then and had been a widower for nearly a year." Laura squeezed Asha's hand. "You were shy and didn't want to join the other children until your father encouraged you. Then he sat on the bench beside me and we started talking. And I watched you. Your father and I met in the park each day after that. You'd play for a while and then you'd sit beside me and hold my hand just like you are now and talk so seriously. You'd lost your mother and I'd lost my child and someone I'd loved deeply. I think we each sensed the sadness in each other. Your father and I married, and here we are."

"I wish there'd been a happily ever after for you, too, Mum."

Laura stood up then paced to the window again. "I don't for a minute regret marrying your father, Asha. Not for myself. I gained you and Michelle. But I regret it for your father's sake. He deserved someone who'd love him unconditionally. I never had that to give him. That's why I'm so pleased he's found Karen. He deserves to be happy. Your father's a good man."

"I know. And you're a wonderful mother." Asha went to her stepmother and hugged her.

"Yes, well, that remains to be seen."

"What happened to him?" Asha asked softly. "Your first love?"

"I don't know." Her stepmother paused, nervously tucked her hair back, and then seemed to gather herself together. "It wouldn't have worked out."

Asha gave her stepmother another hug before she stepped back.

"I'll make another pot of tea, shall I?" Laura asked.

"You sit down and relax, Mum. I'll do it. You sound like Vivienne. She always says a cup of tea—" Asha stopped then turned back to her stepmother, ready to apologize.

"A cup of tea will cure all ills," her stepmother finished as she followed Asha into the kitchen. "How is Viv? Is she keeping well?"

"Pretty much so. She's eighty-six, I think. Did you know her husband and her daughter-in-law were killed in a car accident two years ago?" Asha asked, filling the electric kettle.

"Yes. I saw a report on television. It brought it all back for me. Luckily you were at the Coast, and Michelle was spending the weekend with your father. He was a nice man, Dickie Chaseley, and very protective of his family. Sara was a wonderful person. She and Richard were so much in love. He must have been devastated."

"He was," Asha told her. "And still is, according to Vivienne."

"It's a beautiful house, isn't it?" Laura said, concentrating on setting out cups for their tea. "So big." She paused slightly. "Does Viv live there alone?"

"Richard and his family still live in the separate unit, but they're in Melbourne at the moment. And Peri's been staying with Vivienne for a while."

"And the daughter? Rosemary, wasn't it?" Laura asked.

"Yes. She works in Melbourne. I haven't met her yet, but I believe she's coming home to visit her mother. I don't know when exactly but I'm sure it's fairly soon."

Her stepmother was silent, watching as Asha poured hot water on the tea leaves.

"Mum? About the man you fell in love with—"

"I don't think I want to talk about this anymore, Asha. Let's just leave it." Laura held up her hand when Asha went to say more. "Please, love. I really don't want to talk about it. And I want you to give me your promise you won't discuss this with Viv or anyone else. Don't tell them I'm your stepmother. All right?"

"Of course. If it's what you want, Mum."

"How long will you be working on this research for the

Chaseleys? Can't you do it from home here rather than stay in their house?"

"It's just more convenient for me to stay there. And I'm not sure how much longer the research will take me. I've done quite a bit, and the information Vivienne found in the box in the attic saved me heaps of work. The old journals—"

"Journals? The ones you mentioned before?"

"Yes. They're so fascinating and contained so much information. Anyway, I have a template for the book, but there's a lot of information to be entered so . . ." She shrugged. And then she suddenly realized when she left Tyneholme and the Chaseleys she'd be leaving Peri. "I can't say for sure," she said as regret filled her heart. "But not too much longer."

"I feel so tired now." Laura sat down and sighed. "I've wanted to tell you both for so long. Clear my conscience I guess."

"You have nothing on your conscience, Mum. You were young."

A faint shadow passed over Laura's face. "Yes. Young. And very foolish. But now, it's been very freeing somehow."

"I know what you mean," Asha said with feeling. "I've hated lying to you. Even if it was lying by omission."

"I can understand how difficult it was for you, Asha. I . . . There's . . ." Laura gave a small shake of her head. "I suppose I should tell Michelle when she comes home later."

"I'm sure there's no hurry, Mum. If you'd rather take time to, you know, recover a bit from all this. But I'll stay if you do want to tell her tonight. Michelle will be fine, you'll see."

Laura patted Asha's hand. "I know." She brushed away a tear. "I must have done something right with the two of you. I'm very proud of both of you."

"We're proud of you, too."

"And you said you've told Michelle about you?"

"Yes. This morning. She liked Jack, too."

Laura laughed softly.

"At lunch I thought you'd pick up on some of Chelle's not so subtle 'tell Mum' looks."

"I'm afraid I didn't, Asha," Laura's fingers played with her tissue. "Jack's sister, the one you said you cared about . . ."

"I've fallen in love with her."

"And she feels the same?"

Asha hesitated. "I don't know. It, well, we're new to each other. We haven't really talked about it. But it would have been so much easier if it had been Jack."

"Yes, I suppose it would," her stepmother said. "It's so complicated, any association with the Chaseleys," she added softly and Asha sighed.

"I can see that. But I don't know that it will come to anything. With Peri and me, that is."

"Oh, Asha." Laura West shook her head. "I don't know what to tell you. I certainly don't want to ask you not to see this young woman if you really care about her. I just . . . I can't make any contact with the Chaseleys. I just can't."

"I can see that, Mum." Asha felt her heart sink. How could she choose between her stepmother and Peri? It was too difficult and it would tear her apart. There had to be a way.

"Believe me, Asha, it's all best left in the past. And I—" Her stepmother swallowed and shook her head again.

Asha waited, instinct telling her there was something her stepmother wanted to add, but Laura remained silent and began to pour their tea.

When Asha left her stepmother and returned to Tyneholme she was surprised and inordinately pleased to see Peri's car parked in the garage. She refused to allow herself to dwell on her stepmother's revelations and she hurried inside, finding Peri with Vivienne in the morning room. Vivienne immediately asked about Asha's mother and sister, and Asha managed to make the correct responses. Then Vivienne stood up.

"I was just saying to Peri that I felt a little tired, so I might excuse myself and have a little rest."

Asha quickly handed Vivienne her walking stick. "Can I help you upstairs?" she asked.

"No, thank you, my dear. You stay and talk to Peri." She moved slowly out of the room.

When they were alone, Asha turned back to Peri and smiled. "This is a surprise. We didn't expect you back until tomorrow," she said, wishing she could simply cross the room and take Peri in her arms. She desperately wanted to do that.

Peri had walked over to the window, away from Asha, and Asha's heart sank.

"I didn't expect to be back either," Peri said evenly, turning to face Asha. "I rearranged some appointments because I wanted to get home as soon as I could." Her lips twisted self-derisively.

Asha swallowed, her mouth suddenly dry. "Is something wrong?"

"You tell me," Peri replied.

Asha frowned slightly. "I don't know what you mean. Are you upset about something? If it's about last night, we can talk about it if you like."

"What would you suggest we say?"

A dull ache settled in Asha's chest. "I would say it was wonderful. And that I haven't been able to get you out of my mind," she said honestly, knowing she was putting herself in the very vulnerable position she'd told herself to avoid.

"I was thinking about you, too," Peri said. She bit off a soft laugh and shook her head slightly, folding her arms across her chest. "Then I was sitting on the plane coming home and suddenly, on the TV screen, there was your face." She leaned back against the windowsill. "I was thinking about you and there you were, looking absolutely incredible. I thought I was dreaming."

"You saw the segment on the Sporting Awards?" Asha felt

herself flush. "I haven't seen it yet, but it seems everyone else has."

"And then the cameras panned to Jack." Peri shook her head. "Of all people, my brother, Jack."

Asha laughed, embarrassed. "He looked very dashing in his tux, didn't he? I didn't realize the cameras were on us. Michelle's been teasing me mercilessly ever since."

"I can understand that. You and Jack seemed to be . . ." Peri paused almost imperceptibly. " . . . enjoying yourselves," she finished in that same flat tone.

"We did have a good time. I like your brother. He's great company." Asha studied Peri's face, her downcast eyes.

"I couldn't . . . I can't quite work out why you were with him," Peri said almost absently.

"It was a special night and my father got the tickets. Jack was just here at the time and I knew he liked cricket, too."

Peri was silent for long moments while Asha could only watch her, trying to read Peri's closed expression.

"He reminds me so much of you," Asha said.

"He reminds you of me? And that makes it all right?" Peri said. "My own brother, Asha. You went on a date with my brother. How could you do that?"

"It wasn't like that. I asked him to go with me because I needed a partner for the Awards Dinner. Jack had called in to see you and Vivienne suggested it."

"Vivienne?"

"I wanted to ask you," Asha said thickly.

Peri shook her head again.

"It wasn't a date," Asha repeated. "I told you I wanted to ask you, but you had left for Townsville."

"You could have gone on your own."

"Peri, you can't think there's anything between Jack and me. It's ridiculous. I scarcely know him and—"

"You scarcely know me, too." Peri swallowed and began walking toward the door. "Why did I think it would be different this time?" And she walked out the door, leaving Asha to stand staring after her. Asha stood still, trying to understand Peri's reasoning.

By the time she moved out into the hallway to follow her, Peri was in her car and driving away.

Asha headed downstairs the next day, trying unsuccessfully to tell herself she was simply looking for Vivienne, when her thoughts were filled with Peri. Not that Peri would want to see Asha. According to Vivienne, Peri had left for work before Asha was up this morning, and she'd certainly stayed away until late last night. She'd made it very plain that Asha was the last person she wanted to be around. And yet, that night, it had been so different.

As Asha approached the morning room, she heard voices and her lips rose in a spontaneous smile. Just being near Peri was bittersweet, but she was determined not to show how hurt she was by Peri's mistrust. She turned into the doorway expecting to see Vivienne and Peri.

Vivienne was there, but the woman with her definitely wasn't Peri, and Asha stopped, mortified by her lack of manners. "Oh. I'm so sorry, Vivienne. I thought it was Peri with you. I didn't realize you had company. If you'll just excuse me, I'll—"

"No. No. Stay." Vivienne smiled and waved Asha forward. "Come on in, my dear. I want you to meet someone."

Asha slid a glance at the tall, elegant woman standing by the window. She must have been admiring the view, but she'd turned on Asha's entry. The woman's dark hair was cut short, shaped into the back of her head to feather on her neck. When she turned, Asha saw the front flopped onto her forehead and sat back close to her head on the sides.

She wore a tailored white shirt and dark slacks with a belt that featured a small antique pewter buckle. She was a poised, attractive woman, and a prickle of recognition ran over Asha. She was almost certain the woman was a lesbian although she couldn't have pinpointed why she felt this was so. As far as guessing the woman's age, Asha decided she could be anything between thirty and fifty. And her eyes looked vaguely familiar.

"Asha, my dear." Vivienne's voice claimed Asha's attention. "I want you to meet my daughter, Rosemary. She arrived home this morning. Rosemary, this is Asha West."

Of course. Asha mentally chastised herself. This could only be Vivienne's daughter.

Rosemary Chaseley crossed the room with long-legged strides and held out her hand. Asha took it and was rewarded by a firm grasp.

"Nice to finally meet you, Asha." Rosemary smiled. "My mother's told me so much about you."

The smile transformed Rosemary's face, and Asha found herself smiling spontaneously back.

"She has?" Asha grimaced. "All good, I hope."

"Oh, yes. Mother and I chat on the phone regularly and she's been singing your praises."

"Vivienne's far too kind. I think my shares went up when I discovered the journals, which, by the way, was simply pure luck on my part."

"Ah, yes. The journals." Rosemary sat down and indicated for Asha to do the same. "I'm really looking forward to reading them."

"Asha's typed them up for us," Vivienne said as Asha sat down. "So we don't damage the original journals. I've finished reading them, and Peri took the second part to read last night, so you can begin on Part One, where Richard and Georgie leave England."

"Wonderful! And such a good idea to transcribe them, Asha. I've been dying to read them since Mother rang to tell me about

176

them. I can't believe they were hidden away in a secret compartment. Sounds like a movie plot."

Asha laughed. "It does, doesn't it?"

"Have you worked out who might have put the books in the box and why?" Rosemary asked and Asha shook her head. "We've all been speculating. It may have been for safekeeping, which points to Georgie putting them there. The journals end in 1897, when Georgie and Margaret came down from Charters Towers to Brisbane, and Vivienne tells me Georgie lived on until 1950. However, as they were in the false bottom of the box, it does look as though the books were hidden away."

"Would Georgie's wife have put them there?"

"I wouldn't have thought so." Asha frowned. "Georgie mentions the music box as a gift Richard gave to his wife, Susannah. Perhaps Susannah put them there, or one of the children. And it would have had to have been after the mechanism that played the music was removed. That poses another question. Did the mechanism actually break, or was it removed on purpose so the books, et cetera, could be hidden?"

"It's quite a mystery," Rosemary said.

"If my Internet server hadn't been down, I'd have had a chance to look into the family before they left England. I know Vivienne wanted the book to cover the family in Australia, but I'm curious about their life in England, too, especially since Georgie refers to it in his journals." Asha told Rosemary excitedly. "And the old photo with the books is unusual, too, in that not many families in the mining villages would have had the money to spend on photographs. The Bolam family Georgie mentions living at The Hall were well off apparently, so perhaps they had the photographs taken. I've looked in my reference books, and the fashions in the photo are in keeping with the date on the back. It appears to be Richard's family at his sister, Mary's, wedding. That's one of the things I want to check, a marriage between Mary Chaseley and Enoch Bolam."

"I just can't wait," said Vivienne.

"And it's really amazing," Asha continued enthusiastically. "The journals, I mean. Especially when you consider children would most probably have had only limited schooling in the mining villages. This would have been so with Richard and Georgie, but Georgie mentions in one of the journals that his father saved one of the Bolam children from drowning, and in appreciation, the Bolams allowed the Chaseley children to be tutored with their own children."

"When will you be able to do this research, Asha?" Vivienne asked, as excited as Asha.

"They tell me the problem with my server will be solved by this afternoon. Fingers crossed." Asha held up her hand.

"Perhaps Peri could help when she gets home from work," Vivienne suggested. "She's a whiz with those computer things."

"Ah, it's okay, Vivienne," Asha said quickly. "The problem's with the Internet provider rather than the software."

Vivienne looked perplexed. "I just can't understand all this modern technical jargon."

Rosemary chuckled. "At least you recognize it as technical jargon, Mother."

Asha's gaze went from mother to daughter, and she could see the resemblance between them now. She remarked on it. Vivienne looked pleased and Rosemary laughed.

"The acorn, as they say, hasn't fallen far from the tree with my mother and me. I just hope I look as wonderful when I'm Mother's age." Rosemary paused and looked at Asha with studied casualness. "And what about you, Asha? Do you resemble your parents?"

"I suppose I look a little like the photos of my mother. She died when I was four years old. But I think I get my coloring from my father. My half sister, Michelle, is the image of her mother. My stepmother, that is."

"And you're a librarian as well as a qualified genealogist?"

Rosemary said.

"Yes. And Michelle's doing Arts at the University of Queensland."

"Your parents must be proud of you both."

Asha looked across at Vivienne's daughter. "I suppose they are. Dad's not one for saying much, but Mum's great."

"I know your father has sports stores, and Mother told me your parents are divorced. Did your stepmother remarry?"

Asha was beginning to wonder if Peri and Rosemary were sisters. And lawyers. They both seemed to enjoy interrogation. She found herself smiling wryly and Rosemary stiffened.

"I didn't mean to pry," she said quickly.

Asha shook her head. "That's okay. Really. I'm staying here in your mother's house. It's only natural that you'd be wary. So, to answer your question, no, my stepmother hasn't remarried. She went back into the workforce when she and my father were divorced. She started out doing clerical work, but now she runs the office of a large timber company near where we live. Office Manager, she laughingly calls herself."

The mantle clock chimed and Vivienne glanced across at it. "My goodness! Is it that time already?" She turned back to Asha. "Rosemary and I are going down to a local coffee shop for morning tea. And I'm going to stop off on the way back so I can post this copy of the journals off to Grace. Why don't you come along with us?"

"Oh, no. But thanks. I don't want to intrude. You must have lots to talk about, seeing as Rosemary has just arrived home."

Both women laughed.

"Mother and I talk all the time," Rosemary said. "Do join us, Asha. I'd love to hear more about Uncle Georgie's journals."

Half an hour later they were seated in a trendy little coffee shop overlooking the river. Rosemary glanced at her watch. "Should we wait a few minutes before we order? Peri should be here any minute."

CHAPTER ELEVEN

Asha stilled. Peri was joining them, too? Her nerve endings danced in anticipation. But what if Peri turned and walked away when she saw Asha? Peri had been studiously avoiding her, Asha knew, and the heavy weight of despair hung over Asha. She'd have to find a way to talk to Peri. Asha suddenly realized Rosemary was watching her, her sharp eyes probing. "It's a wonderful view, isn't it?" She said the first thing to pop into her mind.

Distracted, Rosemary turned to look out over the river where the huge ocean liners now docked, and Asha wrinkled her nose.

"Of course, it's not as nice as the view from the verandas at Tyneholme," she added with a smile.

Rosemary laughed and shrugged. "Still, it's nice to go out for coffee. Very bohemian I always think."

"Here's Peri now," Vivienne said and they all turned to watch her approach.

Asha wanted to remain calmly nonchalant, but she couldn't stop herself from turning to gaze at Peri. Her heartbeats tripped all over themselves as she watched her move down the aisle between the clusters of tables.

She had obviously been at work. She looked every inch a successful businesswoman. She was wearing a light gray skirt that hugged her hips, and a dark blue tailored jacket with the sleeves pushed up her arms to halfway between her wrists and her elbows. High heels showed off her long, slender legs. Her fair hair was clasped back at the nape of her neck.

A warmth washed over Asha and her mouth went dry. In that moment, watching Peri walking toward her, Asha knew, for better or worse, that she had fallen desperately in love with Peri Moyland. She wanted together like her maternal grandparents who were married for nearly sixty years, and like Georgie and his Margaret. Asha wanted together forever with this woman. A great sadness gripped her and she shivered slightly. She knew there wasn't the chance of forever in any equation that contained herself and Peri. And as her stepmother had said, it was so complicated.

Regardless of that, she had to face facts, she told herself firmly. Until that wonderful night in Peri's arms, Asha would have said Peri was straight. Maybe she felt the need to experiment and Asha was simply there and available. No. She'd never believe that. Peri had said that wasn't the case. No, Peri in Asha's arms was nowhere near experimental.

But then how *did* Peri see it? The question intruded with a brutal attack on her self-possession. Perhaps . . . no, it was definite. That night hadn't meant anything to Peri. It was blatantly obvious she regretted it. Otherwise, why was she so quick to believe Asha had dated her brother? Peri must know Asha could have no romantic interest in Jack. That had to be a convenient excuse to put something Peri regretted behind her.

181

Face it. She told herself. She'd broken her own rule, the one she'd made after Tessa, about never again letting anyone close enough to hurt her. A deep, aching pain grew inside her. She suspected this hurt, even though her relationship with Peri had ended before it had begun, would far outweigh what she'd felt after Tessa. Asha could barely contain a moan of despair.

She coughed softly and then realized with dismay that Rosemary Chaseley was watching her again. Had the she seen the pain Asha clutched inside her? Asha made a show of studying the drinks menu. Latte. Cappuccino. Herbal tea. Frappe. The words spun before her eyes.

"Peri!" Rosemary stood up and gave Peri a huge hug. "You look great. I knew a few weeks with Mother would do you the world of good."

"I'm fine, Rosie, and welcome home." Peri returned the hug. "It's great to see you again. I was so surprised when Viv rang me to tell me you were finally home."

Chairs were moved, and with horror, Asha looked up to see Peri sitting opposite her, far too close for Asha's peace of mind. She knew her knees would almost be touching Peri's. She shot a quick glance at her before drawing herself back a little, hoping Peri wouldn't notice.

Peri was adjusting her sunglasses, the darkness of the lenses disguising her expression, so Asha had no way of knowing what she was thinking.

"Hello, Asha," Peri said lightly before turning back to Rosemary. "How long are you staying, Rosie?" she asked, and Vivienne laughed.

"I'd like to know that, too."

Rosemary relaxed back in her chair. "Ah, now that's part of my big surprise. You're looking at an old retiree."

"You've given up your job?" Vivienne exclaimed, amazed. "I know you've been talking about retiring, but I thought you were just thinking about it."

"I've been thinking about it for a long time, Mother." Rosemary caught the eye of the waitress. "I'm financially secure now, so I had no excuse. I went ahead and did it. So here I am, a lady of leisure. Although I'll probably take on some consulting work occasionally, just to keep my hand in, as they say."

"Bravo!" exclaimed Peri. "You've been working too hard for too long."

"Now look who's talking," Rosemary teased.

Peri smiled and nodded. "Touché. But although I'm back at work I'm not putting in the hours I used to."

"And you've discovered a secret," Rosemary said lightly.

Peri's face colored slightly. "A secret?"

"That while you were away the business moved on very well without you," Rosemary explained.

"Oh. Yes. I guess I can't dispute that. It did. I realized now I should have had faith in my staff."

The waitress joined them and they all decided on what they were having. Asha had no idea what she ordered. All she recalled was the fleeting touch of Peri's knee as she passed Vivienne the menu.

"Oh, and scones," Vivienne added as the waitress went to leave. "With strawberry jam and cream. Nothing like Devonshire tea," she said as Rosemary laughed.

"You and your scones, Mother. You know they won't be a patch on the ones you make."

Peri and Rosemary exchanged a few family memories of Vivienne's scones until the waitress returned with their orders.

"So what do you plan on doing in your retirement?" Peri asked, adding sugar to her coffee.

Despair swelled inside Asha. After that first quick glance, Peri hadn't so much as looked at Asha.

Rosemary ran her hand through her short hair. "Firstly, I'm going to treat myself to a well-earned rest for a while and spend some time with Mother." She leaned across the table and gently squeezed Vivienne's hand.

"That's wonderful, Rosemary." Vivienne beamed at her daughter. "But are you sure it won't be too boring for you after your job, and Melbourne?"

"Once a Brisbane girl, always a Brisbane girl. Don't you agree, Asha?" Rosemary drew Asha into the conversation.

"Oh, yes. Definitely," Asha said quickly. She'd been surreptitiously watching Peri lift her latte up to her lips to sip her coffee, and she drew her attention back to Rosemary and made herself smile at Vivienne's daughter. "I've only been living an hour away at the Gold Coast and I've missed home."

"There you are then." Rosemary spread her scone with jam and added a dollop of cream. "I thought I might catch up with a few friends I haven't seen in ages. If they remember me," she finished wryly.

Asha sensed Peri's eyes were on her, and she let herself glance across the table at her. What was Peri thinking about? Was she seeing them as Asha was? Bodies naked, legs entwined, the deep, drugging kisses. Asha's lips parted and she moistened her dry lips with her tongue tip. Peri's head went down, her fingers rubbing at the faint smudge of lipstick on her cup.

"You know, I'm nudging fifty, and I see downhill all the way from now on." Rosemary laughed.

"Go on with you. You don't look thirty," Vivienne told her. "And you're only as old as you feel."

"Thirty is stretching it, Mother." Rosemary sighed. "I've been feeling much more than my age lately. And in the past year I've lost two colleagues to heart attacks. It's pretty sobering."

"My stepmother was saying much the same thing not long ago," Asha said and Rosemary paused, her cup halfway to her mouth. Asha saw her swallow.

"Was she?"

Asha nodded. "She's been working for the same firm for about nine years or so, and she thinks it's time she took a break.

184

She's been talking about wanting to travel for ages."

"She never went overseas with your father when he was on the Australian Cricket team?" Vivienne asked.

"She usually stayed home with Michelle and me. We all went to England on one tour, but it was pretty hectic and Michelle was only about three or four, so it wasn't much of a success. I did get to go to Lords, though. That gave me a certain amount of clout at school, especially with the boys."

"I'll bet it did," Rosemary remarked, while Peri seemed to find her coffee cup fascinating.

"I had quite a business going at one stage," Asha continued with a quick laugh. "I'd introduce the boys to Dad and they'd pay me with books, CDs, or by buying me hamburgers. Business was brisk until Dad got suspicious and put a stop to it. I was grounded for a month."

They all laughed with Asha and then Vivienne exclaimed in surprise.

"For heaven's sake, there's Penny Jenson." She stood up and leaned on her cane, waving at an elderly woman at another table. "Will you excuse me for a few minutes, girls? I have to see how Penny's getting on since she had her hip replaced." She walked off and Rosemary shook her head.

"Mother looks so well."

"She is usually," Peri said. "She's sensible about what she can and can't do. She's remarkable for her age." She grinned at Rosemary. "So it must be genetic."

Rosemary pouted. "And my clean living has nothing to do with it?"

"Maybe a little," Peri conceded.

"The best way I found to gauge it is to see how you're faring at school reunions," Rosemary said.

"You went to that school reunion you were talking about last year?" Peri asked and Rosemary nodded.

"Oh, yes. And no one was more surprised than I was when I

ended up thoroughly enjoying it." She chuckled. "There we all were, forty-something matrons with over eighty grandchildren between us. Not that I did anything to help that total."

"Did you ever consider getting married, Rosie?" Peri asked softly and Rosemary shrugged.

"No." She sipped her coffee.

"What about that persistent suitor Richard always talks about? Neville Harding, wasn't it? He sounded very keen. And I do believe I heard he was free again."

Rosemary groaned and gave Peri a playful shove. "I can't believe Richard was so unkind as to tell that story. I'll never forgive him." She turned to Asha. "My brother takes great pleasure in telling the story, *ad nauseam*, of the tenacious Neville. When I was in my teens I couldn't get him to believe I found him to be a very unattractive man. Thank heavens he eventually married someone else."

"As Richard tells it he divorced her," Peri said with a grin. "And married again and divorced number two. Now I hear he's been deserted by number three."

Rosemary wrinkled her nose. "Then I'd best keep a low profile in case he hears I'm back in town."

They all laughed with her.

"Did Viv tell you Lance and Janet are expecting a baby?" Peri asked and Asha looked back at her, but her dark glasses still hid her expression. Then Peri reached up and took her sunglasses off, then rubbed at her eyes tiredly. "They suit each other, you know, Lance and Janet. More than Lance and I ever did." She grimaced. "Pity I didn't realize that before we booked the church, wouldn't you say?"

"Only with hindsight," Asha said before she could stop herself, and she flushed.

"Asha's right," Rosemary agreed softly. "We still thought Lance and Janet could have acted with more integrity."

"I suppose so." Peri sighed. "But, to be fair, I didn't give him all that much chance to explain anything, even if he'd wanted to. I was caught up in the arrangements for the actual ceremony and working so hard we barely saw each other, let alone had the chance to talk about anything."

"Maybe so," said Rosemary. "However, I still think he could have spoken to you about not wanting to go through with the wedding before he did. He must have known he had feelings for Janet way before the wedding day."

Peri bit her lip. "I should have told him, too."

"What about?" Rosemary frowned. "That you had second thoughts as well?" She looked a little disconcerted, and Peri shot a quick glance across the table at Asha before looking away again.

"Looking back, I think I threw myself into the arrangements for the wedding so that I wouldn't have to face the fact that I really didn't want to get married."

"But you and Lance had been together for so long," Rosemary said.

"I know, Rosie. Out of habit, I think. And I don't really blame him for wanting more out of a relationship. I know I wasn't in love with him."

Rosemary sighed. "Was there someone else? For you, I mean."

"No. Not then. It was just that I thought I had to get married. It was what everyone did."

"Some of us didn't." Rosemary laughed softly.

"The sensible ones." Peri grinned crookedly.

"Not necessarily. Marriage isn't for everyone, Peri," Rosemary said and Peri shrugged.

"And as you said, it's in the past now and I'm okay with it."

"You're sure?" Rosemary said gently.

"Very sure. Janet aside, I know now it would have been a mistake for me to marry Lance."

Rosemary nodded sympathetically. "I'm so pleased you've

finally put it all behind you."

"But seriously, Rosie, what about you?" Peri persisted. "You haven't left any broken hearts behind in Melbourne?"

"Hardly. It was a case of all work and no play. In fact I probably wouldn't have recognized an attraction if it had done a dance in front of me." She laughed and then sobered. "There was someone once. A long time ago. But"—she turned her coffee cup in its saucer—"it didn't work out."

"I'm sorry," Peri said and Asha nodded.

"That's how it goes sometimes." Rosemary took a steadying breath. "Actually, this is a fairly good opening for me to tell you—"

"Can you believe it?" Vivienne returned to the table and sat down. "Penny's going off on a tour of Canada with her son and his wife. Maybe there's hope for me yet."

"I didn't know you wanted to travel, Viv," Peri said and Vivienne laughed.

"Oh, I wouldn't mind, but I'm not sure my old heart is up to all that flying. Dickie and I went to England by ship you know. That was a lovely voyage."

"With Gran and Grandpa, before Grandpa died, wasn't it?" Peri remarked.

"Oh, yes. We went to England and Europe. We were all in our seventies, but we had a marvelous time."

"It's a pity you hadn't known about Richard and Georgie back then," Asha said. "You could have visited the area where they came from."

"So we could." Vivienne smiled. "Dickie would have loved that."

They went on to talk about other subjects, and had Asha not been so upset about Peri, she would have thoroughly enjoyed herself. Rosemary Chaseley was such interesting company.

Another of Vivienne's friends joined them and Peri stood up. "I should get going. I have to call in at my unit for a file and then get back to work, so I'll leave you to it."

"And I feel I should get back as well," Asha said. "With all the excitement of the journals, I'm way behind with the actual book. I'll take a taxi."

"There's no need for taxis, Asha, or for you to hurry with the book," said Vivienne. "But if you do want to get back to the house I'm sure Peri can drop you off."

Asha glanced at Peri, but she'd slipped her sunglasses on again and Asha couldn't see her eyes. "Oh, no. I don't want to hold Peri up. A taxi will be fine."

"It's all right, Asha," Peri said. "I go right past Tyneholme, but I will need to stop off at my place on the way."

"And do you think you could post this off to Grace?" Vivienne pulled the manila envelope holding the journal transcripts out of her bag. "I want her to get it as soon as possible."

"Sure." Peri took the parcel. "We pass the Post Office as well."

Rosemary laughed. "And can you do some grocery shopping and pick up the dry cleaning in your spare time?"

"We don't need groceries." Vivienne tapped her daughter on the arm. "Oh, you! I'd forgotten what a tease you were, Rosemary."

Asha giggled. "For a moment I was getting ready to make a grocery list."

"Don't encourage her, Asha," Peri said. "Let's get going while we can."

"We'll see you back at the house. Drive carefully," Vivienne called after them.

Asha lengthened her stride to keep up with Peri. "I can still take a taxi if you want to get to work."

"It's okay, Asha." She held up the envelope. "We'll call at the Post Office first."

In the car Asha fiddled with her seat belt, her mouth dry. Peri was far too close and she had to fight the urge to reach out and run her hand over Peri's thigh.

Without a word, Peri pulled out into the traffic and headed along the busy road. She turned into the Post Office car park and switched off the engine. "Do you want to come in with me or wait in the car?" she asked with little intonation in her voice.

"I can wait here," Asha said, and she swallowed the heaviness of tears that rose in her throat. Angrily she brushed at her damp eyes and told herself to get a backbone. She hadn't done anything wrong. The misconception was Peri's. But her heart ached for what could have been.

Peri returned and Asha watched her surreptitiously as she strode across the pavement. She was so attractive she literally took Asha's breath away. As she climbed into the car, Asha made a show of adjusting her seat belt in case Peri saw the wanting she knew was reflected in her eyes.

Soon they were driving into the underground car park of a modern block of units. Peri used her security card and the door moved up. She drove in and parked, switching off the engine. "There's no aircon down here, so if you'd like, you can come up with me."

Asha nodded, climbing out of the car and walking across to the elevator with Peri. Standing in the lift cubicle was more torture for Asha. Could Peri feel the heightened tension? She must.

An eon later, the elevator doors slid open and Asha followed Peri to one of two doors. "Come on inside," Peri said cordially enough, but Asha sensed her reservations.

The unit was large and airy and Asha expelled a breath in awe. "It's beautiful," she said.

The living room was antique white and the comfy-looking lounge suite was upholstered in a soft sage green. An amazingly vibrant abstract painting hung on one wall and large plate glass doors opened out onto a covered balcony. The view, from a slightly different angle, was as wonderful as it was from the front veranda at Tyneholme.

Asha crossed the room. "Can I go outside?"

"Sure." Peri joined her and unlocked the doors. "While you're looking at the view I'll just get the file I need from my study."

Asha walked out onto the balcony and leaned on the rail. They were about ten floors up and a cooling breeze blew across from the river. She gazed about with interest, picking out a few landmarks, and then she sighed.

"I find the view very restful." Peri's husky voice came from behind Asha, and Asha's skin tingled as though Peri had touched her.

"I can understand that," she said as evenly as she could. "Have you lived here long?"

"About three years. It's a new block and I bought the unit off the plan."

"It must be lovely at night, with the city lights." Asha turned to face Peri, only to find she was much too close, and Asha was far too attracted to her.

"Yes." Peri had removed her sunglasses and her eyes held Asha's. "Lovely," she said softly.

They stood like that for an eternity before Peri swallowed and turned back toward the living room. "It has two large bedrooms and a study, and a good-sized kitchen," she added as they went back inside.

There was a sideboard near Asha and she stepped across to look at the photographs arranged on the top. Asha was drawn to one, a head and shoulders studio portrait of a teenaged Peri smiling happily into the camera. She wore a deep blue dress that left her shoulders bare, and the color of the dress accentuated the smoky gray of her eyes. Her fair hair was piled in curls on the top of her head.

"That was taken at my formal dance," Peri said behind Asha.

"And these are your parents?" Asha asked, drawing her eyes from Peri's portrait. She'd not seen a photograph of Peri's parents, although she had a box of photographs to go through that Vivienne had sorted out for her.

"Yes. That was at their thirty-fifth wedding anniversary last year."

Off to Asha's right she could see across a hallway and into the pale blue and lemon of what was surely Peri's bedroom. She swallowed. Visions of Peri in her arms, the feel of her smooth skin, the sound of her heady murmurs, took hold of Asha and her nerve endings danced crazily. "You do look like your mother," she said, her voice thin in her ears.

"So I'm told." The silence stretched tautly between them and then Peri's hand reached out, her fingers running lightly up Asha's arm from elbow to shoulder. Asha shivered.

"I'm blown away by the softness of your skin. Do you know that?" Peri whispered brokenly and Asha's heart raced. "When I'm near you I can't think of anything but the touch of you, your kisses—" She leaned forward and her lips found Asha's, nibbling tender, enthralling kisses against her mouth.

Asha melted into her, drowning in a wave of arousal that left her weak and trembling. Her nipples hardened where they brushed against Peri's and spirals of desire surged through her, making her moan into Peri's mouth.

"I can't seem to not touch you," Peri said raggedly. "It's as though I'm totally bewitched by you." Her arms slid around Asha, holding her close, and their kisses deepened.

Asha's hands shakily slipped Peri's jacket from her shoulders, her fingers molding Peri's breasts through her light, silky top. Peri gasped and leaned her hips against the sideboard, upsetting one of the framed photos. She pulled Asha against her and Asha's leg moved between Peri's as they strained together.

"Asha! I need to—"

The buzzing of the intercom made them both jump in fright. Asha stepped guiltily away from Peri, her face pale. "What's that?" she asked, her voice thin with shock.

Peri took a steadying breath and smiled crookedly. "Saved by the bell." She reached down and lifted her discarded jacket from the floor before she crossed to the door. She pushed the button. "Yes?" she said tersely.

"Does that mean yes I can come up?" said the disembodied voice of Jack Moyland.

Peri pushed the button to let her brother through the security door below. "So how could we forget my brother, Jack?" she said cryptically as she shrugged her arms into her jacket.

"Peri, I—"

Peri held up her hand. "Don't Asha! Let's just say we needed that timely reminder about everything."

"Peri, I've explained about Jack." Asha crossed the room then put her hand on Peri's arm.

Peri took her hand, kissed it gently and then let it go. "It's easier this way, Asha. Jack's—" She shrugged.

"Jack's not you," Asha said softly, and then there was a sharp knock on the door.

"I was hoping I'd catch up with you." Jack stepped through the door Peri opened and stopped when he saw Asha. "Asha! Hi!" He moved forward and wrapped his arms around her. "What a nice surprise to see you, too."

Asha caught the sideways glance Jack shot at his sister and she gave a faint smile. "Yes. Peri's kindly dropping me at Tyneholme on her way back to work."

"Did Asha tell you about the fantastic night we had at the Sporting Awards, Peri? It was a total experience, rubbing shoulders with the mega-famous, including her father."

"Yes, I heard," Peri said evenly. "So what brings you here in the middle of a working day?"

"Apparently, Gran's been trying to reach Viv and no one's answering at the house. When she couldn't get you on your mobile, she rang me. You weren't at work, and as I had to visit a client around the corner, I took a chance on finding you here."

193

Peri slipped her phone from her pocket. "Flat battery. There's nothing wrong with Gran or Mum and Dad, is there?"

"No, they're all fine. But it seems she wants to read the copy of the journals Viv promised her, and they haven't arrived."

"We just posted them." Peri sighed. "I'd better give her a quick ring back." She crossed to the telephone and punched in the number.

"Gran's a bit like Peri and me. When she wants something, she wants it now." Jack laughed. "Have you been admiring Peri's view? Fantastic, isn't it?" He lowered his voice. "Or did I interrupt her showing you her etchings?"

Asha blushed. "Jack! It was nothing like that," she said with as much conviction as she could muster.

He chuckled softly. "Don't worry, I'll make my exit ASAP. Don't want to cramp your style."

Asha glanced across at Peri, but she had her back to them so she gave Jack a shove. "Will you please stop it? Peri will hear you and misconstrue."

"Is that before or after she challenges me to a duel at dawn?" He grinned.

"Jack, it's not amusing. Peri thinks, well, that there's something between us and—" Asha shook her head.

"If I thought I had a chance there would be," he said, "but I know when I'm a beaten man. Still, a little competition won't hurt. What do you reckon?" He put his arm around Asha's shoulders as Peri replaced the receiver and turned back to them.

Jack's movement didn't go unnoticed by his sister, and she folded her arms across her chest. "I think I've sorted that out. I sent the parcel by express post, so she'll have it in no time." She looked at her watch. "And talking about time, I have to get back to work. How would you like to drop Asha home, Jack, if you're going that way?"

"If I wasn't I am now," Jack said cheerfully, giving Asha a squeeze. "It would be my pleasure. Shall we go, Asha? We'll leave this workaholic to her, well, work."

"Thank you," Asha murmured, not looking at Peri as she followed Jack from the unit.

Later that afternoon, Asha was in the study trying to work on Vivienne's book, waiting for her Internet server to come back online, when Rosemary knocked on the open door. She welcomed the diversion, as she couldn't seem to prevent her thoughts from returning to Peri, the feel of her, her kisses.

"Am I interrupting?"

"Not at all," Asha said and Rosemary came in and sat down. "I thought it would be your mother. She often spends some time with me in the afternoons."

"Mother's having a rest. She's so pleased you're doing the family history, Asha."

"I'm enjoying it, too, especially since I found the journals," Asha said with a smile. "That's a researcher's dream come true."

Rosemary laughed softly. "I imagine it is." She picked up the glass paperweight Peri always seemed to find so fascinating. "The Chaseleys are an interesting family I guess."

"You certainly are. And reading Georgie's journals shows how resolute and hardy the brothers were. Living in the colonies can't have been easy."

"No. I suppose not." Rosemary twisted the paperweight in her fingers, then she replaced it carefully on the desk. "You really do enjoy researching, don't you?"

"Of course. I love it," Asha said sincerely.

Rosemary remained silent and glanced almost nervously around the study.

Asha felt a stab of disquiet. "Is something wrong, Rosemary?"

"No. No, not really. Not with you," she said quickly and sighed. "The problem's mine. I just—" She shrugged. "I needed to talk to you about something. In private." She stood up. "Do you mind if I close the door?"

Asha shook her head, and Rosemary returned to her seat. "What did you want to talk about?" Asha asked, perplexed.

"Did my mother tell you it was my idea for you to do this family history for my brother?"

"Yes. She told me."

Rosemary nodded. "When Mother brought Betty Peterson's book home to show me and I saw your name, I recognized it straight away. It was an amazing coincidence."

"But, I don't understand. You mean you knew of me because of my father?"

Rosemary smiled crookedly. "No. I'm afraid I'm not a cricket fan. But I did know his name. And yours."

Asha watched her as she picked up the paperweight again and then put it down. "You saw photographs of us in the newspapers?"

"Not exactly. But I . . . we knew your stepmother. A long time ago."

Asha felt herself flush. Her stepmother had impressed on her not to mention her name to the Chaseleys, but it seemed the Chaseleys had known all along.

"Did she? Has your stepmother told you she used to work here?"

Asha looked at the mountain scene on her screensaver. "Mum only found out where I was working a few days ago," Asha said carefully.

Rosemary nodded. "How did she feel about that?"

"She wasn't convinced I should be here."

"I could see how she mightn't."

If the Chaseleys knew she was Laura's stepdaughter, why would they want her working in their home? Asha was disconcerted. "Then what you're trying to tell me is that it wasn't a coincidence I got this job?" Asha asked.

"No. Not strictly a coincidence. It was—" Rosemary gave a

shake of her head. "I should explain. How much did your stepmother tell you about?" She hesitated. "About that time in her life?"

Asha knew Rosemary was choosing her words carefully. "I know she had a child, if that's what you mean." She held Rosemary's gaze. "And I know the circumstances."

Rosemary nodded again. "So she told you who the father of her child was."

"I really don't think we need to dredge all this up again," Asha said levelly. "Mum certainly doesn't need any reminders of it."

"No. I agree. It's a sensitive subject." Rosemary ran her hand through her hair. "As you've probably noticed by now, my mother rarely mentions my brother. My brother, Nicolas, that is."

Asha remained silent. So Rosemary knew Nicolas Chaseley was the father of her stepmother's child.

"When I found out your stepmother had been pregnant, Mother told me the baby was put up for adoption. I just wish I'd known . . ." Rosemary sighed. "Nicolas should have gone to jail for what he did to Laura," she said with feeling.

Asha looked at Rosemary. Her subtle change of tone when she said Laura's name was illuminating. Asha's mind spun. Could she have imagined it? Her mouth went dry. Her stepmother had said she had loved someone but that it was unacceptable, that it would never work out. Asha also suspected Rosemary was a lesbian. Was it possible? Could Rosemary have been her stepmother's lover?

But Asha had never considered the possibility that her stepmother was a lesbian. Wouldn't she have told Asha when Asha had unburdened herself the other day? Why would she? Asha asked herself. Laura West had kept secrets for over twenty years. Perhaps this was something she could never tell.

To Asha's knowledge, her stepmother had never been involved with anyone since her divorce from Asha's father. She

197

belonged to a number of clubs and she sang in a women's choir. She had a large circle of friends. But all of her friends were women, Asha realized.

Asha thought back to the day her stepmother had discovered she was working for the Chaseleys. She'd been totally shocked when Asha had come out as a lesbian. Then she'd gone so white when Asha told her she was living with the Chaseleys that Asha had thought she was about to faint. But what had her stepmother said about Rosemary Chaseley? She'd asked Asha about Rosemary, of that Asha was certain.

"Does your mother know who I am?" Asha asked.

"I'm not sure. She doesn't care for subterfuge, so I would say not."

"Will you tell her?"

Rosemary moved her shoulders slightly. "I don't know. Probably. But it doesn't affect all this." She waved her hands at the work on the desk. "We think the job you've done on our research is wonderful."

"But—"

A knock on the door interrupted them and they both turned as Vivienne peeked around the door. "I suspected I'd find you here, Rosemary."

"And I thought you were having a rest, Mother," Rosemary said lightly and Vivienne shook her head.

"I was, but now I'm miraculously revived. Have you got a moment to look at the swatches I've chosen for the new living room curtains?"

Rosemary smiled. "Sure, Mother. As long as you're not leaning toward green. I never did like those green curtains Dad chose." She turned back to Asha. "We'll see you a little later, Asha," she said, and then they were gone.

Alone again, Asha turned over in her mind all the information she had about her mother and the Chaseleys. Could she ask her stepmother or Rosemary about her suspicions? Of course she couldn't, she told herself. And she had nothing more than a momentary flash of intuition to base those suppositions on, if the truth be told.

With a sigh, she turned back to her computer and exclaimed when her server came up. Now she could distract herself by checking the census returns for the Chaseleys. She logged onto the site she used to search the English census returns and went into the 1851 census. Richard Chaseley would have been about a year old. Only two possibilities came up, and only one Richard Chaseley was born in Sacriston, Durham. She smiled as the family appeared, living on Ninth Ave. The father, Michael Chaseley, was a coal miner, and he and his wife were born in Northumberland, as were Richard's older brother, Michael, and sister, Mary.

She then checked the 1861 census, knowing Richard's brother, Georgie, would now be about eight years old. The family had apparently moved back to Benwell in Northumberland.

Some time later, Asha reached excitedly for the old photograph that had been with Georgie's journals. She carefully set it under the light and lifted her magnifying glass. Yes, there was the Chaseley family in 1867. Michael, the father, was by then a widower. And there stood Richard Chaseley with his older brother, Michael, who was killed later in the same mining accident as his father. And young Benjamin, also killed in the mines.

Asha moved her magnifying glass to the daughters. Mary in her wedding dress. And the other sister, older than Benjamin but younger than Mary, Michael and Richard. She carefully set the old family photograph beside the wedding portrait of Georgie Chaseley and Margaret Gaines and excitement clutched at Asha. The features were the same. Georgie Chaseley was, in fact, Georgina Chaseley, Richard's younger sister. Asha hurriedly scanned and repaired both photographs before she printed them out and examined them again.

Her fingers flew over the keyboard as she delved into Church Records. Then she searched the Births and Deaths registers. There was no recorded birth or death for George Chaseley in Durham or Northumberland, but there was a birth recorded for Georgina Chaseley in the second quarter of 1852 in the right registration district.

Fragments of Georgie's journals flooded into Asha's mind, and the whole thing fell into place. She sat looking at the fine features of Georgie Chaseley and she couldn't decide whether to laugh or cry.

She printed out all the relevant information and hesitated. What was she going to do with it? Should she tell Vivienne Chaseley? She was an elderly woman, from an earlier generation. Could she cope with this particular secret?

Asha swallowed nervously. Perhaps she should broach the subject of Georgie's gender with Rosemary before she spoke to Vivienne. Maybe Rosemary would be able to decide how much Asha should tell her mother.

Although she sensed that Rosemary may be a lesbian, Asha wasn't confident enough to take it for granted. She knew she'd have to tread carefully over this difficult subject. She walked downstairs in search of the mother and daughter and found them in the morning room, the material swatches abandoned on the coffee table.

"Any success?" Asha asked, indicating the patterns.

"All done." Vivienne chuckled. "And not a smidgen of green to be found."

Rosemary smiled as Asha sat down.

"So you've started reading Georgie's journals?" Asha asked, indicating the typed pages also resting on the coffee table.

"Yes. I'm halfway through the second one. I can't seem to put it down." She glanced longingly at the remaining pages in her hand.

"Don't let me stop you," Asha said hurriedly. "And I'll avert my gaze if you have a little weep at the end."

Rosemary nodded sheepishly. "I've been close a couple of times."

"It made me quite bleary-eyed, not to mention playing havoc with my sinuses."

Asha and Vivienne talked quietly about the new curtains while Rosemary finished the journal. Eventually she gave a little cough and wiped her eyes, setting the pages aside with a sigh.

"That's unbelievable," she said reverently.

"Compelling reading, isn't it?" Asha said, worrying again about what she was going to tell them and if she should. If only she could speak to Rosemary on her own.

"Such a hard life they had," Vivienne said, "compared to our creature comforts."

"Yes." Asha bit her lip and her fingers moved restlessly on the folder on her knee, the folder containing the census printouts and the copies of the photographs.

"Is something bothering you, Asha?" Vivienne asked. "You seem a little concerned."

Asha came to a decision. It was Vivienne's project, after all. "Actually, I do need to talk to you about something I think I've uncovered. About the Chaseleys." Asha swallowed. "It's something you may or may not want included in your son's book."

"Something unsavory, you mean?" Vivienne frowned. "I can't imagine what it could be. What is it, my dear?"

"It's a little difficult to explain," Asha began and paused.

"Concerning Dickie's grandfather, Richard Chaseley?" Vivienne asked.

"No. It's not Richard. It's about Georgie," Asha said quickly.

"Uncle Georgie?" Rosemary sat forward.

"What could there possibly be about him?" Vivienne asked. "My memories of him are of a kind, generous man who adored his wife and son."

"Has this got anything to do with Margaret's husband, Will

201

Gaines?" Rosemary asked and Asha shook her head in surprise.

"No. Not at all. Why do you ask?"

"In the journal, it was plain no one liked Margaret's husband, and I wondered if someone had killed him and put him in the abandoned mine shaft." Rosemary shrugged. "He was certainly a drunk and a wife beater."

"You think Georgie killed him?" Vivienne asked in amazement before she turned to Asha in horror.

"No." Asha shook her head. "It's not that at all. I did suspect Will Gaines was murdered, but I don't think Georgie had anything to do with it."

Vivienne shook her head. "No, I don't see Georgie as a murderer either. He was such a gentle man. You should have seen him with us as children. He'd do magic tricks and smuggle us sweets while Margaret admonished him about them rotting our teeth. Grace and I loved him so. Why, he taught us to ride on the old carthorse he kept in the paddock.

"Grace said her mother had told her that when Robert, her father, was killed in the Great War, they had great fears that it would kill Margaret and Georgie. Then to lose Bobby, their grandson, in World War Two, they were devastated. Georgie was in his nineties and worried so about Margaret. I really feel if they hadn't had Grace, Bobby's twin sister, they would never have coped."

Asha glanced at Rosemary and back to Vivienne. She had taken a lace-edged handkerchief from her pocket and dabbed at her eyes.

"Perhaps you should just tell us, Asha," Rosemary said quietly.

"Well, I checked the census returns in Durham, where Georgie and Richard were born, in a mining town called Sacriston. The family left there between eighteen fifty-two when Georgie was born, and 1856, when their brother, Benjamin, was born in Northumberland.

"You see, in the eighteen fifty-one census, Michael Chaseley and Mary Nolan were married and had moved to Sacriston, Durham. Michael, the head of the family, and a coal miner, was born in Newcastle-upon-Tyne in eighteen twenty-six. Mary was born in Hexham in eighteen twenty-nine. The first two children were Michael, born in eighteen forty-six, and Mary, born in eighteen forty-eight in Newburn. Richard was born in Sacriston in eighteen fifty."

Asha passed Vivienne the census printouts and Rosemary moved to look at them over her mother's shoulder.

"Georgie doesn't appear until the eighteen sixty-one census," Asha continued. "The family had moved back to Northumberland by then. Mary, the mother, had passed away, and Michael was a widower. It all fits in with Georgie's journals." She paused. "The children are listed as Michael, Mary, Richard, *Georgina* and Benjamin."

"But where was George?" Vivienne asked. "He would have been about nine years old in eighteen sixty-one, wouldn't he?"

"The Chaseley's didn't have a son called George." Asha looked at Rosemary and away again. "But they did have a daughter, Georgina, born in eighteen fifty-two."

CHAPTER TWELVE

"Georgina?" Vivienne said and then realization dawned. "But Georgie said he was Richard's brother."

"I know." Asha nodded. "But I believe Georgie had disguised herself as a man. She was Richard's sister, and I think some of the cryptic things she says in her journals prove that."

"Georgie was a girl? But she married Margaret and—" Vivienne turned startled eyes to her daughter. She closed her eyes for a moment, and a fleeting expression of pain passed over her face. "Oh, dear God," she said softly before turning back to Asha. "Are you saying Georgie was a lesbian? And Margaret?"

Asha knew a flush washed her face. "I think, reading the journals, that they were," she said as evenly as she could. "I've ordered some certificates, but I'm sure I'm right."

No one said anything for long, tension-filled moments.

"But why would Georgie disguise herself?" Vivienne asked as

Rosemary checked the 1861 census and then the birth record printouts Asha handed her.

"I can't know for sure." Asha shrugged. "Richard and Georgie were all that was left of their family. As single people, they would have been separated on the ship coming out to Australia, Richard with the men, Georgie with the single women. Maybe Richard felt it was the only way he could protect his younger sister. Just reading the journals makes me think Richard took his responsibilities as the older brother very seriously."

"But when they arrived in Brisbane, surely Georgie would have—" Vivienne shook her head and Asha picked up the typed transcript and turned to one of the entries she'd marked.

"For example, Georgie says, 'I can say I have never felt such freedom, and I enjoy it so. At such times I am much convinced Richard and I have made the best choice.' Then, 'After much quiet discussion, Richard had finally come to see that it is best to keep up our story,' and, 'I am wont to say I have almost forgotten my life before we left for the new land. I am sure I am living the life I was meant to live.' I think Georgie valued the freedom of being a male in what was certainly a man's world."

Vivienne was silent.

Rosemary had quietly crossed to the open windows to stand with her arms folded across her chest, her back to them. Was she upset? Asha wondered. "As I said, Vivienne, I can leave all this out of the book if you prefer," she said, feeling as though her mouth were filled with ashes.

Both Vivienne and Asha turned as Rosemary gave a soft exclamation. She'd turned back to face them now. "Don't, Mother! Don't leave it out. Please. It would only negate Georgie's wonderful life." She held her mother's gaze, and Asha sensed their emotions ran deeply.

Then Vivienne sighed. "I know it would," she said thickly. "And I wouldn't do that. I couldn't. I wouldn't make the same mistake again," she added softly. "But I suppose I deserve that you think I would." She dabbed at her tears with her handker-chief.

Rosemary went to her, then leaned down and held her. "I'm so sorry, Mother."

"Don't ever be that, darling." She looked up at her daughter. "You have nothing to be sorry about." She patted Rosemary's cheek. "I'm far better informed than I used to be. But the most important thing is that you're my daughter and I love you. If I denied Georgie's life it would be like denying my daughter again."

Asha watched them, feeling like an intruder, not knowing what to say as her mind slowly turned over the conversation between mother and daughter.

Rosemary hugged her mother again and then straightened, turning to Asha with a crooked smile. "I suppose you're wondering just what's going on. So, it appears the time is right for me to tell you why I feel so strongly about Georgie's life. I don't hide the fact that I'm a lesbian, but I don't exactly shout it from the rooftops."

Vivienne squeezed her hand. "And, I'm ashamed to say, in my ignorance and small-mindedness I almost lost my daughter because I couldn't accept that was who she was."

"Mother," Rosemary said gently. "There's no need to—"

"Yes, there is." She turned to Asha. "When Rosemary told me she was in love I immediately saw a grand white wedding, a beautiful bride and a handsome groom."

"Mother!"

"When she told me she was in love with a woman, I behaved very badly, in the worst possible way. So badly, in fact, that Rosemary decided to leave home. And I didn't stop her."

"There was more going on than just that," Rosemary said gently. "We were all caught up in an emotional turmoil. We were all overreacting. With hindsight, I see I should have known the timing wasn't right. The situation was so painful for all of us."

Vivienne glanced at Asha. "We're being rude, speaking of family things in front of you, but we were all going through a bad time. Which doesn't excuse the choices I made."

"Mother! Don't!" Rosemary put in quickly. "You'll only upset yourself."

Vivienne looked at Asha and quickly away again. "Perhaps you're right, dear. But I feel so responsible for your unhappiness."

"It was all a long time ago," Rosemary said tiredly.

Asha saw the pain on Rosemary's face and suspected it wasn't so long that she'd come to terms with it. Had Rosemary's broken heart never mended? She thought again of her stepmother, sure now that it was Rosemary that Laura had been in love with all those years ago.

"I know it was a long time ago. But I sometimes think she— that you—I've so wished to see you settled with someone who cares for you." Vivienne's tears fell again, and Rosemary held her.

"Mother, I'm fine. I've had a wonderful job and life. I'm not complaining."

"I want you to be happy."

"I am, Mother." Rosemary turned back to Asha. "Did you have any ideas about how to present Georgie's story?"

"No, not really. I wanted to check with you first."

"Oh, dear," Vivienne said. "We've forgotten something here. This isn't just our family's secret. Georgie's wife, Margaret, was Grace's grandmother, and Peri's great-great-grandmother. They should be consulted, too, don't you think?" Vivienne pushed herself to her feet. "I should go and ring Grace, although she won't have received the copy of the journals yet. I have their mobile phone number, and it's to be hoped they're within reception range. I'll leave you and Asha to tell Peri."

"Tell me what?" Peri asked, appearing in the doorway as Vivienne left them.

Asha watched Peri's face as Rosemary told her what Asha's

research had uncovered. Amazement. Disbelief. She slid a glance at Asha and her face flushed.

"I can't take this in," she said at last. "Georgie was a woman?"

They sat quietly as Peri read Asha's printouts for herself. Then she stood up. "I think I need to reread my copy of Georgie's journals. I'm going upstairs to do it straight away." With one glance at Asha's face, she left them.

"How accurate are the census returns?" Rosemary asked Asha when they were alone.

"Reasonably accurate. There are lots of mistakes with ages or places of birth, which could have been the information the census collectors were given or what was transcribed. And occasionally children were left out of family groups, I'll admit. But the census returns aside, all the other Chaseley children were baptized, including the last child, Kate, who died not long after her birth and after her mother had died." Asha raised her hands and let them fall. "I see no reason why they wouldn't have baptized their son, George, if he had been born."

"Could George and Georgina have been twins?" Rosemary asked.

"Perhaps. He could have been mistakenly left off the register but it's a huge coincidence that he would be left out of the census as well. And I checked to see if he was away from home on the night of the census, but I came up with no possibilities." Asha took a steadying breath. "And, most importantly, in the journals, when talking about his family, Georgie made no reference to a sister, Georgina."

"And Georgie said Richard had named his daughter Georgina, after Georgie," Rosemary said reflectively. She sighed. "What a revelation. I think I should go and check on Mother. Will you excuse me, Asha?"

Asha passed Rosemary the two photographs she'd scanned and reprinted. "Maybe you should show Vivienne these, too, Rosemary. This is the most telling proof, I think. It's Georgie's wedding photo and the one of her in the family group taken at her sister Mary's wedding. I think it proves the research beyond doubt."

Rosemary looked at the photographs carefully, then nodded and left the room. Asha could only return to the study.

Asha stepped out of the shower later that evening and toweled herself dry. With a sigh, she reached for her T-shirt then pulled it over her head. She gave her hair another vigorous rub, not wanting to use her noisy hair dryer so late at night.

She looked at herself in the mirror and sighed again. She was drawn and tired, and the past couple of days were catching up with her. There was that wonderful night with Peri, the late night at the awards, and then the emotional discussions with her stepmother. And, of course, the excitement of uncovering Georgie Chaseley's secret. Add to that the scene with Peri, and Asha felt like a piece of chewed string.

She couldn't believe Peri could have misconstrued Jack accompanying her to the awards. Her heart ached. There had to be some way she could make Peri understand. Perhaps if Peri talked to Jack . . . Yet part of Asha wished Peri had simply trusted her.

Her fluctuating thoughts were interrupted by a knock on her door.

"Asha?"

The soft voice was Peri's, and Asha stilled before crossing to open the door. Peri stood there looking pale and hesitant.

"I—" She shrugged slightly. "Can I come in?"

Asha held her gaze for a moment before standing back so Peri could come into the room. Peri closed the door behind her and leaned against it. She wore light shorts and a black sleeveless tank top, and her feet were bare.

Asha desperately wanted to tell her how beautiful she was, but her vocal chords wouldn't seem to work. Uncertainty bade her be cautious, but her attraction to Peri had her defenses crumbling.

Peri drew a shuddering breath. "I was lying in bed. I couldn't stop thinking about you. Since the other night. And this afternoon. And I had to come."

"I was thinking about you, too," Asha said huskily.

"I can't cope with being like this, wanting to touch you, needing to feel your lips on mine. I've thought of nothing else." Peri's voice broke on a sob.

Stepping forward, Asha gently drew her into her arms, holding her close as she cried. Asha murmured soothingly.

"I've never felt like this before," Peri said into Asha's shoulder. "I've never wanted anyone as much as I want you. Don't send me away. Please."

"Never." Asha found Peri's lips and kissed her softly, gently. Then their kisses deepened as passion took hold of them.

Somehow they were on Asha's bed and Peri's fingers and lips were moving over Asha's skin, setting her aflame. She reveled in Peri's touch, the taste of her, the familiar scent of her.

Asha moaned and her mouth settled on the hard peak of Peri's breast. She ran her hands over Peri's smooth skin, lingering over the line of her hip, her thigh, her fingers finding the dampness of Peri's center.

Peri murmured low in her throat, the sound of her arousal, the magic of her fingers sending Asha tumbling over into orgasm. Peri held her, nibbling tingling kisses along Asha's shoulder and the curve of her throat, then found her lips and kissed her deeply, druggingly.

Drawing a steadying breath, Asha moved over Peri, her lips finding Peri's responsive places. She exalted in the heady catch in Peri's breath, the sweet, low sounds she made as her desire rose, the soft sobbing sigh as she cascaded, dissolving into Asha's arms.

After a while, Asha leaned on her elbow and looked down

into Peri's smoky eyes, part of her taking in Peri's long, dark eye-lashes, the very faint oval scar above the arch of one eyebrow. She touched the scar lightly with her finger. "I don't even know how you came by this scar," she said huskily, knowing that wasn't what she should be asking.

"A difference of opinion with Jack when I was seven," Peri said softly, her expression telling Asha she knew they were evad-ing the subject on both their minds. "I wanted a toy he had, there was some shoving, he conceded, and I hit myself with the spoils. It was my own fault. He was mortified when I started to bleed and was unfairly punished by my parents." She wrinkled her nose. "I suspect that happened a lot when we were kids." She held Asha's gaze. "Jack always took the blame."

"I made it clear to Jack that I . . . I didn't lead him on. You have my word on that."

"I know. I was still shifting the blame, I—"

Whatever Peri was about to say was left unsaid when there was a soft knock on Asha's door.

Asha looked at the time. Three a.m. Asha's bedside lamp was on, so whoever was knocking would see the strip of light below the door. Peri and Asha looked at each other for long seconds before they both climbed hurriedly off the bed.

The knock came again. "Asha? Are you awake?"

"It's Rosemary," Asha breathed. "Just a minute," she said louder, as she scrambled to pass Peri her top and boxer shorts. She struggled into her oversized T-shirt. As she smoothed it over her bare hips, Peri hurried into the en suite, clothes in hand, the dim light illuminating the curve of her buttocks and thigh.

Asha took a steadying breath and opened the door. "Sorry. I was just, uh, going to take a shower," she said, her face hot.

"When I saw the light under your door I hoped you were still awake," Rosemary said with a frown. "Do you know where Peri is? She's not in her room and I didn't know she was going out."

"Is something wrong?" Asha asked, concerned now.

211

"Mother's had a heart turn."

"Is she all right?"

"I hope so. She says she is. But I'm going to take her to the hospital just as a precaution, and I wanted to tell Peri."

The en suite door behind Asha opened and Peri appeared, her brow creased with concern. "What's wrong with Viv?"

Rosemary's dark eyes went from Asha to Peri, and Asha swallowed, her blush deepening.

"Is she okay?" Peri pressed and Rosemary seemed to recover from her surprise.

"She insists she's fine, but I think it gave her a fright."

"I'll come to the hospital with you," Peri said, moving out into the hallway. "I'll just throw some clothes on." She jogged down the hall toward her room.

Rosemary's gaze followed her before she turned back to Asha. "I don't know how long we'll be. They might decide to admit her." Her eyes moved past Asha, taking in the tumbled bedclothes.

"But you'll let me know what's happening? You have my mobile number?"

Rosemary nodded, went to walk off and then turned back to Asha. "I think maybe you and Peri and I need to talk, hmm?"

"Rosemary, I—" Asha swallowed and simply nodded, watching as Rosemary disappeared after Peri.

Asha was desperately worried for Vivienne. She always seemed so full of life. Surely she would be all right. Had Asha's exposé about Georgie had anything to do with her heart turn? Asha wondered. Although she was surprised, Vivienne hadn't seemed concerned about anything except Rosemary.

And what would Rosemary be thinking finding Peri in Asha's room? What could she think? Asha asked herself mockingly.

Left alone, Asha tried to gather her scattered thoughts. There was no way she'd be able to convince Rosemary that she and Peri hadn't spent the night together. If she wanted to, suggested a small voice that surfaced inside her.

She had a quick shower, forcing thoughts of Peri moving with her on the bed from her mind. There was no way she could sleep, and the tumbled bed looked lonely, so she pulled on a pair of baggy shorts and a T-shirt and went across to the study.

Vivienne had sorted out a pile of recent photos from the family album that she wanted in the book, and Asha needed to scan them. It would keep her mind off waiting for Rosemary's call about her mother. She powered up her notebook and her scanner and took the pile of photographs from the drawer.

Picking up the first photo, she slipped it into her scanner and listened to it whirring to life. It was a studio portrait of Richard Chaseley and his late wife, Sara, on their wedding day. There was one of Richard, Nicolas and Rosemary as small children, and another of them when they were in their teens.

Asha looked at the smiling face of Nicolas Chaseley. On first inspection he was like his father but with Vivienne's fairer coloring. Asha studied his handsome face, seeing the arrogance in his expression. She saved the file and told herself she was reading that into the photo because she knew how badly he'd treated her stepmother.

There was a photo of Rosemary, aged twenty-one, showing a strong, attractive face. Her hair was swept up and she was smiling confidently. There was certainly nothing to indicate she was a lesbian. Asha laughed self-derisively. What would there be? A large letter "L" in the middle of her forehead?

Since Asha had discovered Georgie's journals, Vivienne had decided to officially add Peri's family to the book. She had a photo of Susannah Reid, Richard and Susannah's granddaughter, at her marriage to Robert Gaines, before he left to fight in World War I, never to return. There was also a later photo of Susannah and her second husband, Edward Ward.

She scanned a photo of Grace Gaines Moyland and her husband and their two sons, and then the sons with their families.

She lingered over a shot of David, Jack and Peri as children. David was the image of his father, while Jack and Peri were so obviously Gaineses. She ran her fingertips gently over the photo of the young, vibrant face of Peri Moyland, and she sighed softly.

She worked steadily, the only sound in the room the whirr of the scanner. She picked up a photo of Richard and Sara and their children and slipped it into the scanner, waiting as the photo was transferred to her computer. Sara Chaseley had been an attractive woman, petite with shoulder-length fair hair. Her daughter, Megan, at three years, was definitely her mother's daughter with her wide smile and fair curls.

Asha turned her attention to Timothy, their adopted son, and, Asha suspected, a favorite of his grandmother, Vivienne. Going by the date, he would be thirteen years old in the photo, as tall as Richard, and if Asha hadn't known he was adopted, she would have said he took after his father.

Timothy Chaseley had the same coloring and square jaw, but his eyes . . . They were as blue as the Chaseleys were brown. He looked vaguely familiar. Asha searched through the remaining photos. Megan, aged twelve years, taken earlier in the year. She found one of Timothy, aged twenty-one. Asha studied his features, and a sudden stillness held her immobile. She went hot and then cold.

Her wallet was in the top desk drawer, and her unsteady fingers fumbled for it. She drew it out, flipped it open and stared at the photos in their plastic sleeves. She put the photo of Michelle alongside the photo of Timothy Chaseley. Surely she was imagining it.

The eyes. The bright blue eyes Michelle had inherited from her mother. Their shape. How could she have not seen the resemblance before?

Asha's heartbeat intensified. She glanced at the time. Just after seven. Her stepmother was an early riser. She'd be sitting reading the newspaper with an early cup of tea.

214

Asha lifted the phone and dialed, swallowing when she heard her stepmother's voice. "Mum. It's Asha."

"You're an early bird, love." Laura West paused. "Is there something wrong?"

"No. Yes. Um, Vivienne had a heart turn last night."

"Oh, no, Asha," said her stepmother. "Is she all right?"

"I hope so. I'm waiting to hear. But Mum, I'm scanning some photos and there's something I . . ." Asha changed the phone from one ear to her other. "When did you?" She drew on all her courage to continue. "Your baby, was it a boy?"

There was a moment of heavy silence. "Why do you want to know?"

"Do you know who his adoptive parents were?"

"How would I know that?"

Asha knew by her tone, the unsteadiness of her stepmother's voice. "Oh, Mum. I'm right, aren't I? I know who adopted him."

"How could you know that, Asha? The records are sealed and . . ." Laura West's voice faded away, and she made a soft, sobbing sound. "Does he . . . ? How does he look?" she asked, her voice heavy with tears.

"You haven't seen him?" Asha asked, wiping tears from her own cheeks.

"Not since he was five days old," she said softly.

"He looks so much like Michelle. And you. Only darker like the Chaseleys. He's away in Melbourne with his father and sister, so I haven't met him."

"I wanted so much to ask you about him, but I didn't dare in case you, well, in case this happened."

"Vivienne says he's a wonderful young man."

"She never knew, Asha. Vivienne, I mean. So you mustn't tell her," Laura said, clearly upset.

"But, Mum. How could she *not* know?"

"It was her husband, Dickie, and Richard who arranged it all. And they swore me to secrecy. I had already decided to put my

215

baby up for adoption when Dickie came to see me. There was no way I could keep him, but this way, at least, I knew he would be safe and loved. I liked Richard and Sara and I knew they would make wonderful parents. And my baby, he was their blood. It was his place with the family."

Tears tumbled down Asha's cheeks. "What will we do, Mum?"

"Do? Asha, we can't do anything. Unless he, unless Timothy," she said the name softly, "wants to know about me, and he hasn't shown any signs of that, so there's nothing to be done."

They talked together for some time, and when Asha eventually hung up she rubbed her eyes. She looked again at the handsome face of Timothy Chaseley, Michelle's half brother. So many secrets. And little did she know the depths of the secrets she was about to unravel when she took on what had started out as a straightforward research project.

A short time later Asha heard the sound of soft footsteps in the hallway. Rosemary came into the study and sank tiredly into the chair by the desk.

Apprehensively, Asha tried to read the expression on her face. "How is she?" she asked quickly.

"Fine now," Rosemary reassured her. "It seems she forgot to take one lot of her tablets. They've given her loads of tests, and now they're letting her come home. Peri's staying with her until I get back with something for her to wear. She doesn't want to come home in her night attire."

Asha smiled. "No, I suppose she doesn't."

"I have to get back, but I wanted you to know Mother was okay. I also wanted to tell you, while we waited for Mother's tests, I had time to talk to Peri."

Asha worked to school her expression. "What did she say?"

"Not much. You haven't known each other long, I take it?"

Asha shook her head.

"She said you were her first." Rosemary gave a small sigh. "I never even suspected Peri was a lesbian. Fine gaydar I've got."

Asha gave a faint smile. "I didn't either. I hoped, but . . ." She shrugged slightly.

"But we knew about each other, didn't we, you and I?"

Asha thought back to her first meeting with Rosemary, and she nodded again. "I wouldn't do anything to hurt Peri," she said quickly. "I just . . . we . . ." She shook her head.

"She said the same about you. I think she wants to talk to you."

Asha's heart constricted. She knew she'd fallen in love with Peri. If only she could be sure Peri felt the same way. What if Peri decided it was all too difficult?

"Does your stepmother know that you're a lesbian?" Rosemary's voice broke into Asha's thoughts.

"She does now. I went to my father's Sporting Awards Night with Peri's brother, and Mum thought Jack and I were involved. I didn't want to pretend any longer."

"Congratulations," Rosemary said gently. "It took me so many years to get to that point." She paused. "What did Laura say?"

"She was worried, but she accepted it." Asha thought about her suspicions about her stepmother and Rosemary. "She said she'd been in love with someone years ago, someone unacceptable, when she worked here with Vivienne."

Rosemary stilled and her fingers fluttered nervously to smooth the collar of her shirt. "When she worked here? She told you that?"

"She was upset when she found out I knew Vivienne. I thought when she said she'd loved someone, someone unacceptable, that she meant she was involved with a married man. But I was way off base." Asha swallowed and forged on. "It was you, wasn't it?" she asked softly.

"Laura mentioned me?" Rosemary asked.

217

"No. I worked it out. It was the way you said her name."

Rosemary was silent until she regained her composure. "We met when she came to work with Mother. I fell in love with her at first sight." She smiled wryly. "It really was the first time I saw her. She said she felt the same. My whole life came together. But we were both absolutely terrified someone would find out. The tragedy of it was, that someone was my brother, Nick."

"Where is he now? As you said, your mother rarely mentions him."

"Somewhere around the world. Nick broke my parents' hearts. He was always selfish, spiteful, even though my parents didn't treat him any differently from Richard and I. But he could be so charming when he wanted to be." She shook her head. "He caught us making love. We'd thought we had the house to ourselves. We were terrified, but he said he understood, that he'd keep our secret. And he did for some time.

"Having Nick know about us put a strain on our relationship. We both felt the pressure about being different, about being labeled as lesbians. We quarreled. I don't even remember what it was about, but we decided to make the break, which we did, and we were both so miserable.

"I made plans to go overseas. I begged Laura to come with me. We ended up quarrelling again. Then Nick—" Rosemary rubbed a hand over her face. "I let her down again. I knew Nick could be cruel, but I never believed he could rape someone. When Laura told me I—" She grimaced. "Like everyone else, I thought she'd slept with him, and I left her to deal with the rape on her own." She looked across at Asha. "Not my finest hour. I selfishly couldn't see past what I thought was her betrayal of our love. So I went overseas for about four years as planned, and then transferred back to Melbourne."

"Thank you for confiding in me, and I'm sorry," Asha added inadequately. "You didn't know she was pregnant, I take it?"

"No." Rosemary shook her head. "Not then. Not for years.

Mother let it slip eventually, and I felt impossibly worse. Mother told me Laura put her child up for adoption."

Asha nodded. So Rosemary hadn't seen the resemblance between Laura and Timothy either. Like Asha, she wouldn't have been looking for it.

Rosemary sighed and glanced across at Asha. "Does she still hate me?" she said softly, and the sadness on her face, the regret in her voice, pierced Asha.

"I really don't know," she said honestly. "I'm sorry."

Rosemary nodded. "I tried to run from what I was, but eventually I admitted to myself I was a lesbian. I had a few relationships, but your stepmother . . ." She swallowed. "Laura always stayed with me. Then last year something changed my entire outlook on my life. I had a health scare and the doctor talked cancer. While I waited for the results, I reevaluated my life, my mistakes. I was working far too hard, just like my colleagues, and I'd seen some of them succumb to heart attacks and other stress-related problems. Apart from my family, I had no one who cared if I lived or died. I decided it was a very sad obituary."

"Were you all right? I mean, with the cancer?" Asha asked and Rosemary nodded.

"I was lucky. But I decided I wanted to find your stepmother and at least apologize to her. I hired a private detective to make some discreet inquiries."

Asha murmured in surprise. "You said you didn't know my stepmother was married to my father."

Rosemary shook her head. "Not before the private detective told me. When I found out, I could only wonder, considering how well known your father is, how I'd never even seen a photograph of them together. And I wondered what I would have done if I had."

Asha was speechless.

"I was trying to decide how I was going to approach Laura, when Mother mentioned Richard's sixtieth birthday and said she was wondering what she could possibly get him that was special. We talked about his interests, and somehow family history was mentioned. I knew you were a genealogist, and I was toying with the idea of hiring you to do some research when Mother brought home the book you did for her friend Betty. I couldn't believe my luck. I suggested Mother ask you to do a similar book for Richard."

Asha tried to take it all in. "Knowing who I was?"

Rosemary nodded. "Oh, yes. *Because* of who you were. But I didn't realize there were more skeletons in the family closet besides my own," she said derisively.

"What will you do? About my stepmother, I mean," Asha asked carefully.

"I don't know," Rosemary replied candidly. "I want to see her, but I also don't want to rake up old memories for her. When I started out looking for Laura, I didn't realize the ramifications of it all. My intentions, I see now, were purely selfish. Again," she added derisively. "Now I see how much it's affected everyone. I didn't think about how Laura's family—how you—would feel. Or my mother. I feel like I've played with fate and disrupted the scheme of things."

"It wasn't all bad," Asha said, thinking about herself and Peri, how much she loved her and how much she wanted to make a life with her. A lump of tears welled in her throat, and she swallowed. "The family should have known about Georgie and Richard and their amazing lives."

"Yet someone must have wanted it kept secret," Rosemary said. "Or why would they have hidden the journals away?"

"Have you considered it might have simply been to keep them safe? If they'd wanted the truth to remain hidden, they would have destroyed them, don't you think?"

"Perhaps you're right. And that would have been terrible."

Asha nodded. "We knew Richard gave the music box to his wife. She could have given it to Georgie and Margaret, or to her granddaughter Susannah. Any of the family could have had access to it. But I like to think Georgie or Margaret put the journals in the box for safekeeping, so the story of their love could live on."

Rosemary smiled. "So you're a romantic, hmmm?"

"I suppose I am." She thought of Peri. "I guess I live in hope."

"Don't we all?" Rosemary stood up. "I should get back to the hospital."

"Should I . . . ? Is Vivienne not well because of what I told her about Georgie?"

"Of course not," Rosemary said quickly.

"How do you think she really feels about it?"

"Not much fazes her these days." Rosemary shrugged. "What with Nick and a lesbian daughter, she's about seen it all, don't you think?"

"She loves you, Rosemary."

"I know. I love her, too. I'd better go."

"Rosemary?"

The other woman paused in the doorway.

"Do you want me to speak to Mum? About you, I mean."

Rosemary shook her head. "Thanks, but no. I think I need to make my own peace with Laura. I'll phone her first, once we get Mother home and I know she's all right."

With that, she left Asha to her own thoughts.

Asha made herself concentrate on finishing scanning the photos. If she let herself think about Peri, she felt sick at heart. What if Peri . . . ? She pulled herself up, admonishing herself. She needed to wait until she spoke to Peri.

Realizing she was hungry and that she hadn't had breakfast, she made herself tea and toast. She kept working, the French doors open now so she'd hear the sound of the car on the gravel drive below. When she did hear it, she rushed outside to look down as Rosemary and Peri helped Vivienne from the car. Vivienne looked up and gave Asha a wave.

221

"Welcome home," Asha said.

"Thank you, my dear. I'm such a nuisance causing all this fuss."

Asha's gaze went to Peri and her heart raced. She wanted to laugh and cry at the same time, but mostly she wanted to race downstairs, slide her arms about her and feel Peri's arms around her.

"We'll see you inside," Vivienne said as she started up the steps.

By the time Asha reached the top of the staircase, Vivienne was moving upward on her chairlift, and Rosemary and Peri were walking up with her. Asha took Vivienne's arm as she stood up, and she gave Asha a hug.

"I'm so sorry I frightened all of you," she said. "And it was such a silly mistake." She kept hold of Asha's hand. "Come with me, dear. I promised the doctor I'd rest and I will, but I also need to talk to you."

"Mother, don't you think it would be better if you talked to Asha later?"

"Now, don't fuss, Rosemary. There's a dear. Why don't you fetch me a cup of tea? I'd love a decent cuppa. It was very good of the nurses to bring me some in the hospital, but it wasn't very nice tea."

Rosemary sighed. "All right. A cup of tea coming up."

"I'll help Asha get you settled," said Peri, and Asha felt she was studiously avoiding meeting Asha's eyes.

When Peri left them to make a call to her office, Vivienne patted the side of the bed and Asha sat down. Vivienne took her hand again. "I admit I gave myself a fright with this, Asha, and it made me realize there are things I should tell you."

"What sort of things? Can't they wait, Vivienne? I'm getting along very well with the book. I have plenty to keep me occupied while you recuperate," Asha said.

"Not about the book." Vivienne paused. "I need to, what is it young people say? Come clean? Yes, that's it. Come clean. You see, Asha, I've been a bit of a fraud."

"In what way?" Asha asked, puzzled.

"I've known for some time who you were, that Laura West is your stepmother."

"You knew?" Asha was taken aback. "Then you must have recognized my stepmother when I showed you her photograph."

"Yes. I recognized Laura immediately." She made an agitated movement with her hand. "But that's not all. You see, when Dickie and Sara—" She swallowed. "In that dreadful accident, poor Sara was killed outright, but Dickie lived for a week before he succumbed to his injuries. We had moments when he was conscious and we could talk. He told me something he'd kept from me all these years. At least, he thought he'd kept it from me, but I knew. He told me how Richard and Sara came to adopt Timothy, my grandson."

"Vivienne, there's no need to upset yourself worrying about all this," Asha said.

"I need to make it right, Asha."

"I already know," Asha said and Vivienne looked at her in surprise.

"Laura told you?"

Asha shook her head. "I saw the photograph of Timothy. He's so much like my sister, Michelle."

Vivienne nodded. "I thought you might see the resemblance. When you showed me that photograph of your sister, I was absolutely stunned. You see, Dickie and Richard arranged for Richard and Sara to adopt Timothy without telling me. And I really don't think Sara knew, either. Rosemary and Nicolas weren't even aware Laura was pregnant. They'd both gone overseas. And at the time I didn't question any details about Timothy's adoption. He was a beautiful baby, and I was simply pleased that having him made Richard and Sara so happy.

"It was Dickie who went to see Laura, offered to have

223

Richard and Sara adopt her child, and Laura agreed. I do remember the moment I began to suspect Timothy was Laura's son. He turned and smiled at me one day. He was about sixteen I suppose. I was reminded so vividly of Laura, it took my breath away. I didn't know what to do. I couldn't bring myself to ask Dickie or Richard. I've kept silent all these years but—" She paused and wiped her eyes with her handkerchief. "Then Dickie told me about the adoption before he died. He also told me that Laura had married your father."

"Vivienne, I don't think you should be upsetting yourself like this. We can talk about it when you're stronger."

Vivienne shook her head. "Last Christmas Timothy asked me if I knew anything about his biological parents. He said he was going to find them because he wanted to ask his girlfriend, Kylie, to marry him. He thought he should know about them before he did. I've been worried about what I should do ever since. I so yearned to be able to talk to Dickie about it. Eventually I decided the right thing would be to talk to Laura, to ask her how she felt about Timothy knowing, but I couldn't begin to see how I could do that. Then Rosemary suggested the family history book. I knew your connection to Laura, and it seemed a far more natural way of making contact with Laura and her family. Through you."

Vivienne clutched Asha's hand. "I'm so very sorry for deceiving you. Please, Asha, say you'll forgive me for not being honest with you."

Asha slid her arms around her thin shoulders. "Oh, Vivienne, there's nothing to forgive. I've had the time of my life working with you, and I can tell you I think my stepmother really wants to meet Timothy, too."

"Oh, Asha, I'm so glad." Tears rolled down Vivienne's cheeks.

"Mother! Asha! What's wrong?" Rosemary set a tray with her mother's tea on the dresser and hurried across to the bed.

Asha stood up and Vivienne took her daughter's hand.

"Nothing's wrong," Vivienne said. "Not now."

"I'll leave you then, Vivienne, to have your tea," Asha said, "and get some rest."

"Thank you, my dear. I have a lot to tell Rosemary now."

Rosemary raised her eyebrows. "More family secrets?"

Asha could only smile as she headed for the door.

"Oh, Asha." Rosemary made her pause as she was leaving. "Peri's waiting to talk to you. In Father's study, I think."

Asha nodded, then made her way along the hallway toward the other end of the house. She went into Dickie Chaseley's study, but it was empty, and neither was Peri waiting for Asha in her room. With a sigh of regret, Asha returned to the study, slipped into her chair and gazed desultorily at her screen saver. It would seem Rosemary was wrong. Peri didn't want to talk to Asha.

CHAPTER THIRTEEN

Asha slipped on her cotton gloves and tidied the desk, carefully returning the photographs to the drawer beside Georgie's journals. So much had happened since she found them in the music box.

She lifted the first one, reread the last entries, smiling at Georgie's expression of love for his—for her—Margaret. Setting it back in the drawer, she picked up the second journal, turning it over in her hands. She noticed the flyleaf at the back was coming adrift, and she made a mental note to get it professionally repaired.

After examining it she decided it was undamaged. The glue had simply given way. But there seemed to be something caught behind it. Asha checked it with her magnifying glass and used her soft tweezers to carefully prize the paper loose. She unfolded it with utmost care and saw that it was a letter, the ink faded and smeared in places. She began to read.

My Dearest Mother and Papa,

I take this opportunity in this rare moment of quiet to write this letter to you. I am huddled in the trenches and the cold night air begins to settle over us. We find it difficult to get warm and yet, in the daytime, we swelter in the heat. For weeks, we have been choked by dust and smoke, but yesterday it rained, a storm much like the one we experienced in Townsville when we went South by steamboat to meet Uncle Richard. With the rain we are now knee-deep in mud. We are all miserable but try to be cheerful.

The noise here is unbelievable and brings back my memories of the Towers, only the constant shelling is far worse and more deadly than the batteries in the mines.

Yesterday I lost my mate, Dave. I believe I told you of him in my last letter. He was a shearer from down South and had a wife and two little girls. I'll write to his wife when I finish this letter, as she may find comfort in knowing what a great bloke we thought her husband was and that he died trying to save a mate. Each day brings acts of unbelievable heroism, and I feel honored to fight alongside these boys.

I got the parcel you sent this past week. The sweets were a treat. And thank you, Papa, for the book. I don't get much time to read, but I carry it in my coat and the feel of it brings me closer to you both somehow.

I try not to be maudlin, but there are things I want to say to you in case I don't make it home. I thank you both for the wonderful life you have given me. Mother, for your love. Papa, for being such a grand father to me. I want to say to you that I have always felt I was your true son. If I get the chance to see my own child, I hope I can be as good a father as you have been to me.

If my time is up in this truly awful land I know you will take care of Susannah and the baby for me. She is a dear, sweet girl and I miss her so. I miss you all.

Your Loving Son,
Robert Gaines

Asha set the letter on the desk. Young Robbie's short life had been documented by Georgie in his journal, and Asha felt as though she had actually known him. Playing in the dirt at the mining camp. Reading stories with his stepfather. Tears coursed down Asha's cheeks.

"Asha? What's wrong?"

Asha looked up at a sound of the familiar husky voice, and then Peri was around the desk, had sunk to her knees and had wrapped Asha in her arms.

"Please don't cry, Asha," she begged, her own voice tight with tears. "I'm so sorry. I didn't mean to hurt you." Her lips found Asha's and she kissed her tenderly, then deeply.

"I'm not . . . I wanted to . . . It was a letter I found, in the back of Georgie's journal. It's from your great-grandfather, Robbie Gaines."

Peri sat back on the floor and slowly read the letter. She too wiped away tears as she carefully handed the letter back to Asha. "My grandmother will be absolutely overwhelmed to see this. It's incredible. A voice from the past."

Asha replaced the precious paper with the journals and then looked down at Peri. She'd obviously just showered, as the ends of her hair curled damply and fell loosely about her shoulders, and she'd changed into a pale blue T-shirt and denim shorts. "If I hadn't been crying, would you still have kissed me?" Asha asked softly.

Peri grinned crookedly. "Let's say it gave me the excuse I was desperately searching for."

"You didn't need one, you know. An excuse, I mean," Asha said and Peri shook her head.

"Can you ever forgive me?" Peri asked. "For being such a coward."

Asha shrugged, her heart singing. "It was all so new to you. I can understand it would be frightening."

"How I felt about you, Asha, it terrified me." Peri stood up, sat on the edge of the desk and took Asha's hand in hers. "When I opened the front door the day you arrived and I saw you standing there smiling at me, I was completely disconcerted. It's a wonder I could even speak."

"You asked if you could help me," Asha said, squeezing Peri's hand.

"I was the one who needed help." Peri rolled her eyes expressively. "I'd never felt that way about anyone, let alone a woman."

"And you couldn't even think straight, hmmm?" Asha asked and they both laughed. "You did a pretty fair job of covering your feelings. I thought you disapproved of me big time."

"Not of you. Of the way I felt about you." Peri raised Asha's hand, kissing it gently. "And when you began to talk to Viv and me about family history you were so vivacious, so enthusiastic about your subject, I had trouble taking my eyes off you. It's a wonder Viv didn't notice."

"I was noticing you, too." Asha chuckled. "I couldn't believe I was so attracted to you when you so obviously didn't trust me."

Peri sobered. "I admit I have an issue with trust. A legacy from Lance and Janet, I guess. And when I saw you talking to Joe Deneen it seemed to reinforce my misgivings. I kept reminding myself you weren't to be trusted either."

Asha nodded. "I felt the same after Tessa." She glanced at Peri. "So that was you up on the veranda that day?"

Peri nodded. "I couldn't hear what you were saying, but I saw him kiss you."

"It was a big sister kiss. He's far too young for me. And he's not you," Asha said simply.

"Oh, Asha. I'm sorry. For thinking the worst of you."

"You threw me into major confusion. I couldn't understand why you were acting so coolly. Just when I thought you were thawing toward me."

229

"I was hot and bothered, actually."

Asha chuckled and Peri stood up, pulling Asha gently into the circle of her arms. "I kept warning myself to keep away from you, but I found excuses to seek you out. I failed miserably there. Especially that night." Her gray eyes darkened. "That night, those nights, by the way, were incredible."

Asha flushed. "They were, weren't they? And it was so difficult for me to keep reminding myself I was too vulnerable and you were far too sexy."

"Sexy, hmmm?" Peri grinned. "You say the nicest things." She sobered, her finger caressing the dimple in Asha's cheek. "Do you know I'd wait to see the flash of that dimple of yours and then I'd have to stop myself from reaching out and kissing that beautiful spot? It was nothing short of torture."

Asha grinned and Peri groaned softly. She leaned forward, tenderly putting her lips to the dimple in Asha's cheek, before claiming her lips in a deep, sensual kiss. They clung together and then reluctantly drew apart.

"You can't imagine how many times I've wanted to do that." Peri shook her head. "After that first night I knew I was in love with you, but I had no idea what I was going to do about it. It was way out of my field of reference. But you showed me all that was missing, that had been missing, from my life. You made me whole."

"Oh, Peri. I felt the same. But you moved away from me again."

"I was committed to go to those two boring conferences, but I came back as soon as I could. Then I saw you and Jack on TV. I was caught in a cleft stick. I loved you, but I also knew how great my brother was. I reasoned it would be so much easier if you went with Jack. He's a guy. It was all so acceptable. But I desperately wanted you myself, and I didn't know how or even if I should try to make you see that."

"Peri, about Jack. He did just step in because I couldn't ask you, and it *was* Vivienne's idea. You know your brother's a pretty special person. He guessed I was a lesbian, and he also knew how I felt about you."

"Jack knew that? You mean you told him?"

"No. He said he saw the way I looked at you, the way we looked at each other."

"At each other? You mean . . . ?"

"He said he'd wondered about you for a long time."

"He had?" Peri laughed incredulously. "The rat. He could have told *me*. It would have saved me a lot of soul searching. And I wouldn't have had to be so jealous of my own brother."

"There was no need. I love you, Peri, and I want to spend my life with you. No hiding. No lying." Asha swallowed. "How do you feel about that?"

"I don't want anything less. I love you, too, Asha, and I can't live without you."

"Apart from Jack, will things be all right with the rest of your family, do you think?"

"They'll understand that I love you." Peri shrugged slightly. "Because I do, more than I've loved anyone else in my life. You're part of me."

"And I feel that way, too. About you."

"What about your family? Do they know about you?"

"Mum and Michelle do now. And they're okay with it. I still have to come out to my father and Karen." Asha made a face. "Now that will be interesting."

Peri raised her eyebrows and Asha reached up to trace their arch. "You have *the* most expressive eyebrows, Peri Moyland."

"Expressive, hmmm? So are they telling you I desperately need to kiss you again?"

Asha grinned. "I do believe they are. Isn't that amazing?"

They laughed softly and then kissed deeply again, and Peri moaned in her throat. "I want to keep doing this. And so much, much more. But this is far too public. Your room or mine?"

231

"Mine's closer," Asha said as a spiral of desire rose inside her. "And we can barricade all exits."

"Brilliant idea," Peri whispered then nibbled tiny kisses over Asha's throat and along the line of her jaw.

Arms entwined, they went to move out of the study, but Peri paused then lifted the photograph of Georgie and Margaret. "They were a great couple," she said. "I can't believe no one guessed their secret."

"I've decided they didn't want it kept a secret. I think they wanted their story uncovered." Asha smiled.

"Such an inspiring story."

"Yes." Asha thought about another story from the past. Her stepmother and Rosemary's. She hoped there was a future for them as well. Only time would tell there. She kissed Peri again and held her close. "There's so much more I need to tell you, but not just now. Maybe later, hmmm? Right now I need some time alone with you. Just us. Reassuringly in the present."

"Reassurance is good," Peri agreed with mock seriousness, then her beautiful lips curved into her wonderful smile. "Then let's make that much later, hmm?"

"Much, much later." Asha gave a quick laugh. "And I think Georgie and Margaret would surely give us their blessing."

COYOTE SKY by Gerri Hill. 248 pp. Sheriff Lee Foxx is trying to cope with the realization that she has fallen in love for the first time. And fallen for author Kate Winters, who is technically unavailable. Will Lee fight to keep Kate in Coyote?
1-59493-065-1 $13.95

VOICES OF THE HEART by Frankie J. Jones. 264 pp. A series of events force Erin to swear off love as she tries to break away from the woman of her dreams. Will Erin ever find the key to her future happiness?   1-59493-068-6 $13.95

SHELTER FROM THE STORM by Peggy J. Herring. 296 pp. A story about family and getting reacquainted with one's past that shows that sometimes you don't appreciate what you have until you almost lose it.   1-59493-064-3 $13.95

WRITING MY LOVE by Claire McNab. 192 pp. Romance writer Vonny Smith believes she will be able to woo her editor Diana through her writing.   1-59493-063-5 $13.95

PAID IN FULL by Ann Roberts. 200 pp. Ari Adams will need to choose between the debts of the past and the promise of a happy future.   1-59493-059-7 $13.95

ROMANCING THE ZONE by Kenna White. 272 pp. Liz's world begins to crumble when a secret from her past returns to Ashton.   1-59493-060-0 $13.95

SIGN ON THE LINE by Jaime Clevenger. 204 pp. Alexis Getty, a flirtatious delivery driver is committed to finding the rightful owner of a mysterious package.
1-59493-052-X $13.95

END OF WATCH by Clare Baxter. 256 pp. LAPD Lieutenant L.A Franco Frank follows the lone clue down the unlit steps of memory to a final, unthinkable resolution.
1-59493-064-4 $13.95

BEHIND THE PINE CURTAIN by Gerri Hill. 280 pp. Jacqueline returns home after her father's death and comes face-to-face with her first crush.
1-59493-057-0 $13.95

18TH & CASTRO by Karin Kallmaker. 200 pp. First-time couplings and couples who know how to mix lust and love make 18th & Castro the hottest address in the city by the bay.   1-59493-066-X $13.95

JUST THIS ONCE by KG MacGregor. 200 pp. Mindful of the obligations back home that she must honor, Wynne Connelly struggles to resist the fascination and allure that a particular woman she meets on her business trip represents.
1-59493-087-2 $13.95

ANTICIPATION by Terri Breneman. 240 pp. Two women struggle to remain professional as they work together to find a serial killer.   1-59493-055-4 $13.95

OBSESSION by Jackie Calhoun. 240 pp. Lindsey's life is turned upside down when Sarah comes into the family nursery in search of perennials. 1-59493-058-9 $13.95

BENEATH THE WILLOW by Kenna White. 240 pp. A torch that still burns brightly even after twenty-five years threatens to consume two childhood friends.
1-59493-053-8 $13.95

SISTER LOST, SISTER FOUND by Jeanne G'fellers. 224 pp. The highly anticipated sequel to *No Sister of Mine*.   1-59493-056-2 $13.95